NEXT OF KIN

A DI Sarah Quinn Mystery

Maureen Carter

severn House

This first world edition published 2015
in Great Britain and 2016 in the USA by
SEVERN HOUSE PUBLISHERS LTD of
19 Cedar Road, Sutton, Surrey, England, SM2 5DA.
Trade paperback edition first published
in Great Britain and the USA 2016 by
SEVERN HOUSE PUBLISHERS LTD

British Library Cataloguing in Publication Data

Carter, Maureen author.
  Next of kin. –(The Sarah Quinn mysteries)
  1. Quinn, Sarah (Fictitious character)–Fiction. 2. Women
  detectives–England–Birmingham–Fiction. 3. Murder–
  Investigation–Fiction. 4. Detective and mystery stories.
  I. Title II. Series
  823.9'2-dc23

ISBN-13: 978-0-7278-8564-7 (cased)
ISBN-13: 978-1-84751-673-2 (trade paper)
ISBN-13: 978-1-78010-730-1 (e-book)

Typeset by Palimps
Falkirk, Stirlingshir

Printed digitally in tl

Then

I remember everything about the night my life changed forever. Afterwards, even when the water ran cold, I stayed slumped in the shower, the clammy tiles pressed hard against my spine. My scalding tears cooling as they trickled down my flushed cheeks. I felt the hot shame course through my veins. Shame and guilt, fear and revulsion. I soaped and scrubbed until my skin was raw, every cell tingled. I could still smell him, still feel the heat of his fetid breath against my neck, still hear his whisper in my ear.

'Lie still, bitch. You want it really. Gagging for it, aren't you?'

I remember how I tried to fight him off – lashing out, kicking and screaming. He hit me harder, swore if I didn't keep my mouth shut he'd kill me. The pain was searing anyway and so I stopped struggling, squeezed my eyes tightly closed, prayed for it just to be over quickly.

I hadn't wanted to die.

For years I wished I could be like the women I read about in newspapers. The ones who say they refuse to be a victim, that they won't let the attack ruin their life, that they won't allow the attacker to win.

But what if he does? What if you're not strong enough? What if you're terrified of leaving your home? What if you panic every time you hear a strange noise? My physical injuries faded a few months after the rape, but the mental scars remained.

After all, I lived with a permanent reminder.

ONE

Now

The clacking of stilettos on concrete sounded even louder when the girl turned into the quiet side road. At this time of night there was little competition – the occasional motor, a distant police siren, snatches of telly drifting from the odd front room. Most houses were in darkness, people tucked up in bed. Under the next street light, she checked her watch. Boy was she cutting it fine. That last vodka-lemonade might not have been the best idea in the world.

She fumbled in her coat pocket for a mint then picked up her stride. If her dad caught a whiff of booze, let alone smoke, on her breath he'd give her a hard time. Nah. She smiled. He was an old softie really, just dead protective, he'd wrap her in mink-lined cotton wool – if she let him.

She'd bet anything he'd still be up pretending to watch *Newsnight*. And her mum. They rarely went to bed without knowing she was home safe. Plus it was school in the morning and she'd promised faithfully to be back by eleven. If she didn't get a move on, Dad would ground her for at least a week, assuming he didn't kill her first. As if. Her wry smile turned into a snort and culminated in a hiccough. An old man glared at her as she walked past but, given his Alsatian was peeing up a lamppost, Granddad didn't have a leg to stand on when it came to social niceties.

Through the railings and trees she caught tantalizing glimpses of the back of her house, flashes of white brickwork; moonlight glinting off the slates. Taking a short cut across the kids' play park would make all the difference. She'd done it loads of times. On the downside, if her dad found out he'd go ballistic. He'd been even worse since the recent stories in the news, but the attacks had happened miles away on the other side of the city.

The girl heard a car slow down and slipped her phone from her pocket, making as if she was talking to a mate on the line. Out of the corner of her eye she caught the driver giving her the once-over as he cruised past. He'd know her again. And she made sure he knew she'd taken a pic. Why not? No harm in playing it safe. A girl had to be streetwise these days. Something else her dad didn't give her credit for.

Hence the white lies.

Like telling him she'd be at Natalie's tonight, revising. The nearest they'd got to anything scholarly was swapping notes on studenty-types in The Dark Horse. A cute guy, who'd invited her to a gig tomorrow, had scored top marks. She'd turned him down though – had a prior arrangement. She'd not even told Nat much about her new fella. Knowing Natalie, she'd only try and muscle in. She had some bloke anyway. Right sugar daddy, if you asked Lisa.

Bottom line was: being grounded was so not an option.

The girl glanced over her shoulder, scanned both sides of the street and slipped through a gap in the railings. She paused for a few seconds, ears pricked, then headed for the track through the trees. Under the overhang the patchy light dimmed, dipped even further when dark clouds momentarily obscured the moon. Good job she wasn't easily spooked.

The heels were a pain though, walking was even harder going on the soft earth. That problem she could remedy. Clinging to a slimy trunk with one hand, she delved in her bag. If she'd had any sense she'd have changed into the flats before getting off the bus. Should've taken off her face then, too. Another rummage produced a pack of wipes. Dad reckoned girls who wore too much make-up were asking for trouble.

She felt guilty lying to him, but really, he brought it on himself. She'd be sixteen in a few days. Not a child anymore. She had a fake ID, though bar staff rarely asked to see it – thanks to good old Rimmel. Smiling, she chucked the dirty wipe in the bushes. Bare-faced lies from now on then.

A faint creak to the left sent the hairs on the back of her neck rising. Heart racing, she glanced in the direction of the noise. She heard it again. Then made out the silhouette in the dark of a swing which was slowly swaying. She almost laughed out loud with relief. Even when she'd played on them as a nipper, the seats had been warped and the chains rusty.

Walking on she popped another mint in her mouth. The smell mingled with the scent of citrus on her skin and certainly masked the bad egg stink coming from the pond.

Hiking her bag, she picked up the pace again. She'd just spotted a light come on in the bathroom window. She'd be home before she knew it. Home and dry.

It didn't immediately occur to her to wonder how or why only one swing had been set in motion. In fact, it didn't occur to her full stop.

TWO

Early morning and a late winter frost glittered across the park like tiny shards of glass, a weak sun cast spindly shadows from a line of skeletal trees. It was no rural idyll. The traffic buzz and stench of fumes drifting from the main drag through Selly Oak shattered any natural illusions. Not that Sarah Quinn currently registered either the terrain or the extraneous noises. Indeed, the tall, blonde detective was only vaguely aware of the damp seeping through the fabric of her one-size-fits-all white forensic suit. If she'd given the spreading clamminess any thought, she'd have considered it a minor inconvenience, and little wonder given she knelt close to a small, shallow pond and the top half of a near naked body.

A middle-aged jogger had made the triple-nine call. He'd had the nous to keep his distance, not further disturb the already churned ground. The guy was now in the back of a squad car being interviewed again, this time by Sarah's partner DC Dave Harries.

The first attending officer had taken one look at the scene and requested CID backup. Like every West Midlands cop, he had Operation Panther in mind. The inquiry into a series of rapes and attempted rapes had been ongoing for more than a month, with an attack almost every week. As senior investigating officer, Sarah had her doubts – Vickie Park was off the perp's beaten track, the violence here bore little relation to what had been meted out before.

Still, open mind and all that. They had to play it by the book, this time the murder book. Even before she'd arrived the forensic corridor had been established, a more extensive outer cordon staked, its blue-and-white tape flapping desultorily, like limp bunting in a light breeze. Beyond it officers in navy blue overalls could be seen on their knees finger-tipping the grass, breathing out what looked like puffs of smoke. Closer at hand the forensic team congregated round the back of a white transit sipping coffee from steel flasks and waiting for a nod. Given the surrounding undergrowth resembled a beer garden after a stag weekend, they'd have their work cut out. And God alone knew what they might dredge up from the bottom of the pond.

Sarah smoothed her left temple. Saw a long day ahead and simultaneously glimpsed the gathering media. An advance pack of reporters and snappers watched through the railings, cameras and notebooks in hand.

Making mental notes Sarah resumed her visual examination of the slight slender body. Boyish hips and pale splayed legs were just discernible swaying gently under several inches of murky water, the trunk lay face down on wet scrubby grass, the right arm stretched full tilt over the head, the left tightly tucked in.

Irrelevant whimsical notion, but to Sarah it looked like a freeze frame of a young woman caught mid-stroke doing the front crawl. Even the dark hair plastered to the scalp resembled a bathing cap, until a closer stomach-churning look.

Sarah sat back on her heels and lifted her gaze. 'Initial thoughts, Richard?'

'There must be easier ways to make a living.' A mask covered most of the pathologist's face but there was no hint of levity in the dark eyes. Richard Patten's good looks and easy charm generally brightened a crime scene. Right now, not so much. Likely his frequent proximity to the dead had rubbed off some of the shine.

'Maybe give me a steer how she died first?' Sarah asked.

'I'll tell you one thing. She didn't get cramp skinny dipping.' Again, Patten's voice was too clipped to be glib. He'd clearly read the girl's death pose in a similar way to Sarah. 'The head injury alone was probably enough to kill her,' Patten said. 'Then there's the shock, blood loss, possible heart failure, hypothermia.'

Sarah nodded, got the picture. A piece of it at least. She watched him lift one of the waxy hands and gently cradle it in his own latexed fingers. 'Have you seen this?'

She nodded again. The girl's nails were broken, caked with blood, full of dirt. Hopefully they harboured more than that – DNA would do nicely for a start.

'She'd tried dragging herself out of there, Sarah.'

'Poor soul must've been bloody terrified.' Briefly the DI closed her eyes, pictured the young woman's final moments: attacked, fatally injured, flailing in the icy water. Begging for help that never came.

For pity's sake, woman. She urged herself to get a grip. Emotional involvement was no part of detective work. Not the way Sarah operated. Fellow cops called her the Snow Queen for a reason. Dave Harries' Mr Nice Guy approach had better not be catching. She might be closer to her DC in more ways than one nowadays – but not that close.

As Patten continued taking samples, Sarah scouted the lie of the land, took in the tatty bowling green, tired looking clubhouse, children's play area. A weathered statue of Queen Victoria that gazed down indifferently had clearly seen, and overseen, better days. Shame the old girl couldn't talk.

People living in properties overlooking the park wouldn't have that problem though and hopefully they'd have spotted something, someone. A handful of locals had already turned out for a closer butcher's. Not that they'd get past the burly uniform at the gate. But why were people such ghouls?

Wincing, Sarah shifted her weight to the other knee. She was trying to work out why the attacker had struck by the pond when there were less exposed areas close by. She glanced back at Patten.

'Could she have regained consciousness after the blow to the head? I'm thinking she might have come round, say, in those bushes.' Patten's gaze followed her pointing finger.

'She'd be disorientated, staggering about in the dark,' Sarah elaborated. 'Maybe miss her footing?' The theory sounded lame even to her ears but better, surely, than the victim knowing she'd been chucked in a scummy pond like a piece of rubbish. Not that it mattered either way. When push came to shove, she was no less dead.

'I very much doubt it.' Patten sealed some of the nail scrapings in a clear plastic bag. 'No one's going walkabout with an injury like that. Look at it.'

She shuddered, thankful again there'd been no time to grab breakfast. The back of the young woman's skull had caved in, flecks of bone like shattered eggshell. The murder weapon was no blunt instrument, more like a rock, a brick, something jagged, lethal. Whatever they were looking for had vanished along with most of the victim's clothes. An animal print skirt ridden up to her waist and a flimsy tee-shirt was all that protected what little dignity remained.

Sarah narrowed her eyes. Where were her shoes? And surely she'd worn a coat? She must've had a bag with her as well, at least a phone. The more she saw, the less likely it looked that the crime was connected to the Panther incidents. It didn't feel right, didn't fit the pattern. Could robbery be the motive? Some off-his-face smack-head desperate for cash?

On the other hand if Patten was on the money and the victim had been alive – just – and the perp had thrown her in to drown, then as well as being pretty damn callous it was a smart move. Where better – make that worse – than a stagnant pond to compromise evidence, muddy the investigation waters?

Surely the perp believed she was dead, or he'd have finished her off before leaving the scene?

'I can't do much more here.' Patten glanced up. 'Sarah?'

She frowned. 'Sorry, I was—'

'Miles away. I noticed. I need to move her now. You OK with that?' It sounded more like a warning to brace herself than a request for permission. Had he picked up on her uncharacteristic flakiness? She made a mental note: curb unguarded expressions.

'Sure. Whenever you're ready.' She stood and stepped back before turning her head at a growing clamour by the gates.

'I blame all those *CSI* programmes,' Patten muttered. 'Wouldn't you think they'd pipe down, show a bit of respect?' He beckoned one of the forensic guys over. Simon? Steve? No matter. He'd help with hauling the woman's dead weight from the water.

Frowning, Sarah glanced over at the gates again. Just what was kicking off there? The uniform looked to be in some sort of slanging match with a beefy bloke in a grey tracksuit. The way the man's fist was flying, the only place he'd be running to was the nick.

'Sarah?' Patten broke her train of thought.

Tight-lipped, she refocused. The girl lay on her back now, blue eyes gazing sightlessly at the cloudless sky. She looked younger than Sarah had first estimated. With the flawless complexion, full lips, eyelashes so long they could have been false, the girl would've matured into a real beauty.

Except some bastard had stripped her of any sort of future.

'What a waste.' Patten shook his head.

'What the hell was she doing here?' Sarah murmured.

'That's more your territory, detective.'

She hadn't expected a response and gave a distracted nod. At this stage an inquiry was little more than a shed-load of unanswered questions, the victim nothing but a blank sheet. With no ID they didn't even have a name to go on, let alone next of kin. Ducking under the tape Sarah removed the cap, peeled off the gloves, finger-combed her hair. Until not so long ago it had been waist-length, even now the close crop took her by surprise.

'Get your effing hands off me.'

She spun round to see tracksuit man hurtling across the grass shrugging off one of the search team. The guy was so focussed Sarah doubted he heard the officer's shouted warning about it being a crime scene. Gasping for breath, shoulders heaving, he halted just short of the tape horrified gaze fixed on the body.

'No. No. No. I knew it. I knew it.' He sank to his knees, pressed both hands against his cheeks.

Sarah took a step closer. 'Knew what, sir?'

THREE

Ian Webb knew the victim was his daughter, Lisa. Four days shy of her sixteenth birthday. This and the fact the family – wife, Angela; son, Anthony – lived a stone's throw from the park was all Sarah had elicited so far. She and the search guy had helped Webb stagger to one of the benches where he now sat hunched forward, elbows on knees, shaking like leaf jelly.

Perched alongside, Sarah kept close watch on the colour of his skin, the rise and fall of his chest. She gave him ten, maybe fifteen seconds before asking gently, 'When did you last see Lisa, Mr Webb?'

The starter was easy, non-judgemental. Sarah had a bunch of follow-ups that she suspected would be less so: why wasn't Lisa at home last night? Did she make a habit of staying out? Had there been a row?

He either hadn't heard or needed a prompt. 'Mr Webb—?' She watched him lace his fingers, the skin stretched tight across the knuckles looked in danger of splitting.

'This'll kill her mother.'

Sarah stifled a sigh. Not only did they need to establish Lisa's last known movements as a matter of urgency, but the girl's death wasn't doing much for her father's health. Ian Webb didn't strike her as cardiac arrest material, but you could never tell. She thought he probably needed a doctor, but any delay in questioning could further harm the inquiry. The killer already had several hours start on the squad.

Glancing up, she spotted Harries cutting across the grass heading their way. The bounce in his step might mean he'd had more joy with the jogger than she'd so far found with the father, but then Dave's youthful enthusiasm was still intact, not to mention his passion for the job – and her. She masked a smile, not hard when she looked back at Webb.

'I know it's difficult, sir, but I really need some answers.' Even the questions she'd posed hadn't been addressed. Delaying tactics? Deep shock? Unlike his breathing, which was shallow and ragged. In the impasse she studied the man a little further: late forties/early fifties, thick black hair with the merest hint of grey, broad shoulders, strapping build, meaty fists, well able to look after himself.

Diminished now by feeling he'd failed to look out for his daughter?

'Mr Webb? We can talk here, or I can get a colleague to run you home, while—' *I get out of this gear.*

'Did she drown?' He made eye contact for the first time. 'Is that how she died?' His penetrating gaze searched her face for answers, the red-rimmed bloodshot eyes held a plea as did the voice.

Childless herself, Sarah supposed that for parents a son or daughter dying in an accident would be the slightly lesser of two evils. But this man surely knew she couldn't supply the assurance he patently craved. Though he probably hadn't seen Lisa's head wound, the near naked body was more than telling.

'I'm afraid not, Mr Webb. The evidence suggests she was attacked from behind and that she died from her injuries.'

'Not Lisa? Not my poor baby?' He held Sarah's gaze, didn't flinch when a back-firing car startled crows from treetop nests, sending them screeching and circling in the still air. Webb shook his head, probably trying to dispel unspeakable images playing in his mind's eye. 'Please say it's not her.'

She couldn't and he knew it. His first words on seeing the body told her that. 'I'm so sorry for your loss, Mr Webb.'

She spotted Dave in conversation with one of the search team. Why the hell didn't he get a move on? The sooner they got shot of Webb from the crime scene the better. She watched him drop his head in his hands, heard quiet sobbing. The guy seemed in a daze as well as in total denial. Truth, as the DI knew, could take a while to hit home. Anger generally came later too.

'DI Quinn?'

She stayed Harries with a raised finger and a mouthed, 'One min—'

Webb suddenly grabbed her arm. 'You said "attacked"?' He'd straightened now, faced her head-on, dashed away a tear. 'Did he . . .? Was she . . .?'

She knew what he wasn't saying – most parents couldn't or wouldn't voice the big question, the greatest fear. She cleared her throat but before even opening her mouth, he tightened his grip.

'Did the lowlife rape her? Tell me, God damn it.'

'Sir.' Dave took a step forward.

'It's fine, DC Harries,' Sarah said.

Clearly Webb wasn't most parents. She'd read the sequence of emotional fall-out wrong, too. The guy's anger had surfaced within minutes.

'Well, did he?'

'It's too early to say. We need to—' She struggled not to wince when the grip on her arm tightened again.

'The minute you know for sure – you tell me. Got that?' His tongue flicked spittle from his fleshy lips. 'And I don't want my wife to know. Right?'

Or what? Calmly, she gazed down at the offending hand.

'Let her go.' Harries took another step forward. 'Now.'

'OK. OK. Keep your hair on lad.' Webb snatched the hand away, wiped it across his mouth. 'But look, love, promise me you won't say anything to Angie if . . . you know.'

'I can't make any promises, Mr Webb.' Hopefully it wouldn't come to that, but nailing the killer was Sarah's top priority not sparing anyone's finer feelings and that included the mother's.

She rose. 'DC Harries will take you home now.'

Webb stood, too, towered over her. 'I'd rather you were there.'

Given Sarah's six-foot height she rarely looked up to people. 'Oh?'

'I don't think I can do it.'

Do what? As if she didn't know.

FOUR

Shoot the messenger? Sarah had delivered bad news often enough but never actually taken a bullet. Verbal abuse, sure, the occasional stinging slap, but more often than not she'd witnessed the suddenly bereaved slip into a silent stupor of shocked disbelief. Given Ian Webb's barely-contained panic in the car on the way over, Sarah had anticipated hysteria from his wife if not total collapse. She'd been wrong on both counts.

Clutching the lapels of a purple terry dressing gown, a vacant looking Mrs Webb had heard Sarah out, then drifted down the hall towards a room at the back of the sizeable semi. Bemused, the detectives had tailed along and now stood watching while she filled the kettle and prattled on about drinks.

Sarah's quick scan took in pastel pinks and creams, Cath Kidston accessories and a shelf full of Delia cookbooks. Shot glasses drained in the rack suggesting the Webbs were partial to a nightcap. When she looked back, Angela Webb had a damp cloth in her hand and was flicking it over surfaces shiny enough to see your face in.

Facing facts was clearly more of a stretch for the woman.

'Sit down, Inspector.' Ian Webb pulled a wheel-back chair from under the pine table. 'And you, lad.'

The boy wonder – as he was known at work – bristled a touch but did as bid. 'It's DC Harries, sir.'

Sarah's mental smile fled fast when she glanced at the wall clock. Despite the record-quick gear change and rapid issue of tasks to squad members in the park, it was almost a quarter to eight. Time pressed and every second counted. The Webbs wouldn't see it that way, of course. For them, it was already too late.

'Leave it, Angie.' Ian Webb patted the place next to him. 'Come on, love, sit down.'

'That's Lisa's. You know she hates anyone sitting there.'

Sarah glanced at Harries whose right eyebrow rose a gnat's.

'The police need to talk to us, love.'

Reaching for a cupboard door she asked if they wanted tea or coffee. Sarah gave Harries a subtle nod.

'Here you go, Mrs Webb.' Standing, he offered his seat. 'Let me sort that while you—'

'You don't know where anything is,' she snapped. 'Besides you're bound to make a mess and . . . what if . . . what if you break something?' Her brittle voice cracked and in the sudden silence Lisa's death at last seemed to register.

Sarah saw Mrs Webb's eyes well up, noticed how the irises were almost the same sky-blue shade as her daughter's. The likeness didn't stop there – hair colour, slight frame, delicate features, only the dry lined complexion marked her out as the mother.

'Where is she?' Suddenly galvanized the woman chucked the cloth towards the sink, strode towards Sarah. 'I want to see her.' Tears trickled unchecked down both cheeks.

'Mrs Webb. I think you'd be better off sit—'

'No. She needs me.' She glanced down, noticed the dressing gown. 'I can't go anywhere like this.'

Mr Webb restrained her as she headed for the door. 'Love, there's nothing—'

'Don't "nothing" me,' she yelled, shook his hand off her arm. 'You said she could go out. If she'd stayed home, she wouldn't be . . .' Gasping for air she flopped into the chair, hands clamped down on her thighs presumably to stop them shaking.

'That's so unfair, Angie.' He sounded calm, almost cold.

'I'll tell you what's not fair—'

'Both of you,' Sarah raised her voice. *For crying out loud.* 'Whoever killed Lisa is still out there. I want him behind bars. Fast. As in yesterday. This isn't helping.'

She caught Harries tighten his lips, presumably in disapproval at her unminced words. Tough. Watching the Webbs sit round arguing the toss was a spectator sport she could live without.

'Ask him.' Mrs Webb jabbed a thumb in the air. 'He knows everything.'

Sarah didn't bother stifling a sigh. 'I need you to tell me where Lisa went last night, who she was with.' They had to have a starting point before they could take the inquiry anywhere. 'Well?' *In your own time.*

They'd had dinner around six, he said, then he'd dropped her at a friend's. Natalie Hinds. Apparently the girls were best mates and often revised together.

'Lisa's very bright.' Mrs Webb piped up. 'A*s in all her mocks.' The smile was fleeting. Sarah didn't pick her up on the tense – grammar wouldn't be the first thing on her mind. She asked instead for Natalie's address, phone number. Dave glanced up from his pad, needed the number repeating.

Sarah slipped her coat off, hung it over the back of the chair. Was it just her or was the room uncomfortably hot? 'Were you expecting her home?'

Webb bridled at that. 'Course we were. We never let her have sleepovers on school nights. I told her eleven o'clock on the dot.'

'How was she getting back?'

'She said Natalie's mum'd give her a lift.' It had happened once or twice before, he told them, though Webb usually acted as chauffeur both ways. Sarah clocked Dave's subtle thumbs up, which meant he'd texted the Hinds' details to the squad room.

'And when Lisa didn't arrive?' Sarah prompted.

'I swear I heard a car pull up and Lisa come in the front door. About ten past eleven.' He pinched the bridge of his nose. 'I was in bed to tell the truth. I'd had a splitting head all day.'

Mrs Webb had gone up even earlier – took a sleeping pill and went out, as she put it, like a light. The detectives exchanged glances.

'So neither of you actually saw or spoke to her?' Sarah asked.

Webb picked at a loose piece of skin round his thumb. His wife slapped a hand to her mouth as if she was about to throw up.

Sarah took both gestures as a no. 'OK.' She hoped she'd not stretched the syllables a tad too long.

'What's that supposed to mean?' Webb clearly knew where
she was coming from. 'Are you suggesting—?'

'I'm suggesting nothing.' Her icy stare would probably
have quelled further argument, she raised a hand anyway.
'So how and when did you realize your daughter hadn't
come home?'

Mr Webb always took Lisa tea in bed. 'I popped my head
round the door at seven as per and could tell the bed hadn't
been slept in.' He'd charged into the room, missed his footing
and the cup slipped through his fingers. His wife muttered
something about mess. 'For Christ's sake, woman, give it a
rest. Lisa's . . .'

Sarah cleared her throat. 'What did you do then?'

'I knew she wasn't in the bathroom. I checked the lounge
– in case she'd fallen asleep watching telly. I mean I knew
she hadn't really but . . .' Sighing, he dragged a hand through
his mop of hair. 'Anyway, I ran back to the bedroom pulled
on some clothes and when I drew the curtains I saw your lot
crawling over the park. I just knew . . .'

Sixth sense? Father's intuition? She let it go for the moment.
'Were you awake, Mrs Webb?'

She sniffed. 'I heard him banging about but I was tired,
fancied a lie-in. I don't work Fridays.'

So no one had yet had a word with Natalie or her parents.
'Dave, can you give the Hinds a quick bell? Outside, please.'

She waited until he closed the back door then: 'Tell me
about Lisa. Did she have a boyfriend?'

Webb's head shot up. 'She can't be doing with that sort of
thing. Nor Nat. They're more into books than boys, aren't they,
Angie? Besides, our Lisa's only fifteen and she doesn't even
look that.'

'Mrs Webb?' Sarah's cocked eyebrow queried his assertion
as much as asked for Mrs Webb's insight.

'Dunno.' She shrugged but Sarah made mental note of the
woman's fleeting eye contact.

'OK but either way I'm going to need a recent photograph.'
Releasing a pic to the media was the quickest way to get
witnesses, intelligence, pointers. Had its downsides too of
course, and when Angela Webb groaned and dropped her head

in her hands she was probably seeing one: her daughter's face plastered across the nation's tabloids and TV screens while the body mouldered on a slab in the morgue.

'Will this do?' Three heads swivelled to the doorway where a young man stood holding a colour pic. 'I heard you as I came downstairs.' Sarah pursed her lips, wondered what else he'd heard.

'You took it about a month ago, didn't you, Dad?'

'Thanks, Ant. Yeah, you're right.'

Given the youth's dark colouring and pale complexion he couldn't be anyone else, but why hadn't Webb mentioned his son was in the house? Sarah studied the guy as he stepped into the room. Late teens? Early twenties? Classic features that currently looked carved out of stone. He moved with an easy confidence but she noted a slight tremor when he handed the photograph to his father.

Ian Webb's expression softened as he ran his gaze over it. 'We were in town. I'd taken her shopping for a few bits and bobs.' Lisa's long dark locks had lifted in a breeze revealing her lovely heart-shaped face, perfect smile. 'She had her hair cut the next day, didn't she, Ange?'

Mrs Webb gave a tight-lipped nod, her glance flicked to Anthony who was leaning against the fridge, arms tightly crossed. Unsmiling, he held Sarah's gaze. 'All I care is that it helps catch Lisa's killer. It's the only thing that matters.'

That probably answered the question about how long he'd been ear-wigging. *So why hadn't he joined the party before?*

'The necklace?' Sarah asked. 'Did she wear it a lot?' The long silver chain carried letters that spelt out her name.

'We bought it for her birthday last year,' Webb said. 'She loves it. Hardly ever takes it off.'

Sarah frowned. It looked as if someone had. 'Did she have it on last night?'

'Far as I know.' Webb nodded. 'Does that mean—?'

'Boss. A word.' Dave had popped his head round the door.

She stifled a sigh. Talk about timing. She was about to remonstrate when she clocked his clenched jaw and the glint in his eye. Whatever he'd learned she'd swear it wasn't good news.

FIVE

'Shit. Shit. Shit.' Sarah ran a hand through her hair. Natalie Hinds hadn't returned home either. The mother only discovered the girl was missing when Harries' call prompted her to nip upstairs and check. The woman was in bits when she came back on the phone. Dave assured her he'd have officers there within minutes, his earlier text meant a squad car had been en route anyway.

Just for a second or two as she heard Harries out Sarah fantasized about having a nice simple job. Nuclear physicist would be good.

'What do you want to do boss? Stick around here or go on to Stirchley?' He slipped the phone back in his jacket pocket. The black leather looked distressed. Sarah knew how it felt.

'Hold on a min.' She frowned. 'You said Natalie didn't go home last night, but they were supposed to be there revising.'

'Revising, yes. But Natalie told her mum she was going to Lisa's house to do it. She called home just before eleven and asked if she could stay over. Mrs Hinds thought no more about it till just now.'

'Great. Can't think why I was so worried.' Sarah wrapped both arms round her waist wishing she'd grabbed her coat on the way out. The Webbs' back lawn looked as if it had been iced. Eyes narrowed, she tried getting her head round the turn of events. Had Natalie and Lisa cooked up a cock and bollocks story so they could go out on the razz? Hook up with a couple of fellas? What was that song about girls and fun? If it panned out that way then Webb's assertion they were more bookworm than bloke fancier looked pretty dead in the water. She grimaced. *So well put.*

'Problem, boss?'

'Take a sheet of A4,' she drawled, deadpan.

'Hey come on, it's early days.' Smiling he reached out a hand that didn't quite make it to her arm. 'It's not like you to—'

'Back off.' Nothing even remotely personal to emerge at work. It was what they'd agreed. She'd stipulated it even before the fledgling relationship took a test flight. Right now he was dangerously close to crash landing it.

'My bad, boss. It's just—'

La la la. 'Who's heading out to Stirchley?'

Brief pause then: 'Shona and Jed.'

Venus and Mars. Double great. As far as she was concerned the detective constables came from different policing planets. Shona Bruce could talk a jammed clam into telling you its life story; Jed Holmes was no Sherlock and had the empathy of a wilted lettuce.

'So where's Beth then?' Beth Lally, Shona's customary sidekick.

'Called in sick.'

Again? She'd have to have a word. Mind you, if Sarah didn't get inside soon, she reckoned she'd catch her death. She swept her gaze over the back of the house, clocked three upstairs windows that would give a decent overview of the park. Soon as they'd questioned the Webbs again, she'd have a shufti. Take a look at Lisa's room at the same time. The inquiry surface had barely been scratched and layers were already building up.

'Shona's more than capable, boss.'

'Got that right.' Brucie's competence compensated for No-Shit Sherlock's lackings. Plus Sarah knew she had to delegate more, she'd been told enough times. Fred Baker might not be boss these days but it didn't stop him handing down pearls of wisdom from his high horse. She curved a lip. Now he'd retired she quite missed the old boy. On the other hand he still gave her the benefit of his infinite knowledge when they met for drinks. Tried, anyway.

'Give Twig a bell, Dave. Get him to arrange a news conference for, say, 10.30. Till then, we'll crack on here. As priorities go, Natalie Hinds is still a MISPER.' Missing person not murder victim. Please God, let it stay that way.

He tapped a salute. 'Makes sense, boss.'

''Bout the only thing that does,' she muttered, heading for the door.

It beggared belief two teenage girls might've been killed within the space of a few hours, virtually on the same patch. And time-wise surely the same perp couldn't be responsible? Mind, if two crazies were roaming what looked like Birmingham's increasingly mean streets . . . Sarah swallowed hard, wondered if this was how it felt when you were out of your depth. She really didn't want to go there right now.

With a new boss on the block she needed a collar pretty damn quick, or she might find her neck there too.

'She can't be in two places at once, guv.' DS Paul Wood – known to one and almost all at the nick as Twig – had dropped by the new chief super's domain to bring him up to speed. Picking up the phone would've been quicker but the squad's office manager reckoned the boss might appreciate the personal touch, especially as he was still finding his feet. Wood's desire to have a sneaky nose round had nothing to do with it of course. He'd clocked the full-length mirror straight away. Difficult to miss, even with Detective Chief Superintendent Charles Starr standing in front of it.

'I'm sure DI Quinn has hidden . . . depths.' Their glances met in the glass and Starr gave a tight smile. The less charitable might call it a snide smirk. The guy didn't half remind Twig of someone. It had been bugging him all week, but he was buggered if he could remember who.

Satisfied with the hairdo, Starr tucked the comb in a pocket of his sharp dark suit then nodded towards a highly-polished three-sided mahogany desk. 'Take a seat, detective.'

Detective? Very NYPD. Twig took in a few more extras as he walked across the carpet to an upright chair. The gleaming red Gaggia on top of a filing cabinet hadn't come cheap. Nor the executive recliner. Very eau de coffee et leather. Starr might only have been at Lloyd House five minutes – OK, five days – but as far as Twig could see he'd certainly made himself at home.

'So what you're really saying is I'll have to take the brief.' Starr sat back in the chair, fingers steepled under his chin.

The veteran DS bit back a response about generally saying what he meant. Benefit, doubt and all that.

'Someone needs to, guv. Sarah's up against it at the mo.' She'd already asked Twig to step in.

'Want to know the first secret of being a successful SIO?' Starr cocked his head. Paused. In the impasse, Wood – who was a good twenty years older – reckoned Starr would struggle to teach him anything, and as for the patronising . . . water off a duck's backside. Starr's predecessor Fred Baker was a past master.

'Enlighten me, sir.' He had to stop himself winking.

'Delegate, delegate, delegate.'

Not a million miles from buck pass, buck pass, buck pass. Wood gave a sage nod. 'I guess prioritising's in there as well, eh?' He rolled a shirt sleeve up a beefy arm. 'The crime scene's relatively fresh and Sarah's pretty hands-on. She prefers working a grid to being a desk . . .' *Whoops.*

'Jockey?' Starr flashed a smile so fulsome it had to be fake. 'There's more to the job, DS Wood, than getting your hands dirty.'

'Couldn't agree more, sir.' Not talking down to the troops helped.

'Good. You're office manager, aren't you? On top of detail and all that. You stand in for DI Quinn. I have to be at a meeting in five minutes.' The grey silk tie he now smoothed was a shade or two lighter than his eyes. 'I'm only surprised she didn't ask you herself.'

'She did.' As Twig stood, his glance fell on a bulky file: **West Midlands Police and Crime Commission – Strategic Policing and the Community**. *Bollock-speak for sodding politics.*

'I'd best let you get on with it, sir.' Then it dawned and Twig masked a grin as he turned to leave. The 'delegate, delegate, delegate' should have given it away sooner. A tad taller maybe, but the smarmy geezer could be Tony Blair's bloody double. Well, Blair back in the day when things could only get better. Yeah. Well that worked.

'One thing, detective.'

Already at the door, Twig turned again. 'Sir?'

'First names for senior officers? I'm not hot on it.' Never mind the eyes, Starr's smile barely reached a lip. 'Full ranks in future, there's a good chap.'

Wood saluted, but then, he couldn't trust himself to speak. His footsteps down the corridor were eloquent enough.

As he rose, Starr gave his first genuine smile. He tucked the file under an elbow, straightened the remaining papers and lined up a pen with the edges. Standing back to admire the result, he reckoned it wouldn't take long to knock the squad into shape. Baker had let it get slack and though Starr knew how to play the lip service game, at the end of the day, Quinn was a woman. For running a team of detectives you needed a sure touch, a safe pair of hands.

And balls.

SIX

'Get the fuck off my property, sleaze bag.' Ian Webb's screamed command carried upstairs loud, if not exactly clear. Partway through searching Lisa's bedroom, Sarah and Harries paused and exchanged what-the-hell glances.

Muffled low voice, male. 'Please, sir, there's really no need for . . .' Scuffle sounds. More effing and blinding.

Sarah made it to the window just in time to see a meaty fist fly. *Ouch.* 'He's only gone and landed one, Dave.' Grimacing she turned back to find the room empty: her DC had done a runner. Sarah took the stairs two at a time to find Webb struggling to get out of Harries' arm lock and a youngish fit-looking guy getting to his feet, gingerly rubbing a hand down his left cheek.

'That really wasn't necessary. I only want to help.'

'Vermin. The lot of you.' Webb's spittle missed the guy's face by a gnat's nose hair.

Fitty tightened his lips. 'I'm just trying to do my job.'

'Job? Don't make me laugh. You're all muck-raking pieces of shit.'

Journalist then. Sarah stifled a sigh. Faecal matter or not, in a case like this the cops needed the media on board. 'DC

Harries, perhaps you'd . . .?' *Take Webb somewhere to cool down.* Moving into the vacated space, she held the guy's gaze. 'I'm DI Sarah Quinn.' She ignored his extended hand. 'You are?'

'Mark. Mark Slater. *Birmingham News.* I guess I asked for that.' Still rubbing the cheek he gave a wry smile to which she also failed to respond. In close-up she realized she'd seen him before at one of the Panther news conferences. If she recalled right he'd sat towards the back taking copious notes while more hardened looking hacks fired questions. She did a quick scout over his shoulder. It looked like he was a lone wolf today.

'How come you got here so fast, Mr Slater?'

'I'm on what you might call "home ground".' He'd not long moved to a place in Hyde Street, he said. Sarah knew it well but didn't react. An old . . . acquaintance . . . had a house there. The detective and the TV news reporter Caroline King went back a long way, but the term friend was too strong for a relationship that had more spikes than a porcupine in a cactus doing cross stitch. King had now started churning out books on real crime as a side line, but in either capacity she could hack off Sarah like no one else on the planet.

'Anyway.' Slater offered another smile. 'I saw the police activity as I was driving into work.'

She cocked her head. *Lucky you.* It still didn't explain his foot in this particular door. Either way she was about to burst his bubble. 'There's a news conference at headquarters. Half ten. I have nothing to say until then.' Stepping back she made to go inside, almost trod on Harries' toecaps.

'Sure about that, DI Quinn?' The reporter's raised, and what looked like recently plucked, eyebrow reinforced his question. The soft voice held an edge. Not cocky, almost flirtatious. The guy was tasty, but if he really thought she'd bite . . .

'Something wrong with your hearing?' Harries stepped forward sounding seriously unimpressed.

He could've been the invisible man as far as Slater was concerned. 'It's entirely up to you, DI Quinn. Only this isn't

the first door I knocked. And when I say I want to help . . .'
Smiling he pulled a notebook from his jacket pocket. 'I've
found you a witness.'

'Never let the facts spoil a good fairy story, eh?' Harries tapped
a tetchy finger on the wheel. The detectives had just questioned
Slater's putative witness and were now haring back to HQ to
make the start of the news conference.

Slightly distracted, Sarah scrolled through messages on
her phone, paused when she hit the latest from Shona: she's
still missing. The .jpg showed Natalie Hinds in school
uniform: black shoulder-length hair, mandatory teenage pout.
The media had been issued with both the pic and a police
appeal for information along the lines: Have you seen this
. . . Not a peep so far. Nothing from the police Twitter feed
and Facebook page either. Sarah pursed her lips. *No news is
good news?*

The bigger question was whether Natalie's absence had any
connection with Lisa's murder. Scrub that. The really big
question was whether either or both incidents had links to
Operation Panther. Sarah sighed, she had her doubts but Starr
was in overall charge. If he thought differently he might decide
the workload was too big for one SIO.

'Is that a no comment?' Harries asked. 'Or didn't you hear?'

She flapped a hand. 'I'm not deaf, Dave. I think your view's
a touch harsh.'

'Come on, boss.' He reached to tweak the heater. 'Pretty
boy reporter acted like the old guy had spotted the perp up to
his armpits in blood.'

Whereas what they'd actually gleaned from Eric Havers had
been more by way of character assassination – the victim's.
Havers, a pensioner who lived in a poky end-terrace a couple
of streets from the park, had been out exercising his dog just
before eleven last night when he encountered a girl who was
probably Lisa walking down Sycamore Avenue. 'Girl' and
'walking' weren't Havers' terms. He'd used 'slut' and 'staggering
all over the pavement'.

Which, again, was at complete odds with how the Webbs
perceived their daughter.

Sarah slipped the phone in her coat pocket. 'Didn't take to him much, did you, Dave?'

'Slater or Havers?' He didn't wait for clarification. 'Now you come to mention it – both.'

Mind, she could've given Havers a tongue-lashing when he started banging on about 'women with skirts up to their arse asking for it'. The fact he recalled the skirt's material as animal print suggested he'd had more than an eyeful. Though when he'd studied the girl's photograph, Havers couldn't identify it a hundred per cent as Lisa's.

'Yeah, well, Havers was right out of order.' Dave gave one of his telling sniffs. 'I s'pose the crap he came out with is a generational thing.'

What? She cut an incredulous glance. 'So in your book it's only bigoted old gits who write off people on the basis of how they look?'

'Hello? That's not what I said.'

'Good. Because not only would that be totally out of order, it'd really piss me off. *Pretty boy.*' Talk about pot and kettle. His words had proved her point though: age gave no clue to anyone's deep-seated prejudices whether against women, gays, skin tone, religion or class. Smart-arses just knew how to cover their Non-PC backs better.

'Well that put me in my place, didn't it?' The smile in his voice was still in situ when they exchanged glances.

'Yeah. The naughty step.' Smiling too, she shook her head. With dark glossy hair a tad too long these days and those finely honed cheek bones, Dave still put her in mind of a youngish Keith Richards. Maybe that partly explained his antipathy towards the reporter. Slater could only be in his early twenties and in the looks department was in a class of his own – despite Ian Webb's cack-handed bid at rearranging his face. Good job it had been a glancing blow – and not just for the reporter. Webb could probably get by without an assault charge.

Was the guy always so handy with his fists? Frowning, Sarah made a mental note then checked her watch as Dave pulled into the car park at the back of Lloyd House. The racket from the handbrake prompted a wince from her. Little wonder she didn't often let Dave get his mitts on the Audi. Gathering her bits she made a sharp exit hoping there'd be time to grab at least coffee before kick-off.

Dave chucked the fob her way as they weaved through the police vehicles. 'Y'know boss, I still don't see what was in it for Slater.'

She shrugged. 'Angling for a scoop, wasn't he? You scratch my quid pro quo back.'

'That worked then.' Holding the door open, he offered a lazy smile. 'I'd say Mr Backscratcher ended up with a bit more than he bargained for.'

Got that right. In more ways than one. Her vague suspicion had been confirmed when she'd casually asked Slater what number on Hyde Street he'd moved into. Sarah curved a lip. As his new landlady, Caroline King would definitely take no prisoners.

SEVEN

After casually spooning cappuccino into her mouth, Caroline King de-frothed her lips with a practised flick of the tongue. The sometime writer of real crime books sat across a table in Starbucks from a guy who'd spent most of his life fighting it. Fellow clientele in the New Street coffee bar was mostly the shop-till-you-drop variety, plus the odd JK Rowling wannabee tippety-tapping at a laptop. Caroline, dressed to kill – as per – in a snazzy red, black and white ensemble was on full charm offensive. Fred Baker – Sarah's old school ex-boss, the erstwhile Detective Chief Superintendent – was on his second croissant. Elevenses. The reporter's treat.

'I go stir crazy when I'm stuck in the house all day. How do you put up with it, Mr B?'

'Not still chasing tips are we, Kingie? 'Cause if this is a sweetener . . .?' He winked as he shovelled in the last bite of croissant then helped himself to the Danish pastry going begging on her plate.

'I'd be in trouble with the law?' She laughed, tossed an artful head. 'No, this isn't a bribe.'

His mouth was too full for a comeback. His belly must be getting that way, too. Not that he needed to watch his weight these days. Baker's natty charcoal suit – his wardrobe could double as a branch of Hugo Boss – looked pretty roomy to Caroline. She even spotted cheek bones making their debut as he chewed.

'Come on then, Lois Lane, You can't be after a scoop. I heard you chucked your notebook in the bin, got yourself a proper job.'

'Best-selling author, me.' She flashed a wide smile. Best-seller was pushing it but then, Caroline never sold herself short. 'Mind, you know what they say, Mr B . . . once a journo – always a journo. Cut me – I'd bleed Quink.' Holding his gaze, she took a sip of coffee. 'Must be the same for cops? Always sizing people up? Always sit back to the wall? Constantly on the lookout for the bad boys?'

'Mebbe.' He turned his mouth down. 'But don't get carried away. There's a world o' difference twixt thee and me, lass.'

One big difference for sure, and she didn't mean his sudden shit Yorkshire accent. Caroline's in-house incarceration was self-imposed and short-term: she had a book to finish and a fast approaching deadline. Fred Baker's enforced form of house arrest had been down to a deadline that, for the time being at least, had receded. His prostate cancer was in remission, the on-going radiation treatment clearly working. On the other hand, she reckoned the old boy's health had definitely been ruder. Then again so had the old boy. He must be on his best behaviour.

'Why you going all northern on me, Mr B?' She watched him gather errant crumbs then lick his fingers.

'You wanted to know how I stay sane stuck between four walls?'

She was after something a damn sight more interesting than that, but no harm humouring him. 'Go on then. What's your secret?'

'Last o' the Summer Wine.' Another wink. 'I'm glued – re-runs every afternoon. Ee, by gum, 'appy as a pig in muck, me.'

She rolled her eyes. 'Course you are.' *Pig in something.* Just who was playing who here? He'd no more watch daytime

telly than appear on it. Still: gander, goose, beat, join. 'So
where's t'flat cap and that ferret o' yours, then?'

'In't pigeon loft.' Another wink. Unless he'd developed a
twitch. 'Mind, any time you want to stroke my ferret, lass,
you have only to ask.'

'Charm personified you, Mr B.'

'Get it right, Lois, call yourself a reporter? You left out the
wit, the humour, the good looks, the stunning intellect. Get
you another?'

She nodded, curved a lip as she watched him amble to the
counter. His six-foot frame looked to have developed a slight
stoop and the broad white badger-streak in his dark mop of
hair stood out even more noticeably. Nothing seemed amiss
with the old grey cells though. She reckoned Baker was still
as sharp as a filed tack. With little to fill his days – how long
would that last? She couldn't see crosswords doing it for him,
not after crime grids.

Masking a smile she reached for her Gucci bag, rummaged
round for a mirror. Baker was oblivious right now anyway,
blithely chatting up a blonde yummy mummy behind
him in the queue. Caroline touched up the scarlet lippie,
patted her dark sleek bob, not that there was a hair out
of place.

'Looking good, kid.' Baker placed a tray on the table. 'You
always put me in mind of that Hepburn woman.'

'Audrey?'

'Nah, the other one.' He rolled his eyes. 'Course, I mean
Audrey. Anyway Kingie, enough of the chit-chat, cut to the
chase. What you after?'

'Mr B?' Mock-piqued, she pouted. 'Can't a girl—?'

His withering look silenced her, as did the pain au chocolat
pointing her way. 'Girl? Christ, if I called you that I'd never
hear the last of it.'

'Fair enough.' She offered a lop-sided smile.

'So?'

'I just want to see how you're doing, is all.'

'Bollocks.'

'That's nice, isn't it?'

'There's always a sub text with you, Kingie. So give.'

'Mr B. How could you?' She widened her eyes as he pushed the chair back.

'When you decide to stop patronising and pissing around – let me know, yeah?'

'I'm stopping now, OK. Sit down.' Business-like bordering on brusque. He raised an eyebrow. 'Please, Fred.'

She waited until he was back in the chair then leaned across the table and lowered her voice. 'I need your help. I'm contracted to write a book about rape. Something new, something ground-breaking. The definitive work examining the issue from both perp and victim point of view.'

'Good luck with that.' He dunked the pastry in an Americano.

'I'm serious, Fred. I want to find out what drives men to it. The impact on victims, fall-out on families.'

'Read the rag mags.'

'Been there, done that. It's nowhere near enough.' She needed in-depth exclusive interviews with men and women, both sides of the story, laid bare.

'And you're telling me why?'

'Come on, Fred. I shouldn't need to spell it out.' Christ. How many years had he spent collaring scumbags?

'I imagine you want case histories, intros, talking heads?'

'Exactly.' Plus wheels-oiled, doors opened.

'Google it. There's a shed load of stuff on—'

'All done to death. I want original material. Nuanced. Maybe people whose cases never even got to court.'

'Yeah, sure.' He sniffed. 'Must be a bunch of them hanging around dying to tell the world every sordid detail.'

'It's cathartic, Fred, gives people closure.'

'It's codswallop, King, that's what it is.'

'It's so not, Fred.' Was he even listening anymore? She stifled a sigh. This was going nowhere. If not for the deadline, she wouldn't even bother. But getting Baker to dig round while she worked on the current book meant when she was free, she could hit the ground running. 'Trust me. I'll get them to talk. I just need you to find them.'

'Do your own dirty legwork.'

Baker-brick-wall wasn't going to budge. No use banging her head any more. 'Sod you then.' She stood and grabbed her bag. She could maybe press gang her new housemate into lending a hand. Mark Slater was considerably easier on the eye than Baker and, she reckoned, almost certainly easier to manipulate – scrub that – *cajole* into temporary lackey-dom. Besides, it'd be a two-way thing: the cub reporter's investigative skills needed honing.

'Hold your horses, Kingie.' Waving her down with a free hand Baker added a quip, 'Or should that be your hacks?'

She masked a smile, certainly wouldn't mind handling Markie. And she'd no intention of sitting down. 'I'm wasting time here, Fred. Told you, I'm chasing a deadline.'

'How much?'

Time? She frowned. 'Delivery date's three weeks.'

'Not that.' His tone suggested he'd just stopped short of adding 'Dumbo'. 'I'm talking . . .' His thumb rubbing across his finger mimed *cash*.

'You want paying?' She managed to stifle a gasp. 'I thought you'd jump at the chance. That it'd be—'

'Doing me a favour? Yeah, right. Don't make me laugh, Lois. Look, I think the idea stinks, the book's a non-starter and you'll never get it off the ground. But who knows? Either way, if you want my insider knowledge and expertise, it don't come cheap.'

She held his gaze, tapped her lip, ran a few calculations. 'How much?'

'Now you're talking.' The Baker wink was back big time. 'Best sit down, lass.'

Patronising git. Even so, Caroline gave a thin smile. 'Yes, boss. No, boss. Three bags full . . .'

EIGHT

DCS Starr stopped pacing and loomed over Sarah's desk, simultaneously fiddling with a heavy gold cufflink. 'I want the perpetrator behind bars pretty damn quick.'

She clocked the signet ring on his pinkie as well and realized the last time she'd seen anyone sporting that combo, it had been the heir to the throne. Maybe Charles Starr was a closet royalist.

'I think that goes without saying don't you, sir?' Calm, cool. Condescending? *Tough.* It *went* without saying even before the pathologist's call confirming Lisa Webb had been raped pre-mortem. Still craving caffeine Sarah was running late and could do without lectures, let alone self-aggrandizing crap. Every officer in the West Midlands wanted a result and, unlike the newbie head honcho, they'd been working their bollocks off for weeks trying to collar the bastard.

'What is it now?' Starr asked. 'Four rapes, one murder and a missing girl?'

Get it right, man. Rising, Sarah gathered several files and her notes for the news conference. 'I'm about to run through the detail with the media. Perhaps you'd like to sit in?' He definitely needed the up-sum.

'I'll leave that in your more than capable hands, DI Quinn.'

Weasel words? She held his gaze slightly longer than necessary, read only insouciance there. 'I need to get on, sir.' She nodded towards the door. 'But bear in mind there's still no proof the crimes are down to a single offender.'

'It's your job to get proof.' Tight smile.

'And if it's not there?'

Holding the door, he gave a little bow. 'I have every faith in you.'

She heard his tacit, *my dear.* Sailing past head held high she told herself it was a damn good job he'd not voiced it.

Sarah tapped a pen on the conference table to get the hacks' attention. Still standing she did a rough count. Disappointing. Only twelve had turned out plus a regional telly crew with its lens already trained on a recently extended line-up of near life-size colour photographs. Lisa Webb's now added to those of the three previous sex attack victims. Within the last few hours all had waived anonymity, even the women who'd been raped. Though the police invariably withheld ID's in sex cases,

Sarah hoped releasing the names would boost what had become flagging press interest.

As for Natalie Hinds? The missing girl's image was in the public domain on news bulletins, web sites and social media. But unless Shona Bruce had worked magic and was even now driving the girl's mother in to the nick, Sarah had decided to hold back the possible connection with Lisa's murder. A mother's heartfelt appeal on camera would pack more punch than anything any cop came out with. Sarah glanced at the wall clock, reckoned there was still time for Mrs Hinds to show. Fingers crossed.

After taking a sip of coffee – *Thanks Dave, you're a star* – the DI picked up a pointer then strode towards the display. Pin drop silence. No preamble. Making the pointer live up to its name, she walked along the line pausing at each picture. 'Hannah Winter. Zoe Darby. Jessica Silk. Lisa Webb.'

Frowning she was struck by a thought that should have occurred before: the women's height, build, hair colour all differed widely. Yet broadly speaking a serial sex attacker targets a specific type: women with similar physical characteristics. Apart from gender, these women had very little in common. Could there be a link she'd yet to see?

'They need your help ladies and gentlemen.' Sarah turned to face the journos. 'And being entirely upfront . . . so do I.' Well aware the plea could be wildly and wilfully misinterpreted she still thought the risk worth taking. And in one way – in reality, the biggest way – the cops had failed: the perp or perps was still at large. More than four weeks now since the attempted rape of Hannah Winter, and every lead had ended down a dead end street. Ditto with Zoe and Jessica's rapes. The possibility that Lisa Webb had paid the ultimate price was a heavy cross to bear.

Watching closely, Sarah waited until the predictable shifty looks and bum-shuffling died down then: 'For the benefit of the new faces out there I'll run through what we already know. Sum up where we stand.' As she made her way back to the first image she scoped the room again. No late arrivals and it didn't look as if DCS Starr had taken up her offer. *Fancy that.* She did spot Mark Slater though. The reporter was sitting pen poised near the front. She hoped his peers were equally bright-eyed and bushy-tailed. In theory, by feeding everyone the same facts there'd be fewer errors and/ or creative embellishments. Same reason a news release would be handed out at the end.

'Hannah Winter.' Sarah paused. 'Eighteen-years-old, lives with her parents in Edgbaston.' When the attacker struck, the auburn-haired student had been on her early morning run round the reservoir. He dragged her into bushes, beat and assaulted her then tried to rape her. Sarah was pretty damn sure he only failed because Hannah lied about having an STD. Talk about thinking on your back. Even so, the aftermath had left the teenager traumatized.

'Zoe Darby, 24, lives alone in Moseley.' In a flat bought by her businessman father. She'd been violated in her own bed after the attacker broke in through a window during the early hours. He'd threatened to throw acid in her face if she screamed. After raping her twice, he escaped with cash, jewellery, photos and a digital camera. Zoe had moved back to stay with her parents in Harborne and would almost certainly live there for the foreseeable future.

'Jessica Silk, 23, lives in a bedsit in Handsworth.' On benefits. A recovering drug addict. Sarah suspected Jessica supplemented her unearned income by turning the occasional trick. Either way eight nights ago she got into a car in Hope Road and was lucky to get out alive. The attacker drove towards Alvechurch, parked in an isolated country lane and repeatedly raped her. Beaten black and blue, Jessica had been thrown half-naked into a ditch. She'd spent four days in hospital.

Each attack had been more violent, more sustained, more vindictive than the last. And now, Sarah told them, a rape victim had died. 'Lisa Webb, 15, attacked while walking through Victoria Park. Left to drown in a pond.' Sober thoughts, quiet reflection.

'The necklace you see here is missing. She was wearing it when she left the house last night so obviously we're keen to trace it. If you could highlight the detail, I'd be grateful.'

She saw most of them make a note then a hand went up. 'What makes you think the crimes are linked, Inspector?'

Going by the number of nods and pursed lips the reporter had
voiced a question most had in mind.

'We're not sure they are.' Another silence as she walked
back to the conference table, took her seat next to the press
officer. 'Without more evidence we can't be.'

Lumping the sex crimes together may well have been the
wrong call, there were several disparities. Added to which a
single crime generates a massive workload – with four crimes
now under investigation, each with its own actions and admin,
Operation Panther was in danger of getting out of hand.
Assuming it hadn't already.

Sarah again ran her gaze over the gathering. 'It's why we
need more media coverage. Without intelligence from the
public I'll be straight with you, we're struggling.'

Were the hacks impressed with a cop telling it like it is?
Or would they use it as a stick to beat her? Doubtless time
would tell. But with the victims' pictures out there in the public
domain witnesses were more likely to come forward: people
who'd not only seen the women but maybe spotted someone or
something suspicious in the same place around the same time.

'What about a description, DI Quinn?' Slater broke the
silence. 'Have any of the victims been able to help at all?'

Man in black. Leather gauntlets. Ski mask. Muffled voice.
Sarah shook her head. 'Not so much.'

'Is there any DNA evidence?' Nathan Powell. Late-twenties,
dark hair, snazzy dresser, looked more boy band member than
BBC reporter. Albeit local telly.

'No comment.' She'd hardly reveal that buckets of the stuff
had been recovered from the Zoe Darby crime scene, the only
attack where a condom hadn't been used. Problem was,
without a suspect's samples for comparison, the semen, saliva
and skin cells were as much use as a cat-flap in a lion enclo-
sure. There was certainly no match on the police national
computer so the perp had no criminal record. Which meant
either he'd not broken the law before, or was smart enough
not to get caught. Way things stood it looked like the latter.
Given the likelihood, why on earth would Sarah tip the perp
the DNA wink?

'CCTV?' Powell again.

I wish. Not so much as a frame of incriminating footage captured on security cameras. Again it seemed to point to a smart arse perp. 'We've yet to uncover any, Mr Powell.'

Studying his nails he threw in a purportedly casual question: 'The attacker seems to be on the ball forensically wouldn't you say, Inspector Quinn?'

I so wouldn't. She could picture the story, read the headlines now: **Crim runs rings round cops.** 'I'd say he's been very lucky, Mr Powell.'

He muttered something that elicited a few sniggers from smaller fry. Could've been: unlike his victims. She was almost relieved when Slater's hand shot up, drew Powell's fire.

'Is there a danger he'll strike again, Inspector?'

Stock question. She was only surprised it hadn't been thrown at her before. 'I'd be foolish to rule it out, Mr Slater.'

'So you're saying the streets aren't safe?' A bleached blonde seated next to him straightened, clearly scenting a new angle. 'Are you warning women not to go out alone at night?'

Why don't I open my mouth so you can pour in more words? Sarah stifled a sigh. 'My advice is the same for anyone anytime anywhere: always be vigilant, always be aware of your surroundings, people nearby, potential dangers.'

'Sounds like the Martini ad – anytime, anyplace, anywhere.' Blondie's murmured aside to Slater wasn't so *sotto voce.*

He visibly distanced himself from the woman. 'Any chance of the victims talking to us, DI Quinn?'

She shook her head. 'Not yet.' She had STOs working on it though. From day one each victim had been assigned a specially trained officer skilled in gaining trust and building rapport. Without their persuasive talents, Sarah doubted she'd have been in a position to release the names today. But what do they say about baby steps?

Besides before Hannah, Zoe and Jessica had any direct contact with the press, the DI had plans to bring the women together on neutral territory where they'd be more likely to open up. With a little gentle questioning, who knew what might emerge?

'I guess Mr Webb won't be giving interviews either?' Maybe

unwittingly, Slater stroked his left cheek. Sarah ignored what
could've been a conspiratorial glint in his eye. She took a
sip of by now cold coffee, held the reporter's gaze over the
polystyrene rim. 'You guess right.'

Not that she hadn't tried to get Webb to go on camera,
appeal for witnesses; his refusal had been unequivocal. And
how could she blame him? To say he was cut up about Lisa's
death was a statement straight from the school of the bleeding
obvious.

NINE

'I'm sorry, DI Quinn, I can't budge the woman.' Shona
Bruce on the phone reporting back yet again from the
Hinds' place in Stirchley. 'She won't leave the house in
case Natalie shows.' The DC's Glasgow lilt sounded a touch
downbeat to Sarah, but it wasn't like Shona hadn't tried. Christ,
she'd been out there long enough.

'No worries.' Sarah lied smoothly. Mind, if Natalie hadn't
turned up in a few hours, the mother could well have second
thoughts. The news conference was history now anyway, the
DI was currently deskbound digesting latest feedback from
the crime scene. Dave was up in the canteen grabbing
something for her empty stomach to work with as well. Not
that the house-to-house inquiries had produced anything
solid for the squad to sink its teeth in so far.

'While we're here,' Shona said, 'I thought we might
swing by the school. See if any of Natalie's mates can shed
some light?'

'Good thinking.'

'I'll keep you posted.' Slight pause. 'You know . . . I might
be wide off the mark . . .'

'But?'

'I think Mrs Hinds might have an inkling about Natalie's
whereabouts and isn't letting on.' Sarah turned her mouth
down. Brucie's instincts were generally pretty sound and if

she couldn't get Tracey Hinds to open up, then whatever the woman might be privy to probably wouldn't be shared any time soon.

'Why'd you say that, Shona?' Traffic noise. Shona's sharp intake of breath. Horn beeps.

'Bloody hell, Jed. Look out will you?' Laboured sigh then she resumed normal volume. 'Where was I? Oh yeah. For a woman whose daughter's gone AWOL – it struck me she seemed a wee bit laid back.'

'Laid back?' Sarah frowned. Dave reckoned the woman had been in bits that morning on the phone.

'Maybe *out of it* is a better description.'

'As in away with the fairies?' Sarah tapped a pen against her teeth.

'Or on medication. Y' know, tranx, Prozac—'

'Hell, if your daughter was missing, Shona, it'd take more than a few happy pills to—'

'Please. I don't even want to go there.' Brucie gave an audible shudder. 'I know what you're saying though, you'd move heaven and earth with a toothpick to help your kid. Any parent would.' She sniffed. 'Well most.' A string of headline-grabbing exceptions had probably sprung to mind: they would to most cops.

'What about the father? Is he still on the scene?'

'In the wings. He walked months back. They barely talk apparently.'

'We still need an address.'

'Got one, ma'am.' She'd called it in to the squad room; someone would be paying a house call.

If nothing came of the appeals Sarah decided to try and drop by the Hinds' place later, see if she could suss out the state of play. Still pensive she replaced the receiver, reached for the remote and aimed it towards the TV. Timing couldn't be better, or worse depending on your viewpoint.

Lisa Webb's murder led the regional midday news. The school-girl's happy face beamed from behind the presenter's head. Deadly serious the autocue smoothie linked to Nathan Powell's package. Looked to Sarah as if it had been mostly shot in the park: footage of uniformed officers beating undergrowth with sticks, others ferreting through bins, one in waders, exiting the pond. The pics segued into a seemingly compulsory vox pop that consisted mainly of work-shy gawpers demanding extra police patrols until the killer was caught. So far, so same old . . .

Then against a backdrop of uniforms on their knees searching the grass, Powell – all sombre-faced and sad-eyed – popped up and launched into a piece to camera.

'The callous criminal who left Lisa Webb here to drown,' sweeping an arm somewhat superfluously to point out the pond, 'is believed to be behind a series of sex attacks across the city. Police admit they're baffled by the so-called Ski Mask Killer.' *Ski Mask Killer? So-called by who? Was he having a laugh?* Apparently not. Still straight-faced Powell elaborated: 'Baffled and struggling – as within the last hour – the detective leading the manhunt told reporters.'

Cut to news conference. Sarah grimaced. Nothing to do with thinking she looked like Action Man in drag, though the crop-chop had clearly been a big mistake. It was the way Powell had twisted what weren't even facts to portray the police as a bunch of incompetents and her specifically as DI Clueless. A map with red arrows indicating locations of the sex attacks replaced her face on screen, but the relief was short-lived. Almost as cringe-making was the sound of her disembodied voice appealing for witnesses to come forward. The cool clipped delivery came across even to Sarah as more regal than the Queen's.

'Here you go, ma'am.' Harries wandered in bearing a plate of goodies. Lucky that, or she'd have snapped at him for failing to knock, not to mention using the m-word.

Cutting the screen a glance, she snarled, 'Effing toss pot.'

'Hey, that's no way for a lady—' His smile faded when he registered her face. 'What is it, boss?'

She muted the sound, gave him the gist then: 'So-called Ski Mask Killer? Says who? It mightn't be so bad if the guy had got at least one fact straight.'

'Like that's gonna happen.' Harries found an empty space on the table for the plate. 'It's like I told you: never let the facts spoil a—'

'Yeah, yeah. Either way, it's done now.' She gave a resigned sigh then scooted the chair forward. 'So what've we got here?' Not that she was starving or anything.

'That, boss, is a feast fit for a—'

'Stop right there.' *She could do without the royal references.* Her mouth watering at the smell, her eyes widened when she saw two sausage rolls, two Cornish pasties, two Scotch eggs and a limp lettuce leaf. 'Glad you went for the healthy option, Dave.'

'There's more.' He produced two packets of crisps from one pocket – cheese and onion, her fave – and from another, a brace of Red Bulls.

'Who needs Jamie Oliver, eh?' Smiling she dragged the plate closer then held his gaze. 'So what are you having?'

'What?'

She shook her head. Winding him up was almost too easy. 'Grab a pew.' If she had a penny for every lunch she'd either missed or worked through she could do a Baker and retire early. The working lunch with food combo was definitely preferable. Apart from the egg – go figure – she made inroads into her half of the carb-fest while they chatted tasks, leads, follow-ups, the latter mainly to calls and voicemails left on a couple of police hot line numbers.

Warmer now, she slipped off her jacket, made a mental note to open the window when they'd done, let out the food smells.

'Heard anything from Brucic, boss?' Dave popped in the last bite of pasty.

She gave him Shona's take on Tracey Hinds but Dave didn't really buy it, said she'd sounded distraught when he spoke to her.

'Not a single sighting so far though,' she said. 'I'm surprised by that, Dave.' Natalie's picture had been out there around three hours.

'Maybe she and Lisa didn't spend any time together last night?' He gestured at the Scotch egg going spare.

She nodded. 'Be my guest. You're thinking they did their own thing? Used each other as cover stories?'

'Could be. We all told porkies when we were kids, didn't we?' He flashed a grin. 'I mean didn't you ever get up to mis—?' She cocked an eyebrow. 'Fair enough. I know I did. Bags of times.'

Her lip twitched as he told her how he got stuck outside his bedroom window after sneaking out to meet a girl one night. He'd been about twelve at the time.

'It's peeing down and there I am clinging on for dear life with my foot jammed between the wall and the drainpipe. I can't budge it. So I'm wedged there – can't go up, can't go down. Felt like the bloody Duke of York. Anyway, my mum comes out, stands there wetting herself. Says "Who'd you think you are – Spiderman?".'

'Don't tell me, Dave' – laughing, she brushed crumbs off her lap – 'you lived in a bungalow?'

'I'm so glad there's something's amusing around here.' Starr stood in the threshold looking less than thrilled.

Sarah stiffened. The guy could've at least knocked. 'Is there—?'

He raised a palm. 'No, please don't get up. I'd hate to interrupt your lunch.' His glance took in her desk: paperwork littered with pastry flakes, torn packets shedding crisps.

'We're just about finished, sir.'

He sniffed. 'Yes, Inspector, I can see that.'

'Was there something you wanted?'

'A word in my office.' He turned to go. 'In your own time, of course. I mean, it's not like we're under pressure, is it?'

TEN

'Natalie listen to me, love.' Tracey Hinds, phone clamped tight against her ear, strove hard to hide her angst. The line wasn't the only thing breaking up, Natalie sounded pretty close to meltdown too. 'You have to talk to the police.'

'No way. You just don't understand, Mum.'

Mrs Hinds bit her lip, grimaced at the metallic taste of blood. 'All you have to do is tell them what happened.' *Your best mate's dead for crying out loud.*

'I can't. What if they don't believe me?'

'Don't be so daft, Nat.' She took a deep calming breath, tried to keep the tone light. 'I've had them here already. Detectives. Ever so nice they were. They just want to ask a few questions.' Silence. She raked trembling fingers through mussed hair that, like everything else in her life, was having a bad day. 'Can't you see that the longer you stay away the worse it'll get?'

'Not when it can't get any worse, I can't.'

She grimaced, needed to rinse the foul taste from her mouth. Traipsing through to the kitchen, she caught sight of her reflection in a mirror and looked away quickly. Gaunt, drawn, pale; forty going on late-fifties. No wonder her husband had walked out. She loved her daughter, course she did, but Natalie was a daddy's girl and since Pete left her behaviour hadn't so much gone off the rails as laid down new tracks.

'All they want to know is what happened last night, love. Where you went and that.' She opened the fridge, swigged as quietly as she could from an open bottle of wine. From what she'd gathered during the earlier snatched call the girls had been out drinking, Natalie had left Lisa at the bus stop then gone back to some guy's house. Mrs Hinds sneaked another swig. She'd not even known Natalie had a boyfriend let alone that she was sleeping with him – and oversleeping. Natalie had woken in a panic and rung home soon as she checked her phone.

'Christ, Mum, are you boozing this early again?'

'I'm drinking coffee.' Forcing a smile into her voice, she quipped, 'Allowed, aren't I?'

'Feck's sake.' Clearly finding the gag funnier than chlamydia. 'You'd better not have said anything to the cops. 'Cause I meant what I—'

'No. No. Course not.' God forbid. Natalie had sworn to disappear for good if she breathed a word. It wasn't the first time she'd thrown the threat in her mum's face either. Emotional blackmail? Guilt-tripping? Or chemical imbalance? Mrs Hinds wouldn't dare take the risk of pushing Natalie over the edge. Maybe depression was a genetic thing: like mother, like daughter. Carrying the bottle she made her way back to the sitting room. 'Why not come home, love? We could—?'

'Shut up will you. I'm trying to think.'

She curled a lip then took another swig. *Cheers, darling.* She tilted the bottle towards a photograph on the wall of Natalie in Year 6. Blonde Heidi plaits, green eyes, innocent grin, cute dimples. Fast forward five years and the dimples and eyes were about the only things that hadn't changed. When Mrs Hinds pictured her daughter now she saw long black hair, eyes rimmed with thick black kohl and, apart from a seemingly permanent scowl, a woman's body garbed head-to-toe in black. Goth? Emo? God knew.

'I don't know what to do, Mum.' Sounded close to tears. 'I'm scared.'

Mrs Hinds softened her voice. 'You need to tell the truth, love.'

'Silly me,' she snapped. 'Wish I'd thought of that.'

'Come on, Nat.' Silence again – maybe she'd pierced the bravado at last. 'It can't do any harm, can it?'

'What would *you* know?'

Maybe treating people like shit was hereditary too, or Natalie had just picked it up at her father's knee. Scalding tears pricked Mrs Hinds' eyes. Anger. Fury. For years she'd been everyone's favourite whipping woman but they say even a worm can turn. She opened her mouth but bit back the words on the tip of her tongue. *Maybe later.*

'I'm sure you're right, love, but think what Mr and Mrs Webb must be going through. I bet you could help them.' The self-abasement, the wheedling words would be worth it if they brought her to her senses, and back to her home.

'How's that work?' she sneered. 'They only want one thing. And I can't bring Lisa back from the dead. So unless you've taken a crash course as a miracle-worker, I'd say you're talking bollocks. And besides there's—'

'Get lost you cheeky little sod.' She yelled, but by then, she'd already cut the connection.

'Mum?' The girl frowned, raised her voice. 'Mum? Mum?' Sobbing Natalie slung the mobile on the bedside table and perched on the edge of the mattress. She dropped her head in her hands, narrow shoulders heaving, stomach churning. Fact was, her old lady didn't know the half of it and Natalie had just about psyched herself up to tell all. Now what the hell was she meant to do?

Out of the corner of her eye she glimpsed the man's half naked body sprawled on top of the sheet; only the handle of the knife was visible, smeared with dried almost black blood.

She gagged, gagged again. Tears streaming down her face, she shot to her feet, backed slowly into the corner staring at the corpse. She hugged herself in a vain attempt to stop the convulsive shaking. Her scalp tingled, she'd pass out if she didn't cool it, yet sweat trickled down her spine and her palms felt clammy. She breathed in deeply, let it out slowly through her mouth. Then again. And again.

Tell the truth, her mum had advised. Easy for her to say. But what if the cops didn't believe a word of it? She needed a bolthole, fast. Eyes narrowed, her frantic thoughts raced. Who could she trust? Who could she call for help? She had nothing to lose, what the hell. She dashed her damp cheeks with the heels of both hands then, gaze still fixed on the body, tiptoed back to retrieve her phone.

ELEVEN

'A call, boss. Just come in.' Sarah glanced up from the keyboard to see Dave hovering by the door. Something in his expression told her the call was more than routine. Rebus might crack a case in a couple of hours and nip off for a dram down the Oxford Bar, but in real life, breaks are mostly down to people with tip-offs picking up the phone to the police.

'Let's hear it then.' She scooted the chair back a few inches.

'Actually, you really—'

'OK.' She grabbed her jacket, didn't need the import spelling out. 'Squad room, I take it?'

He nodded. 'Twig's sorting the playback now.' She sensed his gaze on her as they kept pace down the corridor. 'Everything OK, boss?' DC Casual. Too casual.

She could respond with an equally disingenuous 'why wouldn't it be?' But doubtless the whole station knew she'd been closeted with Starr this afternoon. The bollocking had centred on how – by playing it straight with the media – she'd opened herself to ridicule, damaged public confidence in the police, undermined the inquiry and started World War Three. Yeah, well, she'd always known it was a calculated risk. Then he'd dropped the bombshell: he was drafting in another DI to share senior investigating officer duties. As if the professional knocks hadn't been bad enough, he'd had the sodding gall to tap her on the forearm as she left and told her not to take it personally . . .

'Just you look a bit peaky.' Harries pushed.

'Not now, OK?' She unclenched a fist. Even if they hadn't reached the squad room, she wasn't ready to share – and that included with Dave. Spreading the workload might make some sort of logistical sense but to Sarah it still felt like a slap in the face.

Twig raised a hand from his officer manager's post by the window. Sarah headed his way acknowledging nods from a couple of detectives en route. Twig half rose to offer his seat but she flapped him down, perched on the edge of his desk. Harries took up a post on the nearest wall.

'Are we sitting comfortably?' Unsmiling, Twig reached out to hit play. 'It sure ain't *Listen with Mother.*'

'*I saw it on the telly. I should've come forward before. I know that now.*'

Female. Tentative. Hint of a lisp. Birmingham accent. Then a shuddering sigh. Eyes creased, Sarah motioned Twig to tweak the volume.

'No need, boss. It takes her a while to get there.' Her. No dialogue then.

Sarah pressed her lips together. What a pisser. It meant they only had voicemail. Why, oh, why couldn't the woman have called one of the hot lines, spoken to an actual person? Dumb question. Her reluctance to talk with a cop could be down to a number of things: guilt, shame, fear, stress. You name it. Whatever her problem – this way she didn't have to give *her* name.

'*The man in the mask? Well. . . .*' – audible swallow – '*he . . . he attacked me too.*'

Sarah cut Harries a glance then looked at Twig who shook his head, put a finger to his lip.

'*He . . . he threatened me . . . said if I told anyone it'd be the last thing I do but what he done to that girl in the park . . . is . . . is wicked.*'

The silence went on even longer this time interspersed with juddering breaths. Sarah pricked her ears, thought she heard a car horn in the background. If so, it could signify the girl was in a phone box, the chances of tracing the call infinitesimal. She flexed a fist trying to get the blood flow back to her fingers. Her initial high hopes continued to fall.

'*Anyway, I know who he is.*'

'What!' She couldn't have stemmed the gasp if she'd tried. Tight-lipped, Twig raised a palm.

'*His name's Larry Drake. Lives in Aston. Foundry Road. If he finds out I told you – he'll kill me. Don't say nothing to him. Please, please, take my word on that.*'

And that was her final word.

'Chance would be a fine thing.' Sarah blew her cheeks out on a sigh. She'd heard the tape twice now. Tempting though it was to take the contents as gospel, second time round she was even more dubious.

'Not with you, boss.' Harries' crossed arms conveyed the difference – and distance – between them as effectively as his words.

'It's not difficult, Dave. We've no clue who she is for one thing.' Sarah rose from the desk, started pacing; thinking it through.

'Your point being?' Harries' tone brought her up sharp. She cut him a glance before responding icily.

'Are you being deliberately obtuse?' For Christ's sake the girl could be anybody. They'd no way of identifying an anonymous voice, a voice that could be heavily disguised anyway. And what about the mask? Unless the mystery caller had X-ray vision, how was she supposed to have clocked her alleged attacker's face?

'You think she's lying?'

This time Sarah halted in front of him, hands on hips. The aping of her question, plus the now overt querying of her lack of conviction on the call being genuine, bordered on defiance, if not insubordination. Her eyes held a warning.

'I'm saying we only have her say-so.'

He held her gaze. 'Sounds like you're splitting hairs.'

'Listen properly then, officer.' The snapped order came out louder than she'd intended. She cleared her throat, lowered her voice. 'I don't know her from Adam. Eve, come to that. She could be a complete fruit loop. But unlike you I'm not in the business of making unwarranted assumptions.'

'So you're writing the whole thing off?'

'No dammit.' What the hell was wrong with him? 'We can't just take what she – or anyone – says at face value.' Faceless value.

'She sounded pretty genuine to me,' Twig weighed in, scratching the side of his face.

'Maybe. Maybe not.' Sarah shrugged. 'She could just have one hell of an axe to grind.'

'So what now?'

'We check it out. Goes without saying.'

'She's right on one score, ma'am.'

Frowning the DI cut a glance over her shoulder. One of the detectives who'd been on the phone was heading over to join the party. He stood, waving a piece of paper. Christ, what did he want? An invitation? 'Go on then.'

'Foundry Road? I checked. There's a Lawrence Drake at number thirteen. Used to be a teacher.'

Sarah, Harries and Twig exchanged lightning glances before chorusing: 'Used to be?'

'Served six months for sexually assaulting an underage pupil. He's still on the offenders' register.'

TWELVE

'He came at me with a knife screaming the devil wanted me to die. He'd have killed me. I know he would. I was so . . . so scared.' Clothes streaked with dried blood, Natalie slumped on a steel stool at the breakfast bar. Her bare feet barely skimmed the marble tiles, she looked tiny, fragile, damaged physically and emotionally.

'Hey, babe, look at me.' Pete Hinds held his daughter's gaze, felt his heart melt. Since the minute she was born, he'd worshipped the ground she walked on. He'd walked out on the marriage, not Natalie, and the guilt still ripped him apart.

'Help me, Daddy.' Her sheet-white face looked as if it had been painted with black jagged tears. 'I don't know what to do.'

He'd sworn on his life he'd do anything to protect her. But this . . .?

She'd phoned him in the van on his way to a painting and decorating job. Hysterical, barely coherent she'd begged him to come over, mumbled something about a dead man and blurted out an address in Edgbaston. He'd expected to turn up at a student dive not some posh detached Georgian. He'd left her nursing a mug of tea and checked out the house.

Until he saw the body he'd prayed she was playing some kind of sick joke. Swallowing bile, he pictured the scene again: good-looking guy on the bed, blade buried in his chest, blood-soaked sheets. The stink. Even now it seemed like a bad dream, except for the empty slit in the knife block near the sink.

'We'll have to go to the police, babe.' He stroked her slender arm. 'I'll make them see sense.' He held no brief for the law, crossed the legal line a few too many times himself for that. But from what he'd gleaned so far she'd acted in self-defence.

'I can't. I can't.' She gasped. 'I'll end up in prison. I won't have any kind of life. Never get married. Never have kids.'

'Hey, come on, that's rubbish.' Nat's lively imagination up
to its tricks again. He forced an encouraging smile. 'Course
they'll believe you: why on earth would you stab him without
good reason?' Sighing, he ran a hand through his short auburn
hair. Natalie had dropped her head to her chest again, crying
even louder.

He walked to the sink, poured a glass of water, shocked,
though God knew why, to see the tremor in his hand. He was
close enough to his daughter to know she wasn't being straight
with him. But if he was going to get her out of this mess,
she had to come clean. He dragged a stool nearer, perched
alongside. 'Come on, babe, what's the score? Who is he?
What were you doing here in the first place?'

Head still down she picked compulsively at a hangnail on
her thumb. She'd been walking home, she said, it was raining
and he'd offered her a lift.

'For Christ's sake, Natalie, what have I told you ab—?'

'He's not a stranger, Dad.' She lifted her gaze, bottom lip
trembling. 'His name's Ivan. Ivan Burton. He ran the news-
agent's where I had that paper round. Don't you remember?'
Pete shook his head. She told him Burton had sold the
business when his wife died last year. 'Anyway he asked if
I fancied a drink, wanted to listen to some music. He said
he got lonely and I always liked him so I . . .' Gave a one-
shouldered shrug.

'So you said, yes.' He sighed. Her bloody mother was to
blame, letting Natalie roam the streets at night, looking like
some common tart.

'He brought me back here, said I could stay if I wanted.'
And she had been flattered by attention from a rich, good-
looking guy old enough to be her . . .

Pete closed his eyes, bit his lip. *Fucking perv.*

'Not like that, Dad. He was dead nice at first. Asked if I
wanted to call Mum and tell her where I was.'

He clenched his fists, could barely get the words out.
'She knew you were here with a guy more than twice
your age?'

'No. I told her I was staying at a friend's.' She wiped snot
from her nose with the back of a hand.

'Go on. What happened?'

'We sat around chatting, drinking rum and Coke. It tasted well funny though.'

'I bet it did.'

'Next thing I knew I was on the bed and he was coming through the door with a knife.'

Pete struggled to see how his slip of a daughter had overpowered a guy built like a body-builder. His gaze searched her face for clues but she looked down at her lap.

'He was on something, Dad. Staggering about, waving his arms round. He dropped the knife, I grabbed it. He ran towards me and went straight into the blade.'

Was it all a bit too pat? And how come his body ended up on the bed? She must have picked up on the scepticism.

'I know what you're thinking, Dad. But I found him like that when I came out the bathroom.' She'd locked herself in there for hours, she told him, scared to make a sound let alone a move.

'OK, babe. No worries.' He reached in an inside pocket.

'What are you doing?'

'Ringing the police. I'll tell them there's been an accident.'

'You can't.' She screamed. 'What if they don't believe me?'

'They will. And we have to report it.'

'Christ, you're as bad as her.' Scowling, she folded her arms.

Eyes narrowed he looked up; index finger hovering over the final nine. 'You've told your mother about this?'

'You are kidding.' She sniffed. 'No. I was with Lisa for a bit last night. The cops are on to me for that, they've already been round home asking questions. Mum keeps banging on at me to talk to them.'

'Lisa?' He frowned. 'Who the hell's Lisa?'

'Christ, Dad, haven't you seen the news? She's the girl who was murdered in Vickie Park?' She pulled up the story on her phone, slid it towards him. 'We were best mates.'

As he read the implication sank in. 'The cops are searching for you, anyway?'

'You bet they are.'

'Do you know what happened to her, Nats?'

'No. We had a quick drink in a wine bar. Some guy chatted her up but he looked sound. Besides he didn't follow us or anything and from what I've seen the cops are looking for a nutter.'

'You have to tell them what you know, Nats.'

'Don't call them, Dad.' She laid her hand on his arm. 'I'm begging you.'

'It'll be OK, trust me.'

'It won't.' He saw it in her eyes then – utter conviction. 'Why not, babe?'

'It wasn't an accident. He raped me so I . . .' Hugging her waist, she rocked back and forth.

Killed him? 'Oh Natalie, no. Oh, love, no.' He closed his eyes, held her close, stroked her hair. Thoughts raced in his head but he voiced only one. 'It's a fucking good job he's dead then. Saves me the effort.'

And sod the police – they could bloody well wait . . .

THIRTEEN

Sarah banged the heavy-duty front door again, stepped back and tapped a testy foot. It was all very well to have reading matter provided by some fading graffiti, but it was brass monkeys out here. Apart from which, muffled music from inside indicated someone was at home either ignoring – or taking their time – to answer the summons. A few seconds after a sudden blast of something classical, the door opened little more than a crack.

'Mr Drake? Lawrence Drake?' Holding an ID card at eye-level, Sarah fixed an impassive gaze on a portly middle-aged man. He didn't look convinced so she added a verbal name check before introducing DC Bruce. She'd brought Shona along to get first-hand feedback on developments in Stirchley. The decision had nothing to do with Harries' earlier strop. And if Sarah told herself that enough times she might believe it.

Drake on the other hand said nothing, merely nodded to confirm they had the right guy while darting several glances between the laminated card and Sarah's blank face, he even threw a couple of sneaky peeks over her shoulder. His beady eyes put her in mind of aniseed balls and the spindly lashes were sparse enough to count. His fine sandy hair with a pronounced widow's peak wasn't exactly lush either.

After copious cross-checking of plastic with person, Drake seemed – if not ecstatic – satisfied the credentials were kosher. 'What do you want?'

'It's cold out here, Mr Drake.' Sarah tightened her belt to underline the point. Near freezing as it happened. Not that cops ever received a warm welcome in Aston's mean little back streets. The local bad guys were generally too busy dishing out hot property, crime sheets carried more clout round here than CVs. 'And it's not getting any warmer.'

Making heavy weather of a sigh Drake widened the gap and stepped back. 'If you're coming in, make sure one of you bolts the door.'

'That'll be me then,' Shona murmured, adding an even more *sotto voce* line about not realising the crown jewels had been re-housed.

Sarah tailed Drake down a dark narrow hallway. His fleshy bare feet spilled over down-at-heel tartan slippers, brown tracky bottoms sagged under his bum and sported a Heinz variety of stains. She'd been spot on about the receding hair line: all she could see – through the odd sandy strand – was pink shiny skull. Eggshell territory again. She suppressed a shudder, Shona still on bolt-sliding duty made no effort to subdue a sniff.

The vague odours that clung in the hall's fetid air crystallized as they entered a small windowless room at the back: cat pee and chip fat. A naked low wattage light bulb dangled from a wonky ceiling rose and did little to dispel the gloom, not helped by swirling wreaths of smoke. Ten B&H and a Dunhill lighter lay on a low table. The four-bar electric fire in an old tiled grate generated enough heat to bring Sarah out in a cold sweat. Unless it was proximity to Drake. She'd nailed her fair share of sex offenders over the years, but she had rarely felt so much revulsion.

She watched the ex-history teacher home in on a Lazyboy chair by the fire. Semi-reclining he reached a hand to retrieve a can of lager from the floor. Maybe it was a late liquid lunch, the starter might have been soup: a spoon still stood in the empty tin balanced precariously on a fake beige leather pouffe. Oxtail could explain one of the stains.

Waving the hand holding the Carling he told them to sit, adding just loud enough for them to catch, 'Like I have a choice.'

If Sarah had the choice, she'd have opted to stand. She'd seen cleaner sofas on a skip. Shona looked to be of like mind. Sniffing loudly again, she shoved a mountain of newspapers and junk mail to the furthest cushion before sweeping crumbs, clumps of cat hair and God knew what else to the manky grey shag-pile. Talk about fifty shades of grunge.

Drake observed the domestic routine tapping podgy fingers on his thigh; thread veins laced his cheeks like tiny red roads that led nowhere. 'Sorted now?' he asked unsmiling. 'Sitting comfortably are we? Shall we begin?'

That phrase again. He'd inadvertently aped Twig's allusion to *Listen with Mother*. Very droll. Drake clearly thought he was in line for a children's story. Like those he'd consistently claimed his victim had concocted. He'd denied every allegation from the word go. Known in the trade as 'doing a Mandy'.

'Soon as you're ready, eh, Inspector? Time's money.' Lifting a frayed cuff, he peered at what looked like a Rolex with a crack in the glass. 'I'm a very busy man – as you can see.' He let out a loud burp then slapped hand to mouth in mock naughty boy mode.

Prat. The guy might look like a slob with special needs, but the slob was no fool. The cultured voice told her that, not to mention the First from UCL. If the guy's circumstances were reduced, he should have learned to keep his body parts to himself. She saw no point in beating around minced words.

'We're looking into some serious allegations, Mr Drake.'

'Old story, officer.' The bored drawl belied the sudden

narrowing of his eyes. 'If that's all you have . . .?' Holding her gaze, he slowly crushed the can in his fist.

Was the macho act meant to rattle her? Good luck with that. 'We're investigating a series of sex attacks in the city including the rape and murder last night of a girl in Selly Oak. You'll have seen stories in the media?'

'I don't do news, Inspector. Waste of time.'

'Would you mind telling me where you were—?'

'Funnily enough I don't get out much. *These days.*' His curled lip told her why – as if she hadn't already picked up on the Fort Knox security, his twilight existence, shifty over the shoulder looks.

'Oh?'

'Sadly not.' The smarmy smile bared slimy yellow teeth and made her skin creep. 'Not with the streets the way they are. Well . . . for men like me.'

The streets were a damn sight dodgier for women. 'Sex offenders you mean?'

He didn't miss a beat. 'Paedos. Perverts. Nonces. Kiddy-fiddlers. Need I go on?'

'I get the picture.' She smoothed her skirt. 'Let's get back to—'

'No, DI Quinn. You don't. You have absolutely no idea.' Tight-mouthed, he flung the can against the tiles. A mangy black cat shot out from under the settee, arched its back and hissed fishy breath towards the detectives. Drake clicked his fingers and the cat slunk over and squatted at his feet.

'Even here I'm not safe.'

'If you're being threatened—'

'*If?*' He snapped the ring pull on another Carling. 'Shit through the letterbox? Rotting vermin on the step? Filthy looks. Hurled abuse. I've even had reporters knock on the door. Muck-raking scum.' She watched his Adam's apple take several dives as he knocked back the drink.

'I take it you've reported the incidents?'

He very nearly choked. Red-faced and still spluttering, he dragged the sleeve of his cardigan across his mouth. 'Are you winding me up?'

'I assure you the police take threats of any nature seriously.'

'Don't talk bollocks. Besides, if it wasn't for your lot and a bunch of bent lawyers I wouldn't be living like this. Other people get away with far worse.' *Pass the violin in the sick bag.*

He snivelled his way through a self-serving account of how conviction had cost him dear. He'd lost everything, he said: job, wife, kids, colleagues, friends. No one wanted to know.

'And all on the say-so of a two-faced malicious little slut.' He took a deep breath then slowly exhaled. 'If I'd touched her – fair dos, Inspector. But I swear I never laid a finger on Emma Vane.'

'That's not the way the jury saw it.' Nor Sarah, and she could live without the history lesson. 'The allegations I have in mind are new, Mr Drake. We've received intell—'

'Who from?' He sat up straight, eyes narrowed.

She sighed. 'Intelligence regarding a serious sexual assault. Your name came—'

'Not good enough, Inspector.' You can say that again. He'd not let her get a word in edgeways. 'This so-called *intelligence* – how did you come by it?' He licked flecks of saliva from his bottom lip.

'I'm not at lib—'

'Course you're not. Because you haven't got a clue where it came from.' *Lucky guess? Or familiar with police fudge?*

'That's not what I said, Mr—'

'Are you arresting me?'

'No.' Or they'd be squaring up across a table in one of the nick's interview rooms.

'Charging me?'

She shook her head.

'Excellent. I'm so glad that's cleared up.' Smiling, he hauled himself out of the chair and headed towards the door. 'Come on, Genghis, time for a nap.'

Open-mouthed the detectives watched him leave the room, followed by the cat swishing its tail. Sarah heard the stairs creak and a few words she couldn't quite make out. 'Did you catch that, Shona?'

She turned her mouth down. 'See yourselves out?'

Sarah thought it sounded like 'Sod off loser.'

*   *   *

Shona hit the gas and shifted the Vauxhall into the off-side lane muttering under her breath. Presumably the Aston Expressway wasn't living up to its name again. Curious, Sarah cut a glance from her phone screen to the wing mirror and saw a slow-moving convoy of shiny black Daimlers bringing up the rear. Bad luck, wasn't it, to overtake a cortège? A few seconds later, Shona said, 'Y'know, Inspector, I can't see any winners in it at all.'

Sarah frowned. Where the hell was she coming from? No winners in what? The coffin? The lottery of life? The Euro-Millions draw? After barely uttering a syllable since they'd left Drake to his beauty sleep – that could take a while – Shona had either just slung in a non sequitur of gargantuan propor-tions or gone all deep and meaningful. Scratch the *meaningful*. And scratch the flea bites. Sarah's ankles were covered in the bloody things. She'd already made a mental note to get cala-mine lotion.

'I'm not with you, Shona.' The DI slipped the phone back in her pocket. She'd checked new texts and emails: nothing had moved in the last hour. 'What are you saying?'

'The fall-out. Drake, his wife, kids, parents. The girl. They're all still suffering to a deg—'

'Whoa. Stop right there. The girl has a name. How about putting Emma Vane top of your list? And leaving Drake out of the equation altogether.' She stared at Shona whose profile gave nothing away. For a cop, her take was barely credible. Emma had been sexually abused by a creepy old perv who'd simultaneously abused a position of trust. To Sarah's way of thinking the only thing Drake had lost was his moral compass. Oh, yes, and a place in the sympathy stakes.

'You don't see it like that?' she prompted. Apart from a fairly explicit one-shouldered shrug, Shona had reverted to silent partner. 'If you disagree – say so.' Dave certainly wouldn't hold back. 'I assure you I don't bite.' Unlike the fleas.

'Forget I said anything, ma'am. Your mind seemed pretty made up anyway.'

Seemed made up? Past tense. Had Shona just accused her of blinkered vision, and biased thinking before they'd even arrived at Drake's pad? 'Meaning?'

'I'm not looking for a fight, ma'am.' She raised a palm. 'I'll leave that to—'

'Who?' Good job Sarah wasn't prone to blushing or she'd be doing fuchsia. 'Dave Harries? Is that where you were heading?'

'How about letting me finish a sentence now and again, ma'am?' She tapped the wheel with a finger.

Sarah opened her mouth to speak, thought better of it and turned her head to stare pointedly through the passenger window. The passing scenery was a mishmash of high-rise flats, church steeples, office blocks, factory chimneys belching smoke. It barely registered with Sarah, Drake still occupied too much of her mind. The house call had been a waste of time; they'd got virtually zero out of it. Partly, she now realized, because he'd kept talking over her too. Great tactic for skirting issues and unpalatable truths. Not to mention evading questions.

Like what his movements had been last night. As an answer, 'Funnily enough, I don't get out much these days,' was neither here nor there. Natalie Hinds' whereabouts were still unknown too – Twig's update had told Sarah that. She massaged her temple, doubted it would do much to stave off the incipient headache.

They were almost back at the station before Shona broke the in-car silence. 'Look ma'am, I'm no apologist for Drake. Like they say, if you do the crime, you serve the time.'

'I read the reports. There's no *if* about it.' She cut Shona a glance.

'Fine.' Slight pause as she turned into the car park. 'What I'm saying is – he's paid his dues. He should be allowed to move on. Prison's about rehabilitation as much as punishment.'

Forgive and forget. Easier said than done. 'Try telling that to the Vanes.'

'The family has my sympathy ma'am but Drake's paid a heavy price too. Especially if he didn't do it.'

'What is this, Shona? A new board game? "Miscarriages of Justice I Have Known"? "Name That Dodgy Verdict"?' She ran her fingers through her hair. God, she must be riled if she was resorting to sarcasm.

'It wouldn't be the first time, would it?' Shona cut the ignition. 'Not when it's one person's word against another.'

'You sound like a defence lawyer, detective.'

Shona's response was another shrug.

Sarah reached a hand towards the door then turned back. 'And talking of words, they were damn thin on the ground back at Drake's place. It may have escaped your notice but the guy failed to answer a single question.'

'I'd say he was royally pissed off. We turn up there with nothing to go on and as good as accuse him of a string of sex attacks.'

They exited the motor in sync, walked in step across the tarmac. Sarah's thinking was on a par with Shona up to a point. With an anonymous informant flinging so far groundless allegations and not even flimsy evidence against him, Drake had every right to protect himself by keeping schtum. Fact was Sarah had gone off half-cock and probably deserved the flea in the ear. Not round the ankles though.

'Yeah, well next time we'll have to try a bit harder.' Sarah held the door.

'What makes you think there'll be a next time, ma'am?'

'He lied to us that's why, Shona.'

'Go on.'

'He claimed not to keep up with the news.'

So why have months' worth of daily papers lying around?

FOURTEEN

Caroline wandered into the kitchen and found a bottle of wine propping up the local rag. She shook her head smiling, reckoned the product placement would be Mark's baby. He was still newbie enough to get a buzz from seeing his by-line, especially on a front-page lead. Sipping what was left of her coffee, Caroline ran an expert eye over the copy, mentally editing as she read.

Park death sparks police fears
By Mark Slater

Detectives fear a fifteen-year-old girl found dead beside a shallow pool in Birmingham's Victoria Park could be the latest victim of a serial sex offender. Lisa Webb's partly-clothed body was discovered early this morning by jogger, Andrew Frome. Mr Frome, 45, a call centre worker from Selly Oak, immediately raised the alarm. Police cordoned off the crime scene within minutes and launched an extensive search of the area.

Mr Frome said he couldn't believe his eyes at first. 'I thought kids had nicked a shop dummy and dumped it for a laugh.'

Caroline sniffed. *Dead funny that.*

Lisa is the fourth young woman to be seriously sexually assaulted in the city over the last four weeks. Police believe the same man could be responsible for all the attacks. They're appealing for witnesses to come forward. They're also keen to trace a necklace Lisa was wearing when she left home last night. The silver chain holds letters spelling out her name.

Detective Inspector Sarah Quinn who's leading the murder inquiry hasn't ruled out the possibility that the attacker could strike again and is urging women to take special care at all times.

Caroline rolled her eyes. *Another quote to die for from the Snow Queen.*

Lisa, a pupil at Grange Road High School, lived with her parents and brother in a house overlooking the park. The family was today too distraught to comment.
Cont. page 3.

Not a bad job, all things considered, but it wasn't going to win a Pulitzer. Caroline couldn't be arsed to read on, she could write this stuff in her sleep. Not that she had to – or would – these days.

Stifling a yawn she sashayed to the sink. 'Hemmingway eat your heart out.'

'That's nice, thanks.'

Her fingers stilled on the tap. *Shoot. Faux pas in mouth.* On the other hand Mark's softly-softly approach had scared the shit out of her. She'd half a mind to spin round and let rip – set a few ground rules. Nothing to do with attack being the best form of defence. But, no, she told herself, stay cool. She still wanted him on board with the research for her book proposal. She took her time rinsing the mug and still with her back to him said, 'I didn't hear you come in.'

'No. Well . . . I was . . . in the shower.' And sounded on the back foot.

As for in the shower, Caroline pursed her lips – now that she would like to see. When she turned there was quite an eyeful on show anyway: drops of water glistened on toned pecs and a white towel kept what was probably a six-pack under wraps. Shame she didn't need to dry her hands.

Unsmiling she leaned against the sink, arms folded, ankles crossed. 'And now you're in my kitchen.' She dropped her eye-line a couple of feet. 'In a hurry, were we?'

With a blush to match the Merlot, he glanced down. 'I just popped in to grab a drink.'

'Don't let me stop you.' She pushed herself off the side. A girl could only have so much fun, and more work beckoned. Not that she could get past the doorway. They mirrored each other's moves in one of those stupid excuse-me-dances until Mark raised both palms and offered a smile.

'This must be God's way of getting you to join me.'

Join him? The wine, of course. 'Yeah, why not?' A quickie would do no harm. She might have touched up the lippie and slipped into something a little less comfy if she'd realized Mark was in-house. The leopard-print leggings and last season's sweater was a combo she'd not normally be caught dead in. Mind, at his age she'd have been mortified at the thought of staying in on a Friday night. The prospect didn't exactly thrill her now but needs must when the deadline drives. Besides, the book was a cracker – or would be once she'd written it.

'Coming right up, ma'am.' Delivering a mock salute, he sauntered across the kitchen. Caroline, observing the hip action, reckoned if he didn't curb it he'd lose the towel. That really would be show-time. Maybe that was the point?

'So, Caroline, the Hemmingway jibe—?'

'The corkscrew's in the top drawer, just to the left.' Distraction technique. The grapes of wrath route was definitely one to avoid.

'Thanks for that. Handy.' Eyebrow arched he opened the fridge, whipped out a bottle of champagne. 'Not right now though.'

Wow. Even better. 'I thought the Merlot?'

'No, the red's for Mum.' *Our gain, her loss.* 'She can still just about manage a few sips.'

Inwardly cringing, Caroline perched on the table: thank God she'd not voiced the thought. 'How's she doing?' *Spare me the gory details.* All she knew was that Mrs Slater had ovarian cancer and the outlook wasn't rosy. Having buried her own ma not that long back, it was all the detail Caroline wanted.

'Oh, you know . . .' – pause while he eased out the cork – 'so-so. Cheers.' He handed her a glass.

'Here's lookin' at ya.' Deadpan, she dropped her gaze.

He glanced down again, lifted a finger. 'Two ticks, don't go away.'

'I live here – remember?' Smiling she watched him dash out, heard his feet on the stairs. At least he was quick on the uptake. And very easy on the eye.

He looked even tastier when he came back: man in black – tight T-shirt and denims; dark hair still damp and smelling of limes.

'I could get used to this.' He popped a black olive into his mouth.

In your dreams, babe. Laying out a few nibbles was the full extent of Caroline's domestic goddess prowess. The bedroom was more her domain than the kitchen.

'Cheers.' She took a sip then dabbed a finger across her lips. 'Me, too, if the Bolly's always going to be on tap.'

He cut a glance at the newspaper. 'I did feel like celebrating.'
Whoops. 'It was only a joke. No need to take it personally.'

He shrugged. 'Coming from you, it's difficult not to. So
where do you think I went wrong?' *How long have you got?*
It wasn't so much the qualifying 'could' in the second line of
the article or the superfluous verbiage further down, it was the
boring angle, bland tone.

'It doesn't exactly grab the reader by the throat, does it?
Why didn't you use the ski mask line? And why trot out a
load of police-speak?' She'd watched the coverage on the
evening news. Sarah Quinn looked as if she'd swallowed a
vat of vinegar through a mouthful of lemons. 'The cops are
on the back-foot, Mark. You should be firing rockets not
bashing out PR pieces.'

'Don't hold back, Miss.' His smile was less than convincing.

'You asked, kid.' Heat. Kitchen. Home truth.

'That I did.' He hoisted himself up on the side. 'But what
if I have a reason for playing it down? Not taking a pop?'

Fact or face-saving fiction? 'Go on.'

'I feel strongly about violence against women.' He dropped
his gaze, swirled his glass. 'I saw that poor kid's body in the
park this morning.'

'And?'

He told her he wanted an inside track on the inquiry and if
he played nice with Quinn she might agree to be interviewed,
throw him the occasional exclusive, even let him talk to some
of the victims.

'Good luck with that.' She raised her glass.

'You don't think?'

Going on past experience with the Snow Queen, Caroline
reckoned an ice cube in a blast furnace stood more chance
than Mark of being granted a royal audience.

'In a word – no.'

'And in several more . . .?' Warm smile. Eye contact.
Cocked head inviting confidences. She recognized the technique, used it countless times herself. Maybe he was a better
reporter than she gave him credit for, or would be.

Holding his gaze, she was almost tempted to share the silent movie playing in her head: a police sting on a London street, the fatal shooting of a DI – the then rookie PC Sarah Quinn's fiancé, a man Caroline casually bedded from time to time. He'd given her off-the-record gen about the upcoming covert operation. What ambitious young reporter wouldn't have used the info? But even now she heard the screams in her nightmares, screams that panicked the killer into opening fire. Mostly they were Caroline's. Sarah had been a tad too busy trying to stem the flow of her fiancés blood.

'Well?' Still smiling, Mark held out empty palms.

She paused a few seconds more then shook her head; decided to keep the screening private for now. 'Let's just say she hates the media, Mark.'

'That's OK.' He hopped off the side, approached bottle in hand. 'I like a challenge.'

'Personal or professional?'

'Both. Why?'

'I'm pretty sure I can help you out then.'

'Business or pleasure, ma'am?'

'I can't see a problem.' Smiling she held out her glass. 'Why not both?'

Standing in the dark Pete Hinds peered through a gap in the side of the curtain. The bedroom window looked out on to the back of the house. Nightfall was long gone. Even less chance now of being seen when they made their move. He'd spotted the gate in the walled garden during a similar recce earlier in the day, already had it marked down as their way out.

He narrowed his eyes. 'What the . . .?' Froze. *Shit a brick.*

A greyish figure stood in the middle of the lawn. For a second or two he toyed with the crazy notion it must have snowed, that kids had sneaked in and built a snowman while he'd been otherwise occupied cleaning up his daughter's bloody mess. Literal and otherwise.

He felt a tug on his sleeve, warm breath near his ear. 'What is it Dad?' Her still-damp hair smelled of apples, the scent incongruous among the foul odours pervading the place.

'It's OK, babe.' He blew his cheeks out on a sigh. 'It's just a statue.' The clouds had lifted and moonlight now revealed a de Milo knock-off standing there in the buff. The relief was so great – or the hysteria rising – that he almost cracked a joke. Something about it being armless enough. Almost but not quite. Not with Natalie's frayed nerves on a knife edge. Instead he put a smile in his voice and ruffled her hair. 'No worries, eh?'

No response either.

Course there were no worries: a decomposing body in the next room, his daughter with blood – albeit metaphorical now – on her hands, the murder weapon stowed in his coat pocket and every cop in the West Midlands and probably beyond on the lookout. *Walk in the park, wasn't it?*

Well, car park. Thank God he'd opted for the NCP round the corner. If he'd risked leaving the van in the drive or taking up one of the resident's bays, all it needed was one nosy neighbour picking up the phone. The police wouldn't even have had to run the plate through the PNC. Not with his name and numbers emblazoned in huge red lettering on both sides of the bodywork.

'All set, Nats?' He put an arm round her shoulders, hoped he sounded more confident than he felt. Again there was no answer. She'd barely opened her mouth all day. He didn't really need a response, not with the shaking and shallow breaths telling him how scared she was.

You and me both, babe.

He steered her to the landing, lit a match and led the way downstairs. 'See all right?' The last thing they needed was to fall, break their necks. In the hallway he stroked a thumb down her cheek, told her to go and wait by the back door. He'd done almost everything he could conceive of to cover their tracks: washed glasses, wiped just about every surface, light switch, door handle, poured copious amounts of bleach down kitchen and bathroom sinks, even more down the shower after Natalie had sluiced the blood off her. Mind, the killing room – as he thought of it – still looked like an abattoir. No way could he have removed every trace of the bastard's blood. Not that he'd tried. But he knew it would take only one drop of Natalie's, one skin cell to put them both behind bars for the foreseeable. And the cops weren't stupid. With the wealth of forensic techniques at their disposal, Pete realized whatever steps he'd taken were probably just a question of buying time.

Listening out, he paused at the bottom of the stairs. 'OK, Nats? I won't be a tick.' He had one more thing to do.

'Don't be long, Dad.'

He crept back to the killing room, opened the curtain to let in street light. The bottle of rum was where he'd left it just inside the door. 'Time, gentlemen, please,' he mouthed as he poured every last drop of booze over his daughter's rapist. Lip curled, he watched it glisten as it ran off the body, soak into the bedding. 'Last orders, you bastard.'

Then he struck a match.

FIFTEEN

'Have you nailed the bastard yet?'

Sarah frowned, couldn't place the voice and caller display had meant nothing to her.

'Who is this, please?' Mr Shouty was bloody lucky to get a 'please'. She had a splitting headache and given her mood, it was lucky she didn't own a cat, or it could be in line for a kicking.

'That's nice isn't it, love? You were supposed to be keeping me informed. I've been sitting round all day waiting for word.'

And hitting the booze by the sound of the slurs. Mind, Sarah had just poured a large G&T – the second since getting home. Normally she avoided spirits. She'd successfully avoided Dave though. Or maybe he'd done the dodging? Probably still pissed off with her. She sniffed. *Join the club.*

'An officer called at the house, Mr Webb,' she said ferrying her drink through to the open-plan lounge. The all-purpose-patronizing 'love' had told her who the caller was.

Normally she'd have pulled him up on it first time round but, given the circumstances under which they'd met, it would have sounded pretty heartless. 'He told me he didn't think anyone was home.'

And Sarah was beginning to think it was time she rationed who she gave her phone numbers to. She gulped a large mouthful before setting down the glass on a low table.

'Well he should've knocked a bit louder then, shouldn't he? Besides, I'm not interested in lackeys, you're running the show, aren't you?'

She traced an eyebrow with a finger. *Moot point.* Starr had graced the late brief with his presence, hung around just long enough to bring on board DI George Brody. In theory, Brody had equal SIO billing with Sarah, but in practise the extra years and experience under his belt gave him the edge. And as Starr had kindly pointed out, Detective Brody boasted the best clear-up rate in the Midlands. Boasted being the operative word: the guy never failed to big himself up, and with the build and swagger of a heavyweight boxer, he had the physique to match. Not to mention the nose.

Bee-atch. Sarah slapped a mental wrist, flopped down on the leather couch and kicked off a shoe. 'I assure you, Mr Webb, any major developments and I, personally, will be in touch.'

'That's big of you, love. But basically what you're really saying is there's naff all moved and my daughter's killer's still out there roaming the streets?'

She winced. The other shoe had ricocheted off the TV. As for Webb's take on the inquiry's current state: *tell me about it.* Seemed like everyone else had. Before exiting the brief Starr had voiced straight out his disapproval at the lack of progress. Squad members had exhibited feelings more subtly with closed body language, minimal eye contact; lukewarm responses when she dished out tasks. Had the tacit criticism – disappointment? – been directed at her, or was she being defensive? Hardly surprising given how marginalized she felt. Either way it barely figured. Sarah was her own harshest critic and her current reviews were crap.

'I assure you, Mr Webb, we're doing everything possible to apprehend Lisa's attacker.' Reaching down to scratch her ankle, she reeled off a few stats: officers on the case, statements taken, doors knocked, hours of CCTV viewed. The sheer force of numbers usually placated grieving relatives.

'If you're doing so bloody brilliantly, how come he's not banged up?'

Usually.

Lost my magic wand, didn't I? 'I've every faith he will be. It's just a question of time before we make an arrest.' That was pushing it given they didn't have a lead.

'I hope to God he is, love.' Quieter, subdued, contrite. She heard him swallow what sounded like a sob. 'It's just . . .' Waiting while he composed himself, Sarah took another sip or two of her drink. Eating something wouldn't be a bad idea either. 'I keep seeing her . . . my little Lisa lying there. I can't . . . I can't handle the thought of him . . . you know . . .'

She did. 'I understand, Mr Webb. I'm sure I'd feel the same.' She'd interviewed more than enough bereaved parents to gain a modicum of insight and empathy. He blew his nose then apologized for balling her out, said he felt helpless, itched to do something constructive.

Scratching the ankle again, she narrowed her eyes. 'There is actually.' She told him how much impact it could have if he appeared on TV, made a personal appeal for witnesses. 'I can call a news conference for tomorrow if you like?' Silence. More silence. At least this time he'd not rejected her request out of hand. 'What do you say?'

'I'd like to, love, but I'd be no good to you. I'd likely dry up or break down or something.'

And that was a problem? The more tears the merrier, as far as the media was concerned. As it happened, Shona had already lined up Zoe Darby's father to do a turn first thing. She mentioned this to Webb and added a jocular line about safety in numbers.

Another pause then: 'No. I don't think so.'

She stifled a sigh. 'No pressure, Mr Webb. Sleep on it, I'll be in touch in the morning.'

'I said no,' he snapped. 'Don't ask again.' *Touch-ee.* She recalled him lashing out at Slater that morning. Had half expected Webb to have a record for violence, but checks had come back blank. 'And one more thing while I've got you,' he said, 'you reckon it's just a question of time before the guy's nicked? Well, you'd best hope your lot get to him before I do.'

Of course his clean sheet could be about to get stained. Sarah straightened. 'Meaning?'

'Read into it what you like, love.'

'I'd strongly advise against taking the law—' A glance at the phone confirmed she was talking to herself. Scowling, she slung it on the cushion, picked up her glass and drained it. She was pretty sure the bluff and bluster was big talk brought on by misplaced feelings of guilt. Besides, if Webb harboured even the vaguest notion about taking on the killer, he'd keep schtum, not broadcast it.

She twisted her leg for a better view of the bites. There was a crop of the sodding things and all the scratching had drawn blood. Would Savlon do? 'Cause she sure hadn't had time to buy calamine.

En route to the bathroom Sarah paused and pressed palms and forehead against the cool glass of the floor-to-ceiling window. Multi-coloured reflections danced on the canal's dark water, a narrow boat drifted slowly by. She invariably found the view therapeutic, certainly better than the telly. The apartment's central location had been a big selling point when she moved to Birmingham. Brindleyplace buzzed with night life: cinema, theatre, comedy clubs, countless eateries and wine bars all within walking distance. So why wasn't the magic working? She sighed. Maybe she should get out more?

Her spirits took another dive when she clocked Dave's toothbrush and razor. Absence makes the heart grow fonder? Or regret she'd allowed him into her personal space in the first place? One thing she did know: if Dave was around tonight he'd chivvy her out of the current woe-is-me-pit. He was always on at her to loosen up, chill out. Easy for him to say, but old habits and all that.

She gave a wry smile when she found the Savlon behind Dave's aftershave. Every time he stayed over, he left more territory-marking stuff. If she gave the word, he'd move in like a shot, but for her it was a no-no. Living together would be too close for comfort.

'Ouch.' The antiseptic stung like crazy. Better than the bites getting infected though. She couldn't afford to take time off work. Not with Brody snapping at her heels.

Holding on to the sink, she gazed into the mirror. Why the hell had she cut her hair? She swore the short style aged her. Or was that the crow's feet? She sure wasn't getting any younger. At thirty-four, she was older now than her parents when they died in the car crash. She barely remembered what they looked like. Her aunt, who she'd lived with after the accident, told Sarah she was the image of her father. Sarah wouldn't know. The only photographs she had were buried at the bottom of a battered old suitcase.

She closed her eyes, and shut her mind. Fully aware Freud would be having a field day.

SIXTEEN

A DC on the night shift made what could be a break-through. Sod's Law. Doug's Law even. Douglas Spencer wasn't even assigned to Operation Panther. He'd been on a trawl through city centre CCTV in connection with another case, some drunken fracas. On fifteen seconds of pretty decent footage, he'd clocked a laughing Lisa Webb and Natalie Hinds walking arm-in-arm out of a wine bar. Spencer might have been chasing brownie points – more likely a place on the murder squad – but he'd alerted Sarah at home first thing.

She'd driven through relatively empty streets and headed straight for a viewing. The incident room was almost deserted too, a couple of detectives on phone calls, a cleaner spraying polish around – the smell of lavender mingling with coffee and sweat. It had been a hectic night though. She'd picked that much up on police radio: hit and run in Handsworth, house fire in Edgbaston, GBH in Small Heath.

Now glancing up from the monitor, she asked Spencer for a replay. This time, she squatted down to get a better view, reckoned he'd done bloody well – the likenesses on the tape bore little relation to the girls' photos already on general release. They looked much older for one thing, heels added height, Lisa had her hair gelled into spikes and so much make-up on even her mother would struggle recognizing her.

'Freeze it there can you?' The sharpest close-up now filled the screen, both girls looking as if they hadn't a care in the world. Sobering thought. Sarah tightened her mouth. *Thank God no one knows what's round the corner.*

'Can we get that circulated ASAP?' She stood, shucked off her coat.

'It's in hand, ma'am. A guy in the press office is sorting it.' She gave him more than a cursory glance this time. Late twenties? Six-two? Looked as if he worked out. A lot. The deep-set eyes were pale blue, piercing. She was surprised he'd not hit her radar before.

'Good.' She gave a fleeting smile, glanced at her watch. Should just be time to grab coffee before the brief, might even stretch to a round of toast. 'So the wine bar? Where is it?'

'The Dark Horse. Just up from the law courts?' His five o'clock shadow went with the longish blue-black hair. Five o'clock? More like eight.

She nodded. 'We need to get on to the owner.' Most of the bars round there had security cameras inside these days. With a bit of luck . . .

He slipped a casual hand in the pocket of tailored black trousers. 'I spoke to him, ma'am and despatched a rider. The footage is on its way now. He seemed reluctant at first but when I pointed out the girls' ages . . .' A shapely eyebrow disappeared under a thick fringe. 'It seemed sufficient leverage.' The guy had initiative. Not to mention a winning smile.

'Excellent, well done.' She ran a hand through her hair. 'Let me know soon as.'

'Tape back from the bar yet, Dougie?'

Sarah felt a sudden draught, stiffened, forced herself not to

turn round. Heavy breathing and a voice with a sixty-a-day
rasp told her who'd hurtled through the door. And if Brody
was that far up to speed, Spencer must have put in a call to
him before her. She cut the young detective a glance. Not such
a blue-eyed boy after all. Well not in her book.

'I'm expecting it any minute, sir.'

'Good lad.' Brody forced a silk tie down a straining waistband. 'Late night was it, DI Quinn?' He must've clocked
Sarah's expression because he dropped the smirk, raised a
palm. 'Joke.'

'Really? Let me know next time.' *I'll be sure to crack a
smile.*

'I've already tipped you the wink once today.'

'Sorry?'

'Early bird, me.' He cocked his head towards the screen.
'Not late like some little birdies, eh?' The line and its flip
delivery shocked her. Brody read the silence differently.

'Keep up, Inspector. I've been in since half-five. It's a
habit of mine – grabbing the juiciest worms. Anyway, I got
Dougie here to give you a bell. Isn't that right, lad?' Spencer
looked none too pleased with the blokey punch to his upper
arm.

She didn't look delirious either. As she walked away, Brody
called after her, 'Cheer up. It might never happen.'

'Black coffee please, Doreen.' Sarah tapped testy fingers on
the metal counter. Sod the toast. In her current mood it would
probably choke her. For a few seconds she fantasized about
having her hands round Brody's bull neck and squeezing.
Hard.

'On a diet are we, Quinn?'

'Chief?' A genuine beam of pleasure crossed Sarah's face
as she turned to find Baker waiting next in line. Decked out
in one of his sharp grey suits, he casually jangled keys in a
pocket. 'Good to see you, Fred.' Who'd have thought it? Her
old boss a sight for sore eyes.

'Missed me have you, Quinn?' He winked. 'And what about
you, Doreen, my lovely? Positively wasting away back there,
I see.'

Wasting away? Amused, Sarah dipped her head. The old dear behind the counter looked like she'd scarfed as many breakfasts as she'd served and she'd worked there since God was in a Moses basket.

'What are you like, Mr B?' Simper, simper. Sarah curved a lip. The woman who must have been in her late-sixties had gone all coquettish, fluttering barely there eye-lashes, rocking on her Reeboks. 'What can I do you for then?'

'How about a night of passion with the woman of my dreams? Mind, I'll need the full Monty first.'

'You are a one, Mr B.' Giggling, she scuttled off blushing, as red as the sauce.

Still smiling Sarah said, 'Glad to see you're cutting back, chief. And no I'm not on a diet.' He'd eased off the Paco Rabanne, too. Baker's lavish aftershave habit had always been a useful early warning signal. It sure hadn't worked this time.

'Good. I've seen more meat on a toothpick.'

He'd lost none of his charm then. 'So what you doing here?'

'Can't keep a good man down, Quinn.'

'And? Thanks.' She took a steaming mug from Doreen who only had eyes for her number one fan.

'Extra sausage, Mr B?'

'You temptress, you. Go on then.' He watched her scuttle off again, dropped the smile, then said: 'To tell the truth, Sarah, I'm not entirely sure I know myself. Ted Willis called, asked me to drop by.' He nodded acknowledgement to a couple of uniforms waving from the far side of the canteen.

'ACC Ops?' Why on earth would the assistant chief constable operations want to see Baker?

'Correct.'

'A working breakfast then?' she quipped. Breakfast? The plate Doreen was currently stacking would keep two men going till midnight. Tomorrow.

'Stick to the day job, funny girl.' He seemed a tad distracted. Maybe mulling over why Willis had issued the summons, too.

'When are you seeing him?' She took a sip of coffee.

'Kick-off's at nine. So I thought I might as well get in early, grab a few worms while I'm at it.'

She snorted. 'Don't talk to me about worms.' Sensed his keen gaze on her.

'Someone rattled your cage, Quinn?'

Had he ever missed a trick? 'Don't worry about me, chief. I'll get over it.'

'Hold on a tick. I'll get the violin.' He rolled his eyes. 'Come on, Quinn, don't be such a bloody martyr. What's your beef?'

'Martyr. Thanks.' At least she always knew where she stood with the chief – the guy didn't do pussy-foot.

'You gonna be around later?' Baker said.

She raised an eyebrow. *In the middle of a major inquiry?*

'Yeah, yeah, OK, dumb question.' He flapped a hand. Shit. She'd caught sight of the time on his watch.

'Look, chief, give me a bell, eh? I'm running late. It's—'

'Brief o'clock. Yeah, I used to work here remember?' He smiled. 'Go on then don't stand there yakking.'

She started backing off, palm raised. 'Really, really good to see you, chief. Let me know how—'

They swivelled in sync when the swing door burst open. Dave stood there scanning the room, his face flushed, tie askew over a shoulder. The second he spotted her, he headed over like a man on a mission.

'Well, well, well . . . if it isn't the boy wonder,' Baker murmured. 'Looks like they've sent a search party, Quinn.'

'I've been looking for you, boss.' He threw Baker a brisk nod. 'Chief.'

'And now you've found me.' She tried to read his expression in the pause. 'What is it, Dave?'

'Triple-nine's come in.'

Sarah sighed. Why couldn't he just spit it out? 'Fuck's sake, Dave. I'm not clairvoyant.'

He held her gaze. 'It's that teacher bloke, boss.'

She frowned. 'Drake?'

'He's dead.'

'Dead?'

'Sounds like he topped himself.'

SEVENTEEN

A postman put in the call after finding Drake with slashed wrists. That was about all Dave had been able to impart so far. Sarah stared through the passenger window, her conflicting thoughts racing. Rain ran in rivulets down the glass and further blurred passing scenery. Not that she gave a toss about the view. Barely saw it. Uppermost in mind was whether her questioning had pushed Larry Drake over the edge. Unwanted images flashed in front of her eyes – the blotchy face, the pink skull, the spittle on his lips as he repeatedly protested his innocence.

Dave had cast one or two sneaky glances her way when they got in the motor, but was currently keeping his cards close. She was pretty sure it was to give her space rather than keep his distance. One thing she'd learned over the years: he was a damn sight quicker than her at picking up on people's moods. Another? He rarely sulked. Apart from a tongue-in-cheek, 'Forgiven am I?' he'd not alluded to her freezing him out yesterday.

'It could be a sign of guilt you know, boss.' Casual testing of the water.

She didn't turn her head 'Yeah, but whose?'

It took a second or two for him to digest that then, 'Surely you're not blaming yourself?' Concern? Incredulity? 'Come on, Sarah. That's utter bollocks.' *A bit of both then.*

'Is it?' She let the Sarah go. Like it mattered.

'Course it is. You were the one who cast doubt on the call's credibility, remember?' She shrugged. 'It couldn't just be ignored,' he persisted. 'The accusations had to be put to him.'

Yeah, but what if she'd not been the right man – woman – for the job. She hadn't exactly sugared the paedophile pill. What had Shona said? We turn up there with nothing to go on and more or less accuse him of a string of sex attacks.

Sarah balled a gloved fist. 'He said he didn't do it, Dave.'

'Well of course he—'

'None of it,' she snapped, turned in the seat to face him. 'Including the offence he was jailed for.'

'And that makes it your fault?' He let the silence ride a while, then: 'Come on, boss, how does that work?'

'Leave it, eh.' She flapped a hand. Her icy aloofness couldn't have helped though. She cringed recalling how she'd barely been able to hide her revulsion for Drake. That would have worked wonders for his self-esteem. Shona hadn't let any emotion show, and she'd actually felt a certain amount of sympathy for the guy. Shona's face had dropped like a stone when she'd heard the news this morning; her wide eyes and sudden pallor spoke volumes. Volumes Sarah could do without dipping into any further. Even if Shona hadn't made prior arrangements with Zoe Darby and her father, Sarah wouldn't want her here now.

She glanced at Dave's profile. Better the devil you know. And DC. She reached forward to switch the blower higher. Wished confusion could be dispersed as effortlessly as condensation. Lack of sleep didn't help, nor the nightmares when she'd finally drifted off. Doubtless Drake's death would provide a few more.

'Shona questioned whether he was guilty you know, Dave.' She waited for a reaction. 'After we left the house.' Waited again then pushed. 'Said either way he'd suffered enough.'

He glanced across. 'I wouldn't know about that, would I?' His half-smile took the edge off the dig.

She couldn't dredge one up in return. Of course Dave couldn't offer an opinion, he'd not been there; he'd been left out in the cold. Like Sarah at this morning's brief. She could picture it now: Brody playing the big 'I am', all blokes together. Just when the case was showing a hairline crack. Funny that. Starr's pointed suggestion that she head out to Aston hadn't bothered her. She felt the need to be there anyway. So how come she also felt side-lined?

Because Drake isn't a major player and has nothing to do with the main event?

Leaning her head back against the rest, she closed her eyes thinking it through. If the anonymous caller hadn't brought

Drake's name to the fore, the squad would have been none the wiser. She'd not have gone haring off to the house yesterday. And Drake would almost certainly be alive and kicking.

So who'd made it and more to the point—?

Dave cut the engine, and glanced across. 'What did she mean, boss?'

'Sorry?' She straightened, glanced round. Christ, they were here, she'd been miles away.

'Brucie. She reckoned he'd suffered enough?'

Sarah grabbed her bag. 'Drake was seen as a convicted paedo, Dave. Go figure.'

He didn't need it spelling out. No cop did.

Someone needed a lesson though: a crash course in English maybe.

FUCK OF PEEDO

'Seen that?' Sarah nodded at the latest wall art. It was difficult to miss: jagged letters four foot high scrawled across the brickwork in – what else? – scarlet paint. More *billets*-not-so-*doux* became legible the nearer they approached.

CuMface Wankarse

'Is it recent?' Dave sniffed.

'It sure wasn't there yesterday.' Neither were the dozen or so ghouls milling opposite the house. Or the police cordon, marked cars, white transit.

'Nor that.' She pointed at shit smeared on the window. Talk about reek. No wonder Dave sounded as if he was coming down with a cold.

Sarah glanced up at the sky – gloom grey. Shame the rain had eased off or the audience might not be so keen on hanging around for the final scene. Mind, with their chanting it was more like a Greek chorus.

'Nonce. Nonce. Nonce. Out. Out. Out.'

She was about to ask Dave to sort it but spotted a couple of PCs on the way over. Thank God. What with the heckling,

she could barely hear herself think or make out what the
uniform on door duty had just said.

'Say again.' She slipped her ID back in her coat pocket.
'Constable Noakes, isn't it?' *Ken? Keith?*

'That's right, ma'am. Kevin.' Big noise in the Police
Federation if she remembered right. Big full stop.

'I missed what you said, Kevin.'

'I can't let you in like that, ma'am. Sorry. You need a
boilersuit.' *Protective gear? For a suicide?*

She asked Dave to grab one from the boot then turned back
to Noakes. 'What's the score, then? I thought he'd—'

Noakes tapped the side of his nose. 'Current thinking's he
might have had a helping hand, ma'am. Maybe even two.'

EIGHTEEN

D rake's body lay flat out on the Lazyboy, an expanse
of lardy flesh on show where the grubby T-shirt had
ridden up over his belly. His wide eyes stared sightlessly at the nicotine stained ceiling. The pathologist held the
left arm aloft in both hands closely examining the damage, a
police photographer reeled off shots like there was no tomorrow.
Which in Drake's case was undoubtedly true.

Neither turned when Sarah entered. Not that she got far,
the sight of the arm brought her up sharp. It looked like a
joint you'd see hanging in a butcher's.

'Inspector,' Patten murmured, focus still on the arm. 'We
can't go on meeting like this.'

Reaching for another lens, the photographer acknowledged
her with a mock salute. She nodded but beneath the white
mask, drew her lips together. Patten's limp gag was old enough
to come with a Zimmer frame. She'd found it vaguely amusing
first time round, might even have smiled when he cracked it.
Not now. Time, place and all that. Besides, scanning the poky,
stifling back room, the DI struggled to find anything even
remotely amusing; struggled almost to breathe.

The sea of plastic sheeting laid out by the FSIs covered the entire floor and indicated massive blood loss. Duckboards were also in place to provide a forensically safe passage.

Still hanging back Sarah continued a mental inventory, knowing the bigger picture would be infinitely more palatable than the close-up. She reckoned the snapper must have an iron stomach. The sight of the arm alone was enough to make most people think about going vegetarian. Vegan even.

Her glance fell on a grimy foot where a slipper had come adrift revealing hard cracked skin like the rind on a cheese. On a ring-stained table close by, half a dozen pale, flaccid chips floated in a lake of vinegar. The number of lager cans in the grate had tripled. And even through the protective mask, the stench of blood and human waste made her want to throw up.

Dave, long straw boy, was al fresco having a word with the postman who – funnily enough – hadn't been in a hurry to resume his round. Mind, even with more space inside, the forensic manager wouldn't have let Dave in – the fewer people trampling a crime scene, the less risk of contaminating evidence. If it was a crime scene? It sure as hell looked like one.

'Just nipping back to the car, Inspector.' The photographer smiled as he passed her in the doorway.

Sarah swallowed then took a shallow breath and moved nearer the corpse. 'What happened then?' Terse. Terser than she'd intended.

Richard's gloved hand stilled momentarily as he cut her a glance. 'And good morning to you, too.'

'Can we get on with it, please?' She let out a laboured sigh.

Taking his time, he laid the arm down gently, almost reverently. The way he treated stiffs was one of the things she liked about him. Usually. Right now she wanted him to pull his finger out.

'If you're in such a mad hurry, take a wild guess,' Patten snapped. He could do sharp too.

'I don't get paid to do guesswork.' Given the congealed pools of blood, the gaping wounds and a bagged and tagged carving knife she'd spotted in Patten's metal case, she probably could. But she was in no mood for games.

'Good for you,' he paused, made a note on a pad. 'Neither am I.'

She mentally counted to ten. 'I take it that's the knife?'

'I'm not paid to speculate either.' The fact he often gave her an early steer was another thing he had going for him. She'd clearly irked the normally amiable Patten, but they were here to do a job, he needed to get over it. 'Look, Richard—'

'No, Inspector, you look.' He pointed his pen at Drake's left arm. Sarah flinched. The flesh had been hacked from wrist to elbow. No. Gouged was a better word, the skin damn near flayed, the wound ragged, wide and deep. And looked as if it had been dipped in paint the colour of liver. Dead meat. The butcher's image flashed in her head again.

She shuddered. 'Christ, Richard. That was no cry for help, was it?'

'Damn right.' Clearly he was shocked, angered even, at the brutality and she'd blundered in and added insult to injury. She started to apologize but he flapped a 'no need' hand.

'As it happens, Sarah, I'm not convinced that knife killed him. It was in his hand when I arrived. But look at the blade.' She saw his point: too thin, too smooth. 'What's more, given the state of him I think there'd have been a hell of a lot of crying going on. Crying, screaming, begging.'

She raised an eyebrow. 'Begging?' *As in, for mercy?*

'I can't see how he did that to himself. Look at the extent of the wounds. Opening up one arm would have been nigh on impossible but two? I don't think so.'

She nodded slowly. 'What if he'd taken something?'

'Like?'

'I don't know.' She shrugged. 'Painkillers? Some sort of anaesthetic? Drugs?'

'A dose big enough to deaden that? No way.' He shook his head. 'He'd have been comatose before he even started.'

'Hold on.' She stiffened. 'You said he'd have screamed?'

'Loud enough to wake the dead if he was conscious.'

And the neighbourhood? Eyes narrowed, she pictured the Greek chorus outside. If neighbours had heard Drake yelling blue murder, why hadn't they called the police? Because no one gave a shit about an aging perv? Thought Drake had it coming? *Even had a hand in his send-off?* No, that was pushing it. Names and addresses wouldn't go amiss though; video, even better. The rubberneckers might disperse before she could ask the pro to do it. She'd get Dave to shoot a bit of footage on his phone. And if walls had ears – so did Drake's neighbours – and a tongue in their head. Another job for Dave.

Telling Patten she needed to make a call, Sarah took a few steps away. The ringtone sounded as she slipped the phone out of her pocket. *Great minds.* 'What've you got?'

He'd finished with the postman, Dave told her, thought it might be worth having another stab later. 'He's still in a state of shock, boss. Wishes he'd never set foot.'

Good point. 'How did he get in? When I came the place was like Fort Knox.'

'Not this morning it wasn't. He found the door ajar, popped his head round, called out a few times. Said the stink nearly made him bring up his cornflakes.'

'Missing breakfast's not all bad news then.' She must have sounded plaintive. Dave told her there was a caff on the corner, he'd pick up a bite if she liked. No way. They'd driven past it, she wasn't that desperate. 'So did the postman think there'd been a break-in?' She'd not spotted anything obvious, but with Noakes' bulk in the way . . .?

'Nah,' Dave said, 'just doing his concerned citizen bit. Probably thought there'd be a medal in it down the line.'

'Talking of concerned citizens . . .' She brought him up to speed, told him what she wanted.

'I'll knock off as many pics as you like boss, but surely anyone with something to hide isn't going to be dense enough to show their face outside.'

'Maybe not.' But the grandstanders might have spotted something, heard something. And one of them might even be a dab hand with a paint brush. He got her drift, said he'd sort it then liaise with uniform who'd already made a start on the door-to-doors.

Pensive, she ended the call. So if the door hadn't been forced and there were no signs of a disturbance, had Drake let in someone he knew? Someone he trusted? She doubted the friends' list would be long.

'I'm about done here.' Patten snapped the locks on the case then stood, lowered the mask and faced her. Either he'd taken to wearing eye shadow or he'd been burning the midnight oil. And lost his razor.

'You OK, Richard?'

'I'm dog-tired as it happens. Got a call out in the early hours.' Scratching at his stubble, he gave her a wry smile. 'I'll live though. Unlike the poor sod in the fire.'

'The blaze out at Edgbaston?' She frowned, recalled hearing a line about it on the police radio while driving in that morning. 'I didn't know it was fatal.'

'The fire wasn't – not for want of trying.' Two fires had been started, he told her. One upstairs hadn't caught, fizzled out before it caused real damage. The blaze downstairs had – fortunately – generated enough smoke to alert a neighbour who'd called nine-nine-nine.

'Smoke inhalation then?'

He took off the cap, smoothed his hair. 'It might well have killed him eventually. If he'd not already died from stab wounds.'

'Who's the investigating officer?'

'Raj Malik?' DCI. Safe pair of hands. 'Anyway, it's not your baby, is it? Getting back to the job in hand, doubtless you want an idea on time of death?'

Time? She frowned. 'Did he have a watch on, Richard? Rollie on the right wrist?'

He shook his head. 'I've not seen one around either.'

'No worries.' She'd ask someone to check. 'Back to time of death then.'

Patten's smile suggested he'd forgiven her earlier brusqueness. 'Trickier even than normal, Sarah. That was on full blast when I arrived.' Pointing his cap at the four-bar fire. The heat, he said, would have affected the fall in Drake's body temperature – usually the best, but still rough, guide to how long someone had been dead. 'Rigor's set in but isn't advanced,' Patten added.

She nodded, knew the best bet would be stomach contents. 'So the sooner he's on the slab . . .'

'Exactly.' Case under arm, Patten headed out, turned at the door. 'Of course, there could be another explanation why no one heard screaming?' It felt like a test, she ran her gaze over his face for clues.

He voiced one: '*He* might not have taken anything but . . .?'

'The killer could've sedated him.'

'Got it in one. Even then, I think he'd have been drifting in and out of consciousness. He'd have to have been gagged and restrained as well.'

She frowned. 'Are we talking rope? Gaffer tape?'

'Nothing to indicate either.' So no abrasions, ligature marks, bits of adhesive. 'I'm thinking hands, as in an extra pair.'

NINETEEN

'It's likely the killer had an accomplice, sir.' Phone to her ear, Sarah paced up and down the narrow pavement outside Drake's house, dodging wheelie bins and dog shit. *Dog. Cat. What happened to Drake's?* And was Starr still on the line? Judging by the silence, the boss was mulling over what she'd said.

Glancing up she saw a couple of uniforms on doorsteps, a third tailing an old man into his house. She presumed the ghouls' absence from across the street was down to the meat wagon's late arrival. No fun goading a dead man, was there? Hold on a min. Had all that 'out, out, out' malarkey earlier meant they thought Drake would be emerging alive as opposed to feet first?

'Inspector? Are you still there?'

'Yes. Sorry, say again.'

She heard a heavy sigh on the line then: 'I *said*: so one minute it's suicide, the next we're talking homicide and hunting two killers.' Like it was her fault. Whereas the way Sarah saw it now, at least she could stop blaming herself for a bit part in Drake's death.

'I'm telling you what the evidence suggests.' She perched on
the Astra's bonnet circling an ankle, the one without the bites.
A couple of kids walked past casting curious glances at her
white suit. Probably thought she was big in pest control.

'I take it there was no note?'

Yeah, signed confession in blood to murder and serial
rape. 'You take it right.' Talk about clutching frayed straws.
Clearly he'd not been listening properly. Prior to the feedback
he'd probably imagined they could tie up Operation Panther
in pretty blue and white tape and file it away in a box marked
'NFA'. Tough. The inquiry was more than ongoing and *all*
fucking action and Sarah couldn't picture how Drake fitted
into it at all. Neither did she want to hang around in Aston
investigating an unrelated case. Not when things could be
kicking off back at HQ.

'He could still be implicated of course.'

'Sorry?' How the hell did Starr work that one out? She
raised a palm as Dave sauntered her way tugging the ring pull
on a can of Coke.

'Think laterally, Inspector.' She heard Starr take a sip of
something. In your own time, Charlie. Don't mind me. 'Say
Drake went to the pub, got drunk, maudlin, the alcohol loos-
ened his tongue and his conscience. He lets guilty secrets slip.
Someone follows him home. Kills him and makes it look like
suicide to point us in the wrong direction.'

Lateral? Fictional more like. She stifled a sigh. 'Can't see
it somehow, sir.' Apart from the fact Drake had been scared
of venturing out, how much booze would he have to have sunk
to drop his guard that far? Enough to scuttle a fleet. Deliberate
misdirection though? Starr had a point there. The knife Patten
had found for one thing.

'OK. How about this . . . Drake wanted to die? Was wracked
with guilt, couldn't live anymore with the remorse.' Sarah
rolled her eyes at Dave who stood there swigging Coke. Starr
wasn't so much warming to a theme – he was in flames. 'He
hasn't got the guts to take his own life so he gets someone
else to do the deed. A career criminal he served time with
perhaps?' Straw? Bale of the bloody things.

Starr was banging on as if every ex-con just happened to

have a tame killer on speed-dial. 'Still not seeing it, sir.' What she saw was an attack so brutal it had to have been executed by someone who knew Drake, hated him to the extent they wanted him to die in agony and watch him take his final bow. It smacked of the personal not some professional hit man. And if she wasn't on the money, she was in the wrong job.

'Keep with it till you do see something then, eh, DI Quinn?'

'But, sir, I need to—' The bastard had hung up on her. She glared cross-eyed at the phone.

'Wrong call, boss?' Dave smiled, all innocent, then sank more Coke.

Call? There's a thought. She tapped a finger against her lips.

'I take it Starr's in no hurry to see us back any time soon?'

Sod Starr. She jumped off the bonnet. 'The woman who rang the hotline? Incriminating Drake. Why'd she do it, Dave? Why then? What did she stand to gain?'

'I thought she was on the level but like you said, boss, maybe an axe to grind?'

'And a bunch of questions to answer.' She nodded towards the house, needed to grab a word with the forensic boss. 'I want her tracked down.'

He fell into step with her. 'Easy for you to say.'

'The woman sure found it easy mouthing off about Drake.' And if she'd blabbed to the police . . .

'Yeah, but . . .'

'No buts. I want the tape released. A few plays on the radio, TV. Who knows?' Someone had to recognize the voice, surely?

'Twig'll sort it. I'll give him a bell.' He slipped a hand in his pocket. 'Want to see the movie, boss? The chorus line?'

'Later. What about the neighbours? Get anything?' The old dear next door was deaf as a post wearing ear plugs apparently. The other side spoke only a smattering of English. A uniform was going back with an interpreter in tow.

'Stick with it then, Dave.'

'Like glue.' Smiling he lifted the nearest bin lid to off-load the can, backed off fast. 'Shit on a stick.'

Charming. The stench reached Sarah first, second, a noise she'd never heard before. She cut a glance at Dave, retraced her steps then holding her breath peered in. Drake's cat, fur

matted with God knew what, lay on its side on a mound of
rotting food, filthy nappies. The sound was its breath struggling to get through what remained of its face. They'd need
to call a vet.

'Poor bloody thing.' She gave its head a gentle stroke.
'Shame you can't talk isn't it, puss?'

'Is it Drake's?'

'Was.'

He curled a lip. 'Animals.' She presumed he meant the
two-legged variety. 'Why'd they have to—?'

'What's that?' Frowning she pointed in the bin, made out a
black handle attached to what looked like a rusty blade with
a serrated edge. 'Don't touch it, Dave.'

He drew his hand back sharpish. 'Looks like an old knife
to me, boss.'

It was rusty, red and blood-streaked. To Sarah, it looked
like they'd found the murder weapon.

TWENTY

'We need to find this . . . this . . . monster before
he attacks again.' Well-spoken voice, measured
pace. The reasoned plea came from a middle-aged
man in a Homburg and a black Crombie. Staring ahead he sat
ramrod straight on a park bench. He could've been a bank
manager, a brief. The caption at the bottom of the screen read:
Michael Darby, victim's father.

Wearing leather driving gloves, he wrung his hands in his
lap as if to keep out the cold. The biting wind might account
for the glistening in his eyes. He shook his head slowly and
the camera panned to show the viewer his sight-line. In the
grey mid-distance, a soft focus now-you-see-me-now-you-don't
image of a young woman trudging along an avenue of trees.
Her head bowed, shoulders slumped and hands dug deep in
the pockets of a shapeless brown duffle coat. Trailing behind,
a police officer in a high-vis vest.

Mr Darby provided a low-key, matter-of-fact, soundtrack. 'Since the attack we take each day as it comes. Today's not good. Zoe's too afraid to talk on camera, too scared to allow a film crew anywhere near where we live. But she never again wants to set foot inside a police station. It brings back the night, you see. The ordeal. Will she ever get over it?' He sighed. 'Who knows?'

'Good, isn't he?' Glancing up at the screen, Angela Webb laid a knife and fork on the kitchen table. 'You'd have to have a heart of—'

'Please, love. Shush.' Her husband sat at the table, gaze fixed on the TV. 'I'm trying to listen.' Trying to place the bloke actually, Ian Webb was sure he'd come across Darby before. Something there he couldn't put his finger on.

The camera cut back to catch Darby slipping a white hankie into his pocket. He cleared his throat then looked straight into the lens. 'If you think you know the man responsible, have any suspicion at all, please come forward, don't stay silent. Imagine his next victim is *your* daughter . . . your sister . . . your wife.' He swallowed hard. 'Please call the police. Don't protect this individual. At the very least he needs help.' Three numbers then filled the screen voiced by a studio presenter.

'Help?' Ian Webb zapped the remote. 'Castration's what the fucker needs.'

'The old bill'll have to find him first,' Angela murmured, handing over a plate loaded with burger and chips.

'Yeah right. They're useless an' all.'

'For Christ's sake quit whingeing, Ian.' She slammed a mug of tea on the table. 'If you're so bloody brilliant why not do something instead of—?'

'Do something?' He barged past her to grab a cloth from the sink to mop up the spilt tea. 'Like what?'

'Like him.' Shouting, she flung an arm at the screen. 'You could tell how much he loves her, the pain was written all over his face. You know what the cops reckon? All it takes is one person to pick up the phone.'

His hand stilled mid-wipe. 'Are you saying I don't love Lisa enough?'

'Don't be so bloody defensive.'

He could've bitten back, instead sat down and reached for the tomato sauce then changed tack. 'Is Ant not eating?'

'Does it look like it?'

'Where—?'

'Out.'

'Come on, love, don't . . .' He stifled a sigh.

'Well why don't we do an appeal then?' Christ, she was like a dog with a bone.

'I've told you once.'

'But it might work.' She raked both hands through her hair. 'I swear if I could help that guy, help anyone in our position, I'd be on to the cops in a flash.'

'Yeah, well, his daughter's still around to help.' The look on her face shocked him. Hurt? Hate? Contempt? 'Angie, I'm sorry. I didn't mean it like that.' He reached out to touch her arm but she spun on her heel, walked away.

He sighed, felt he could do no sodding right. Shovelling food down his mouth, he glanced up to see her picking at a few burnt chips on the baking tray. 'Aren't you hungry, love?' Back still turned, she answered with a shrug.

He couldn't remember the time he'd last seen her eat a proper meal. Drifting round the house in that sodding dressing gown, she'd not washed in days, spent hours lying on Lisa's bed staring at the ceiling or curled up in a ball. Surely Lisa's death should've drawn them closer? Fact was she'd barely uttered a civil word to him since the murder. He was pretty sure she held him partly to blame. Maybe she had a point. If he'd not let Lisa go out that night . . .

Christ, the thought of losing Angie as well as his daughter turned his stomach. Appetite gone, Webb picked up the plate, walked to the bin. Scraping in the leftovers, he wondered if he could bring himself to do what she wanted. But, no, he couldn't put himself out there like Darby. Even if he thought it'd do any good. Nothing was going to bring his daughter back. Again, he tried pinning down where he'd seen Darby before. Sod it. If it was important, it'd come back to him. Most things did eventually.

Most things.

TWENTY-ONE

'We're bringing a guy in for questioning, ma'am. Just thought you should know.'

Paul Wood on the mobile. And on the QT by the hushed sound of it. Good man.

'I appreciate it, Twig.' At least someone was keeping her in the Operation Panther loop. Not that Sarah could act on it. She couldn't see herself pulling out of Aston for at least another hour – the murder weapon hadn't been the only thing to turn up.

Gazing down through Drake's grimy back bedroom window, she watched an FSI wade through a tangle of undergrowth towards a ramshackle shed, knew his colleague was still lifting fibres and hairs from the downstairs rooms. Sarah held a dog-eared address book in one hand and had a journal of sorts tucked under an elbow – Drake's odd jottings, cryptic entries, some on loose scraps of paper shoved in between pages. The guy's watch hadn't turned up. No surprise given it was probably the only thing he'd owned worth nicking. She frowned. Not quite. There'd been a Dunhill lighter lying round on her first visit.

'His name's Zach Fraser?' Twig said.

It didn't set any bells ringing. 'How'd we get on to him?'

'Via The Dark Horse.'

She frowned. 'What? On the tape?'

'In a manner of speaking. One of the barmaids knows him, gave us his home address.' From what she'd said, when Fraser wasn't chatting up the talent, he was ogling big time. His default mode was creep-on-the-pull, the barmaid spoke from personal experience. And on Thursday she'd seen him trying it on with Lisa and Natalie.

Sarah turned her mouth down. 'So the guy's a sleaze?' Big deal. Row of beans. Get the cuffs.

'Bit more than that, ma'am. He left the bar about the

same time as the girls. Anyway we checked him out. He's
been inside. ABH.'

Actual Bodily Harm. She stiffened. 'Who's doing the
interview?'

'I'll give you one guess.'

George Brody observed Zach Fraser's antics through the
two-way mirror. The impromptu floorshow had kept the DI
quietly amused while he stood in front of the glass scoffing a
sausage roll. The rude-to-talk-with-a-full-mouth convention
had clearly passed him by.

'Feast your eyes on that, Sergeant.'

John Hunt, who'd been commandeered as sidekick at the
last minute, glanced up from skimming Fraser's police file.
Pouting and preening, the guy shimmied down an imaginary
catwalk towards his reflection. He studied his face in close-up,
teased slick dark hair into an Elvis-quiff then exhaled heavily
into a cupped hand. A slight moue suggested a Polo wouldn't
go amiss. He still puckered up and blew himself a kiss though.

'Bloody pansy,' Brody sneered as he brushed a layer of
crumbs off his Harris Tweed.

'Narcissus maybe,' Hunt murmured.

Fraser boasted five-ten of toned trim muscle and a sun tan
he probably didn't get in Benidorm. He was twenty-four and
a Zach of all trades: delivery driver, builder, gardener. A regular
odd-job merchant. All very hands-on, including roughing up
an ex-girlfriend in a fight outside a pub two years ago. He'd
served three months of a six-month sentence and kept his nose
clean since release.

Brody wiped his mouth with the back of a hand. 'Yeah,
well that's a matter of opinion.'

Hunt had the distinct impression his input wouldn't count
for much anyway. Not with Brody's opinion of his own capa-
bilities being so high. The way Hunt saw it, Fraser had been
brought in under what amounted to little more than false
pretences after being spun some line about helping make a
witness statement. There'd been no caution and he was free to
walk. Brody's view? If Fraser didn't know what was coming
he'd be less likely to duck and dive. The lack of transparency

struck Hunt as devious, it wasn't as if they had a bunch to hold
Fraser on.

'Right then, sarge.' Brody used both meaty fists to haul
waistband over gut. 'Time to sort the men from the girlies.'

Hunt just refrained from an eye-roll as he tailed the DI's
slipstream. If the stale smoke and carbolic soap mix was
macho, he'd pass, thanks.

'Take a seat, Mr Fraser.' The thud of a heavy file on the
metal table was at odds with Brody's softly-spoken invite.

Fraser sauntered to a chair, sat back cross-legged and folded
his arms across his chest. Hunt presumed the rips in the pale
blue jeans were trendy. Either way both kneecaps were taking
the air. Not particularly fresh right now. Fraser's deodorant
was having a tough time keeping up.

'I'm hoping this won't take long, Mr . . .?'

'Brody. Detective Inspector.'

'Big guns, eh?' Fraser raised a querying eyebrow. The rank's
significance would have registered. He gave an uncertain smile,
glance flicking between the straight-faced detectives. 'I thought
this was a routine inquiry?' A showy earring glinted in a lobe.

'That's right.' Brody leaned back in the chair, hands loosely
folded over his crotch. 'Feel free to fire away.'

'Not big on riddles, me. Let's get on with it, eh?' He held
Brody's gaze, but a jaw muscle clenched a couple of times.

'DS Hunt, if you'd be so kind.' Huntie slipped two ten-by-
eight photographs from an envelope, slid them towards Fraser.

'Recognize anyone, Mr Fraser?' Brody hadn't taken his gaze
off the guy's face since they'd squared up across the table.

'Course, I do. I'm no good with names, but those girls have
been all over the news.' He pointed at one of the pics. 'That
one's missing, isn't she?'

'Correct. Natalie Hinds. The other one's Lisa Webb.'

'And?'

'Dead. Murdered.'

Fraser shook a tetchy head. Hunt watched the quiff list to
the left. 'I don't mean that. I'm saying why ask me?'

'You knew she was dead then. Didn't need me to tell you.'
Statement not question.

'Again that's not what—'

'So, Mr Fraser. Don't you bother much with names?'

'Sorry?' As if he'd had trouble hearing.

'Aren't names important when you're hitting on girls?'

'Yeah right.' He gave a brittle laugh.

'Wrong, Mr Fraser. Fact, I'd say deadly serious.'

He tried hard not to react but the guy was no Oscar winner. 'Just where are you going with this, Mr Brody?'

'You were seen.' The detective tilted his head towards the table. 'With the girls.'

'Nah. Not me, mate.'

'In The Dark Horse. Thursday night.'

He gave a double-take straight out of the ham school of acting. Then he snatched both pics, held them close to his face, studied them for a while before saying, 'You know, you could be right.' He glanced up. 'Yeah, I did see them. But I wasn't *with* them with them, if you know what I mean. I was sitting at the bar waiting for a mate.'

'And the mate's name?'

'What's it matter? He didn't show anyway.'

'Leaving you foot-loose and fancy free to pal up with Lisa and Natalie. By all accounts you were getting on like a house on fire.'

'Bollocks.' He chucked the pictures back. 'What accounts?'

'I told you: witnesses.'

'Had white sticks, did they?'

Brody shook his head. 'Nor golden Labradors. Now try again, sunshine.'

'I might've glanced their way now and again.' The sniff was way too casual. Hunt suspected that under the bluff and bluster, Fraser was shitting himself.

'What did you talk about?'

'I've told you—'

'Sweet FA is what you've told me. What did you talk about?'

'For fuck's sake.' Fraser threw theatrical arms in the air, the deodorant definitely didn't work – the shirt looked as if it needed wringing out. 'How many more times?'

'What did you talk about?'

'Read. My. Lips. I did not—'

'What did you talk about?' Brody slammed his fist on the

table. Fraser wasn't the only one who jumped, but unlike Fraser, Hunt didn't follow through by scraping back his chair and getting to his feet.

'Where do you think you're going?' Brody snapped.

'Disneyland.' Deadpan. 'Place has a better class of Mickey Mouse. Laters.' Fluttering a finger, he headed for the exit.

'Hey, funny man. It's on camera.' He paused to let the import sink in.

'Must be *You've Been Framed* then.' But Fraser's hand stilled on the door.

'You cosying up to Lisa and Natalie. And needs be, sonny, I'll get a lip reader in.'

The line of sweat oozing above Fraser's top lip when he turned was already pretty telling. 'Believe me, it's not how it looks.'

'Really, Mr Fraser? So what exactly is it?'

TWENTY-TWO

F raser had done work for the Webbs just before Christmas, a plastering job, only a couple of days. Lisa had been off school with a stomach bug or something, just the two of them in the house. Not that the illness had cramped her style. She'd brewed endless mugs of tea, sat round chatting for ages, paraded up and down in skimpy outfits. The fact she was making a play for Fraser couldn't be much clearer. Well, it could. After he left, she texted images of herself semi-naked. Fraser panicked, didn't want to know, he'd messaged threatening to tell her dad. She'd backed off pronto, he claimed. And until three nights ago, he'd caught neither sight nor sound of her since.

Sarah circled an index finger round the rim of her glass. 'Do you believe him, John?'

'He said he'd deleted the pics but showed us the exchange of messages on his phone. So to a degree, yes. Not Brody though. He reckons it's only a question of time before the guy coughs.' Hunt shrugged. 'Fact is Fraser lied till he was blue in the face about not talking to the girls in the bar.'

So telling porkies wasn't exactly against his religion. She wished she'd caught sight of him before they'd had to release him. 'Good point, John. And if, as he claims, it was just casual flirting, why not come forward after the appeals?'

'Reckoned there was no point. Couldn't offer a steer, hadn't a clue where the girls were going on to. And he sure didn't want to draw attention to himself.' Hunt took a mouthful of beer. 'Plus, he says he was shit scared.'

'Of?'

'Everything coming out and 'cause of his prior we'd fancy him for it. Swore blind he'd been fitted up first time round. Don't they all?' He drained the glass, then: 'Get you another?'

Sarah gave a distracted nod, watched him weave through a few suits to the bar. Hunt had waylaid her in the corridor after the late briefs. Plural. Starr's call, he wanted the inquiries kept separate: Brody I/C of Operation Panther; Sarah running the Drake case. *Cheers, Charlie.* She took the last sip of Sauvignon, swilled it round her mouth. The wine did nothing to alleviate the bad taste.

She could picture Brody now holding court in The Queen's Head, the squad's local. Not in celebratory mood, Sarah and Hunt had eschewed the general invite, wandered a tad further to The Prince where the clientele was mostly lawyers, the copper element restricted to warming pans on the walls.

Now, after listening to a ten-minute summing up of Fraser's four-hour grilling, Sarah – like Hunt – suspected Brody's brag-fest might be a touch premature. Fraser's alibi checked out and the search team combing his Small Heath digs had failed to unearth anything incriminating.

Sarah sighed, started flicking through a local free sheet somebody had left on the next table. Lisa's murder had been relegated to page three, a few pars below the fold, plus a photo of her in school uniform. She ran her gaze over the girl's face. Maybe she wasn't the wide-eyed innocent her dad fondly imagined? Mind, these days a lot of kids and people old enough to know better saw nothing wrong in sexting – bit of harmless fun, wasn't it? Yeah right. She remembered the hoo-ha when a load of celebrities' accounts had been hacked and intimate images leaked into cyberspace. There'd been much wailing and gnashing of bridgework about gross invasion of privacy, but to Sarah's way of thinking the so-called stars should've had more nous. Kids on the other hand didn't always see inherent risks.

But if Lisa had sexted a guy simply because she fancied him, it begged a question: was Fraser the only name on her mailing list? Because if she made a habit of virtually hitting on guys . . .? Sarah shook her head. Boy, they could do with tracking down her phone. The necklace with her name on hadn't come to light either. Not to mention the best friend, Natalie Hinds. How could a girl just vanish off the face of the earth? *Unless?* For whatever reason she needed to go to ground?

Sarah recalled how Shona had reckoned from the get-go something smelled off, that the girl's mother possibly had an inkling of what was going on. *And Sarah had intended having a word with the woman face-to-face.* Best laid plans and all that, but what with the workload . . . Either way, it wasn't her bag, like a bunch of other stuff she'd have to mention it to Brody first thing.

'There y'go.' Hunt handed her another wine, flopped down on the bench next to her. 'What's with the big sigh?'

Where shall I stop? 'Don't mind me, John. A little tired is all.' With dark shadows and fine lines round the eyes, Hunt looked pretty knackered too. The inquiry was enough to put years on anybody. 'Cheers. Here's to an early break.'

'I'll drink to that.' He did – several swigs. 'And here's to Shona. The girl done good, didn't she?'

She frowned. 'Has Natalie Hinds surfaced then?'

'I wish. No. Nor her Dad. I mean with the Darby appeal. Did you not see it?' Hardly. She'd been stuck at Drake's place most of the day. Zoe Darby had thrown a last-minute wobbly, Hunt said, and the only way they could get a media appeal in the can was to sweet talk the BBC crew into meeting on neutral territory, no Q&As and no close-ups. Shona had literally called the shots, more or less written the script and coached the girl's father into delivering a star turn. 'They're calling her Steve back at the nick.'

'Steve?'

'As in Spielberg.'

She smiled. 'Let's hope for a close encounter then. Preferably
with the perp.'

'I'll drink to that too.' Straight-faced he held her gaze for
several seconds. 'Haven't seen that smile of yours in a while,
Sarah.'

Seemed to her he was offering an opening for more than
small talk. Not personal, Hunt was happily married, but
work-wise he was nobody's fool. He'd be fully aware of the
old boy network, the machinations, the macho posturing of
cold-shoulders. Sharing her thoughts was a tempting prospect. She'd little doubt Hunt was trustworthy, he'd been her
bagman long before she teamed up with Dave, might even
be watching her back. But . . .

'I'm fine, John. You know me, always a glass half-full girl.'

'It's up to you, Sarah. I'm a good listener.'

What had she said about nobody's fool? Should she bend
his ear? Eeny, meeny, miny . . . no. Not worth the risk. She
rarely criticized colleagues in front of junior officers.
Besides, if she really wanted a slagging-off session, the best
bad-mouther in the business was filed in her little black
book. Under B. She smiled again at the voice mail Baker
had left hours ago. *'Give us a bell, Quinn. And you know
what they say? Illegitimi non carborundum.'* Not a word
about the meet with Willis. And she'd not had a minute to
get back yet.

'You're a good man, John. I'll bear it in mind.' She took
a sip, changed tack. 'So tell me, what's the feedback been
since the appeal went out?' Thirty calls and counting, he told
her; four maybe five worth following up. She nodded. 'Sounds
about right.' Once detectives had weeded out the nutters and
fruitloops.

Hunt nodded. 'Yeah, it's gone down so well Brody's told
Shona to arrange the same sort of thing with the other victims.
Nearly forgot.' He delved into a pocket, hiked out a pack of
roasted peanuts.

'I'm OK, thanks.' Daren't spoil her appetite. Not when
Dave would be in full *MasterChef* mode back at the

apartment, assuming he hadn't burned anything – again. Which reminded her. 'The arson attack out at Edgbaston? Is anyone in the frame yet?'

'Not as far as I know.' He split the pack, laid it on the table. 'Plenty of leads though. Thanks to the early shout.'

'Neighbour, wasn't it?'

'No, somebody driving past.' He threw a nut in the air, caught it in his mouth.

'Nice shot.'

'Ta. It meant the fire downstairs didn't have time to spread. And the fire upstairs never really took hold, thank God. The body had been dowsed in booze . . . you can imagine what that would have done.' Burned the poor bloke to a crisp and destroyed a bunch of evidence – the arsonist's track-covering exercise had failed big time.

'We were bloody lucky, Sarah. Well, Raj Malik's team was. Place is an FSI's wet dream.' Hunt scored another own-goal with a nut.

She took one and licked off the salt. 'I reckon it's about time the good guys had a bit of luck.'

'What about the good gals? Any joy out at Aston?'

'So-so.' She stuck with the highlights: two sets of partials had been lifted from Drake's body as well as a substantial number of fibres, hairs, skin cells. Still needed suspects for a match though. They now had a witness who said she'd seen Drake let two men in the house one night last week. For all the cops knew, the callers could be Mormons or UKIP canvassers. Even so, the press bureau had issued the descriptions. They weren't brilliant but with a bit more luck, they might ring a bell.

And still on ringing bells, she wondered if Twig had got round to releasing the tape of the anonymous caller. Surely she'd have heard by now if a punter had recognized the voice? Either way it was another thing to chase in the morning.

'Christ, is that the time, John?' Gone eight. 'I'd best be off.'

'You and me both.'

Standing, she slipped her coat on then helped herself to the last nut while he downed the last inch of beer.

'One for the road is it?' He winked.

'Couldn't leave it like that, could I? Looking all sad and lonely-o.' *Like Larry Drake.* His unbidden image flashed before her eyes. Her smile faded fast.

'You OK?'

She nodded. 'He kept a journal of sorts you know, John.'

'Drake did?' Reaching for his scarf.

'Yeah. We came across it in a bedside cabinet.' She'd not had chance to skim more than a few pages but Dave might have made more headway. He'd taken it with him aiming to do a spot of homework in between the cooking.

Hunt held the door for her. 'So, what? You're hoping it'll give you a pointer or two?'

'You never know.'

'I bloody hope so, Sarah. Sooner you get the case cracked, the sooner you get back on the team and the sooner bloody Brody—' He broke off. Like her, he must've had second thoughts on dissing a boss.

She curved a lip. 'Hard task master is he?'

'Hard? Let's just say he makes Baker look like the sugar plum fairy.'

TWENTY-THREE

'All this lah-di-dah muck . . . what's wrong with pub grub, Kingie?' Baker's lip was curled theatrically as he held the menu at arm's length between podgy fingers.

Caroline was beginning to suspect not only that he was too vain to wear specs but that there'd have been Baker-friendlier places for a meet and greet session. She'd plumped for *Jamie's Italian* 'cause she loved the food and the ambience, but the old boy had already had a go at the music – bloody racket; the other diners – too loud; the prices – you're having a laugh. She was pretty sure it was a case of the detective doth protest too much. And the way he was playing to his audience anyone would think he'd be stumping up for the bill.

Reaching for the Prosecco, Caroline rolled her eyes at the third member of the party. Mark Slater – looking particularly tasty in tight white tee and navy denim – recognized his landlady's tacit plea for a verbal lifebelt.

'I know what you mean, Mr Baker. I'm more of a pie and chips man myself, but try the lasagne verde. It's almost as good as my Mum's.' Caroline found his boyish smile infectious. Baker didn't catch it.

'Italian is she? Or a big fan of Iceland?'

He snickered. 'Never set foot out the country but she knows the way to a man's heart. Cooks like an angel.'

Mark was definitely winging it. Apart from the fact his ma was dying from cancer, having seen the array of photographs in his bedroom, Caroline had little doubt that Julie Slater's exquisite features would have played a far bigger role in the love stakes than any foodie skills she might have possessed. Caroline could see no way how having a dab hand with pasta dishes – however yummy – could have competed with the woman's looks. Think: love child of Cillian Murphy and Natalie Portman. If Caroline was any judge, the young Mrs Slater would have been even more drop-dead gorgeous than her doting son. As for Mark, since the minute they'd sat round the table chewing the cud, he'd done his best to have Baker eating out of his hand.

Refilling the old boy's glass for what must be the third time, he said: 'Trust me, Mr B, the lasagne's awesome.'

'It'd better be, lad. Mind, I'll want a decent bottle of red to wash it down. Right, Kingie?' Baker sat back, folded his arms, fixed his beady eye on Mark. 'So what line's Lois been spinning you?'

'Lois?' Nonplussed. *Not big on Superman then.*

'No worries.' Baker flapped a hand 'Get on with it.'

'No line, sir. Just that she said it'd be useful you and I met.' He proffered Baker a bread stick simultaneously playing footsie with Caroline's calf. 'Always good to have a face to go with a name, isn't it?'

He snapped the stick in two. 'Depends. Doubt Quasimodo would see it that way.'

Mark laughed, even sounded genuine. 'Fair point, sir. But if we're going to be collaborating—'

Pointing with the half that hadn't yet made it to his mouth, Baker said; 'Collaborating's a big word for doing somebody's leg work, lad. And the key word is: *if.*'

'Goes without saying, sir.' Serious face, earnest nod. 'It's entirely your call. I just think . . .'

Knowing what he thought, Caroline tuned out. She had to admire Mark's style though: fawning over the old boy was exactly the way she'd play it. And the main reason she'd brought them together. Despite the fat financial carrot she'd dangled Baker's way, he still hadn't fully committed to helping with the research for the book. Mark was more than happy to be on board. And since they'd become bedmates, she'd no doubt where one of his skills lay: persuading people to open up. Especially women. She twitched a lip. But – and it was a big but – Mark didn't have the ex-detective's vast range of contacts or insider knowledge. If lover boy could cajole Baker into doing business with him – bingo. Caroline would have her dream team. *With Mark being what you might call a sleeping partner.* She gave a lazy smile.

'Something tickled your fancy, Kingie?' Baker flicked his laser beam from her to Mark then back again.

Caroline forced herself not to wilt under the heat, came damn close to blushing though. No wonder he'd reached police chief. Wool over Baker's beady eyes pull? Never.

'Just an idle thought, Fred.' It was one thing for her to pry into private lives but hey . . .

'Idle thought? You, Lois?' He glanced down. 'Pull the other one.'

Smiling, she slowly inched her leg out of Mark's reach. Wouldn't put it past the old goat to have X-ray vision.

'Sorry to keep you waiting, folks.' *Thank God for that.* A blonde waitress, hair tucked behind ears, hovered at Baker's shoulder. 'What can I get you?' Even without the Colgate grin and Aussie lilt, she put Caroline in mind of Kylie. More to the point, by the time she'd taken the order, flirted with Mark and poured the last drop of Prosecco into Baker's glass, the exchange had been forgotten or Baker had let it go.

Instead he spent about five minutes subtly grilling Mark. He teased out bits about his background, tastes in beer, politics, footie. Caroline watched closely, knew what Baker was really getting at: what made Mark tick and, presumably, whether they could get along. She thanked God Mark wasn't a closet Tory, reckoned it would've been a deal-breaker in Baker's book. And hers.

'OK, lad. I'll maybe give it a whirl. See how it goes.'

Caroline curved a lip, did the honours with the Chianti.

'Don't get too carried away, Kingie. It'd be very much a trial period. Your new bestie might not be up to the mark. And I might not have as much time on my hands as I thought.'

'Oh?'

He tapped the side of his nose. 'Anyway, cheers.' After sinking half his wine, he settled back again, arms folded, gaze fixed on Caroline. 'And how's that *old* bestie of yours? Seen much of her recently?' The nonchalant delivery belied the glint in his eye.

She frowned, tried to think who he had in mind. Of course. Talk about over-egging the sweet course. Her relationship with the Snow Queen blew lukewarm and arctic at the best of times.

'I've not had the pleasure of Sarah's company for a while.' She took a sip of her drink. 'How is she? Do give her my regards.'

'Warm ones?' He winked, helped himself to another bread stick. 'I bumped into her this morning as it happens. Looking fit as ever.'

She forced a smile. 'Must be all the chasing round after the bad guys.' *In circles most of the time.*

'In circles?' He chuckled. 'You're easier to see through than a washed window, Kingie. Any road, how come you're not asking Quinn to help with your little project? I'd have thought she'd be only too happy.'

Oh how they laughed. 'Oh, I so would, Fred. But the poor woman must be up against it at the mo, what with hunting panthers and all that.'

'Keeping abreast are we?' He cocked his head like the double entendre wasn't intentional. 'News-wise, naturally.'

Mark leaned forward. 'I'm covering the story actually, sir. I've been keeping Caro—'

'Filled in no doubt.' Baker raised an all-innocent eyebrow. 'Coo, that smells good, sweetheart.' Beaming up at the waitress, he rubbed his hands. 'Love a decent lasagne, me.'

Caroline shook her head. Baker could change gear faster than Lewis Hamilton. Not to mention alter his bloody tune.

'Hope you enjoy, sir.' Kylie gave a mock curtsey before plonking down the food. 'Plates are hot though, folks. Watch out, won't you?'

'No worries. We will.' Baker aimed a crooked smile at Mark. 'Wouldn't want to get our fingers burned would we, lad?'

'Warm enough, Nat?' The girl huddled on a chair, blanket draped round her head and shoulders, pale face peeking out. For a second or two, the image put Pete in mind of news footage shot outside law courts, the sort showing villains being bundled in and out of prison vans. *Now there's a thought to hold. Get a bloody grip, man.*

'Hey, love, I said are you warm enough?'

Apart from a shake of the head – nothing. Again.

Pete rolled mental eyes. Dialogue had been mostly one-way since they'd left Birmingham. He knew she'd had a hell of a shock but even so, he was doing his best. Still squatting in front of the gas fire, he turned the heat up a notch, rubbed his icy hands together. It always took a while to take the chill off the air when the place hadn't been used in months. He'd lit loads of candles and even in the flickering light he could see where some of the pine panelling had warped, mould mottling it like bird shit, watermarks stained the ceiling like yellowing lace doilies and going by the smell he knew damp would have got into the bedding: cosy, it wasn't. *Beggars, choosers.*

His parents had bought the mobile home thirty-odd years ago, kept it pitched just this side of the Welsh border. The campsite was called Fir Trees View – dead imaginative. To Pete, the cheap and chintzy not so alpine chalet was like something out of *Hi-de-Hi*. His mum and dad loved it though. They'd christened it The Haven and regarded it as home sweet home from home. Not surprising given the number of family holidays they'd spent stuck inside paper thin walls playing cards or board games while the rain lashed down.

Happy days. Pete sniffed. Endless fun compared with now. He stood, unbuttoned his donkey jacket, cut Natalie a concerned glance. He might as well not have been there, her haunted eyes stared straight ahead, the shadows round them like faded bruises.

Sighing he made his way to the kitchen area, stiff knees creaking almost as much as the floor. Once he'd got past his teens he'd never wanted to set foot here again, but it was the only place he could think of where they could hide for a while. The Haven might turn out a more temporary refuge than he'd thought. The news on the car radio had come out of the blue, as it were.

Pete tugged at a flimsy cupboard door to get it to open, then ran his gaze along a line of tins. He could rustle up some soup, it would go with the sandwiches and crisps he'd picked up at the garage.

'Hungry, Nat?' Course she wasn't. 'Come on love, you have to eat, keep your strength up and all that.'

'Just leave it, please, Dad.' Sobbing, she gathered the blanket round her shoulders, trudged off to one of the bedrooms.

He opened his mouth to have a go, but had second thoughts. She'd come round eventually. *So might the cops.* Sooner rather than later. He found a can opener in the drawer and stood there stirring tomato soup on the hob. The mindless activity left him free to mull over the bulletin he'd heard during the drive. Nat was still blissfully ignorant, she'd drifted off to sleep by then. It had been one of those 'news just in' type stories. He could recall it virtually word-for-word.

West Midlands police have launched a murder inquiry after the discovery of a man's body at a house in Edgbaston. Unconfirmed reports say two blazes had been started deliberately at the property in Kings Road. Fire crews confined damage to downstairs rooms. The man, who's been named locally as businessman, Ivan Burton, was found upstairs. It's believed he died from knife wounds.

Pete snorted. In journalism-speak, 'it's believed' meant 'we know for a fact'. And the fact they knew Burton's name and that he'd been stabbed meant the body couldn't have perished in the flames. Pete's home-made funeral pyre had failed spectacularly. And despite efforts with the bleach and scrubbing brushes, a shed-load of evidence would have survived.

The fire brigade must've got to the scene pretty damn quick. Which meant the alarm had been raised sharpish. And that rang mental alarms. Pete's hand stilled on the spoon. Had someone been keeping an eye on the place?

Even if he was wrong about that, the cops were on Natalie's tail anyway. He desperately needed to buy a bit of time. Turning the heat down under the soup, he slipped the phone out of his pocket. Had to be desperate if he was going to call his ex.

TWENTY-FOUR

D ave was either on the phone or nattering to himself when Sarah entered the apartment. Either way after years of getting back to silence, hearing a voice made a welcome change. As for the garlic and basil smells wafting in the hall? Good job she'd not pigged out on the peanuts. Lip curved, she shucked off her coat, slipped off the kitten heels and headed for the kitchen. She'd been right first time – Dave still had the handset tucked under his chin. He'd heard her key in the lock though, pointed to a glass of Sauvignon on the side, then mouthed 'Hi' as he popped the bottle back in the fridge.

Smiling her thanks, she took a sip thinking how easy it would be to get used to all this. Glancing round she had second thoughts. The place resembled a tip on a bank holiday. Did she really own that many pots and pans? And as for the plates and dishes stacked in the sink, just how many people was he catering for? He could probably knock up a main course with the overspill.

'I'll need to check.' Dave met her gaze. 'Can I let you know? Cheers.' He slipped the phone in his back pocket. 'Sorry about that.'

'What? The call or the culinary fall out? And check what?' She held out a hand. 'Pass the cloth.'

'No worries, I'll do it later. Honest if I'd not had a load of distractions the place'd be all ship-shape by now.'

'Like the Titanic?'

'Below the belt, Ms Quinn.' He wagged a mock-stern finger. ''Specially when I've been slaving over a hot galley all evening.'

'I'll let you off, just this once. Go on then, check what?' She smiled then narrowed her eyes. Unless it was her imagination, he looked a tad shifty.

'It'll keep. Besides, we're nearly good to go. Sauce only needs a quick stir.' The boyish grin wasn't convincing and wielding the wooden spoon didn't add a lot of credence to his words. 'Can you take the wine? I thought we'd eat in the dining room.'

Lucky that, 'cause he sure hadn't left any space free in here. Still suspicious, she pursed her lips but ferried Dave's bottle of red through anyway. With what she'd sunk in the pub, she needed to ease off. She still had an almost full glass in her hand.

Standing in the threshold, she cast an approving glance. Subdued lighting, soft music: Sade? She didn't realize he was a fan. Everything had been laid out restaurant-style: best cutlery, bread basket, grated parmesan, even Daffodils. Made another change. The table usually doubled as a work surface and was generally snowed under with bills, paperwork and half-written reports. As she took a seat she spotted her files towering Pisa-like against a wall, wondered where he'd put Drake's journal.

'Here we go. *Bon appétit.*'

Staring at the plate she tried working up some enthusiasm. 'Looks . . . delicious, thanks.' Looked like spag bol actually, without the meat. Not exactly fine dining. On a good day even the domestically-challenged DI could knock up a decent tomato sauce.

'Bucatini con Marinara e Ricotta.' *Course it is.* He flourished an extravagant napkin and dropped the cod Italian accent. 'Hope it tastes good. I've never cooked it before.'

'First time for everything.' She'd not eaten it either. Smiling, she popped in a mouthful, chewed slowly. 'Hey, I like it.'

'You could sound less shocked.'

'Well, you know,' – she shrugged – 'what with all the distractions?'

'Tell me about it. My Mum phoned, twice. Had Vodafone

on trying to flog me a new tablet. A mate rang offering tickets
to go see the Villa next month.'

'My. You have been busy.' Nothing work related though.

'Too right. I've not had chance to look at the journal yet. I
left it in the bedroom, thought we might . . .'

She raised an eyebrow. A touch presumptuous. Plus, as
far as bedtime reading went, Drake's jottings didn't do much
for her.

'Point taken.' He winked. 'Oh yeah, and Twig called
wondering if I'd heard about Baker.' *Save the best till last,
why don't you?* 'But you'll know anyway. Horse's mouth and
all that.' He glanced up, registered her puzzled frown. 'You
were in cahoots in the canteen this morning? I thought—'

She shook her head. Even the chief hadn't known then why
he'd been called in. 'Tell me.'

'Gossip has it he's coming back. Part-time initially. See how
it pans out.' He broke off a chunk of ciabatta.

The fork still hadn't made it to her mouth. 'Doing?'

'Not front-line stuff. Hot money's on professional standards.'

Pensive, she popped in the food. The chief rooting out bent
cops? Policing the police. Sounded like a poisoned chalice to
her, shoved in a basket of tetchy snakes. Baker sure wouldn't
be winning many popularity contests. But, then, he never had.
The old boy didn't give a toss what anyone thought about him
and as for getting up peoples backs, as his main form of
exercise he'd taken it to Olympian heights.

She took another mouthful, watched Dave dunk his bread
in the sauce. She could see how Baker's comeback made sense.
He'd always been straight as a die and as a cop who'd worked
his way through the ranks, he knew the force from bottom to
top, never mind inside out. Though he'd retired early on
medical grounds, the cancer was in remission. As long as it
stayed that way, there was no reason why he couldn't do a
good job.

'So what do you reckon?' Dave asked.

She shrugged. 'Bring it on. He's not sixty yet. All that experience shouldn't go to waste.'

'Can't argue with you there.' Topping up his glass. 'Not sure
how the new governor'll take it though.'

She couldn't imagine Starr had ever put a toe out of line. 'Have you heard whispers then?'

'Nah, well nothing dodge. But Twig reckons Baker can't stand the guy.'

Join the club. Mind, the feeling could well be mutual. Baker was so non-PC he made Frankie Boyle sound like the voice of sweet reason. Starr watched every word, even if it was all lip service. 'Their paths aren't likely to cross though are they?'

'That's another thing,' Dave said. 'Again according to Twig, Baker thinks Starr can't detect his way out of a small room with a big door marked exit. In flashing lights.' She masked a smile. 'So the thinking,' he added, 'is that Baker'll be on Starr's case checking up all the time.'

Which reminded her. 'Talking of checks.' She cocked her head. 'In the kitchen earlier? You said it would keep?'

'Ah. Right.' He took a gulp of wine. 'Well . . . I've not committed us or anything but . . .'

Us? 'But?'

'I had the girl on from the vet's.' *Vet's?* 'Drake's cat?' he said. 'I asked her to keep me posted. Anyway, the injuries aren't as bad as they looked only . . .'

'Only?'

'Thing is. If they can't find a home, it'll have to be put down and I said . . .' He glanced up through his fringe.

'You've said very little.' Barely finished a sentence. She placed the fork on her plate. It seemed safer there.

'I offered to take it in, only I'm not allowed pets at my place so I thought—'

'Are you quite mad? I don't believe I'm hearing this.'

'Aw, come on, Sarah. She's pretty sure they'll be able to rehome it anyway. It's only if the worst comes to the worst.'

'For crying out loud, Dave.' She flopped back in the chair. He'd seen the bloody flea bites, knew she'd never owned a pet in her life. Not so much as a tame tadpole.

'It's just a poor dumb animal, Sarah. I hate the thought of it . . .'

'End of. Not another word.' Lips tight, she crossed her arms. They locked gazes for several seconds before Dave broke

eye contact. 'Fine.' He twirled the last strands of pasta round
his fork. 'I knew you'd take that attitude. You're so—'

'What?' she snapped. *Cold? Hard-hearted? Controlling?*

He shook his head. 'Forget it.'

The disappointment in his eyes hurt most, disappointment
in her as much as the cat's uncertain future. She softened her
voice. 'I'm hardly here, Dave, it wouldn't be fair.'

'And the alternative is?'

She took a sip of wine. Could she risk it? He reckoned
someone would probably take the cat in anyway. Chances were
she'd never set eyes on the bloody thing again. And Dave
looked so downcast it wouldn't take much to make him happy.

'Let's see what happens, eh? If no one wants it—'

'Really?'

'I'll maybe give it a trial period.'

'That's brilliant.' Beaming, he shoved the empty plate to
one side. 'You're brilliant, Sarah.'

'Had enough to eat?' She smiled.

'I'm absolutely stuffed.'

'Come on, then.' She stood and held his gaze, still smiling.
'A little exercise will soon work it off.'

'Can't wait.' The light in his eyes wasn't just from the
candles. Probably thought all his birthdays had come at once.

She turned at the door, started rolling her sleeves. 'Bring
the dishes through, can you? I'll run the water.'

TWENTY-FIVE

*When will it end? They'll only be happy when I'm dead
of course. I know what they want. They'd rather I kill
myself. But I won't give them the satisfaction. I won't take
the easy way out. I swear I won't allow lies to destroy me.*

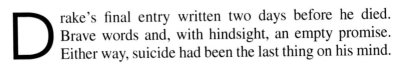 rake's final entry written two days before he died.
Brave words and, with hindsight, an empty promise.
Either way, suicide had been the last thing on his mind.

Sarah sat back, tapped a finger against her lips. Like the rest of the journal, the last page hadn't made edifying reading. She'd risen before dawn to get the job done, jotting notes as she went. Made a list too, dates and times of the worst humiliations wreaked on the poor sod. After a while she'd no longer heard Dave's gentle snores from the bedroom. The toast she'd made to nibble on lay virtually untouched.

Most of what was written down she'd heard from Drake direct: shit through the letterbox, rats and road kill left on the doorstep, verbal abuse, vitriolic letters. He'd not mentioned the time he'd had piss thrown over him in the street, the house brick someone hurled that hit him in the face. Nor had he told her about other items of unconventional post: condoms, used tampons, paraffin soaked rags, maggots, dead birds. Drake's biggest fear was finding his cat nailed to a tree, it was one of the sicker threats they'd made and he'd recorded in neat italic script.

She pictured him cowering in the shadows of a home that had become a prison. Jumping at every noise, scared of every knock at the door. The security measures he'd employed had clearly been underplayed. If only he'd set up surveillance cameras, the cops could be laughing tea cakes. Sighing, she shook her head. There was certainly nothing remotely funny about the torment meted out.

Nothing spur of the moment either. Sarah ran her gaze down the list of dates: weekly incidents over the last four months executed either early morning or after nightfall. Seemed to her the attacks were planned, like some sort of orchestrated campaign. In the DI's experience, vigilantes usually acted after a booze-fuelled night at the pub; blokes, mainly, egging each other on to extremes. Drake's sustained ordeal didn't fit the pattern.

I swear I won't allow lies to destroy me.

Clearly he'd lost the battle. As a final oath it couldn't ring any hollower.

'Can you get that, Dave?' Sarah's shower had taken longer than the normal two minutes. She was getting dressed in the bathroom when her phone rang. She knew her house guest was up and about by the tuneless whistling and door banging coming from the kitchen. It was like living with an adolescent elephant. Still, every silver lining has a cloud and there were compensations. Dave was a more than considerate lover. Though she called the shots at work, from the first time they'd made love he'd led the way in bed. And there'd been none of those awkward silences when they woke. She curved a lip. Even back then, he'd given her no peace and quiet first thing.

Just about ready, she glanced in the mirror. The sight of the short hair was beginning to come as less of a shock these days and considering the late night, she could look worse. She'd eschewed one of her taupe linen outfits for a dark tailored skirt suit and navy courts. The aim was to look business-like, in control. Even though, professionally, she'd never felt more threatened.

As she reached for the handle there was a tap on the door. 'Are you decent in—?'

'Sure am.' He could see for himself now, though he didn't return her smile. 'What is it?'

'That was Twig on the phone. Two points: it looks as if Natalie Hinds has surfaced—'

What! 'You're kidding?' They'd been searching for the girl for days. 'How? When?' *Where? Why?*

He raised a palm. 'All I know is she called her mother, last night.'

Un-bloody-believable. Sarah turned her mouth down. 'So she's safe then?'

'Apparently. And sorry.'

Sorry? She'd regret the day she was born if she'd gone AWOL with vital information about Lisa Webb's final hours. 'Who are they sending out there?' She headed for the hall to pick up her coat and keys.

'Dunno.' He was right behind her. 'Forgetting something?' Smiling, she made a move to peck his cheek. 'Thanks.' He winked. 'I didn't mean that though.'

She frowned then recalled he'd said two points. 'OK, ingrate. Give.'

'The anonymous caller? We've got a name.'

*   *   *

Two people had left the same name on the confidential hotline. Sarah mulled over the implications on the drive to HQ. Even though heavy rain slowed the traffic, she'd left more than enough time to beat the rush hour. Brody wasn't the only cop who could get in early. Dave would be making his own way in. Keeping the relationship under wraps at work was a no brainer: last thing they needed was wagging tongues.

Unless they were informants.

And it looked as if they had two singing from the same hymn sheet.

If they'd identified the anonymous caller correctly as Emma Vane, the question now was why she'd named Lawrence Drake – the teacher who'd sexually assaulted her – as the Ski Mask Killer. Well, it headed a long list of questions.

Just below it was: what the hell had Natalie Hinds been up to?

TWENTY-SIX

DCS Starr stood side-on to Sarah while he poured coffee into a white mug emblazoned with bold black letters. He'd not offered a cup, nor waved her to a seat. He'd beckoned her in from his office doorway as she dashed along the corridor after the Drake briefing. Starr hadn't attended, he'd been otherwise engaged at Brody's brief.

Sarah wouldn't mind the delay so much if she'd not submitted detailed written reports as per, but Starr now insisted on personal updates from her. As if she had nothing better to do. Unless he was scrutinizing her work? Christ, it was like being back at school. Taking the occasional sip of coffee, he'd listened without interruption, until she got to the Emma Vane lead.

'Are you bringing her in?' He held her gaze as he walked to his chair clutching the mug. She still couldn't make out the wording. Shame.

'No. At the house. I'm about to head out there.' She needed

another look at the crime scene anyway and she'd already ear-marked a follow-up interview with one of the neighbours. On top of which, she reckoned Emma would talk more freely on home territory. On the other hand if she had made the incriminating call, her wagging tongue had already been more than loose and she'd now watch every word. Especially if she'd heard her own dulcet tones on the radio. The aim was to get her to drop her guard because if Emma Vane had well and untruly pointed the verbal finger at Drake, careless talk, as the saying goes, costs lives. It was conceivable Drake had paid the ultimate price for a pack of lies.

'It won't be the easiest interview.' Starr pursed his lips.

You don't say? 'I'm aware of that.' Emma would likely be cagier than an aviary of twitchy birds. If – wittingly or unwittingly – her big mouth had led more than a couple of detectives to Drake's front door, wasting police time would be the least of her worries.

'How old is she now?'

'Nineteen.'

'I'm not convinced you shouldn't bring her in. You might get more out of her here.'

Like she hadn't thought of that. She balled a fist. 'If I get nowhere, I will. I see the nick more as a last resort.'

'You make it sound like a holiday camp.' He laughed clearly expecting her to appreciate the lightning wit. Her straight face shattered that delusion.

'If that's all . . .?' She half-turned to go. 'Actually, sir, what's happening with Natalie Hinds?'

'DI Brody's the best person to ask, of course. But I gather from comments at the brief she's been in touch with her mother.'

Tell me something I don't know. 'So where's the girl?'

'She won't say apparently. But as she's safe and well . . .'

Not bloody good enough. Not after launching a full-scale search, wasting God knows how many police hours. 'Surely we—?'

'There are other priorities at the moment, DI Quinn. Determining which to follow,' – Brody gave a thin smile – 'is the secret of being a successful SIO.'

Thanks for that. 'Sir.' She made to turn again but he lifted a restraining finger.

'Who are you going with?'

'I'm sorry?' *Frigging cheek.*

He sighed. 'Are you taking DC Harries along?' Watching her closely over the rim of the mug, he took a sip of coffee. She clocked the legend this time and would've snorted – except she was seething so much she could barely keep a civil tongue.

'Of course I am. He's my part—'

'I'm *well* aware what he is, DI Quinn.' She felt her cheeks flush, fought to maintain eye contact. Starr didn't even blink. 'If you're sure he has the necessary expertise and you won't be playing nursemaid? We need to keep our eye on the ball, don't we?' Lips tight, she treated it as a rhetorical question. Starr lifted a casual cuff, glanced at his watch. 'OK, I'd better get on.'

You had? 'Ditto.' Unsmiling she turned, this time reached the door before his parting shot.

'And DI Quinn? I may take a look at the crime scene later. Fresh pair of eyes. Always a good thing.'

'Have you seen his stupid sodding mug?' Sarah strode across the car park, camel coat flapping in the breeze.

'Whose?' Dave lengthened his stride to keep pace.

'*World's Greatest Policeman?*' She snorted. 'World's greatest wank pot.'

'Ah.'

'Exactly.' Tight-mouthed she chucked her attaché case on the back seat, slammed the door of the Audi. That alone clinched the depth of her fury. The noise pissed off a pair of pigeons pecking round an oily puddle. They squawked and took off in a flap, not just of wings.

Sarah sat in the driving seat, stared ahead, took a calming breath or two. 'And don't even think about it.'

'What?'

'Saying, "don't let him get to you".' She reached to switch on the ignition.

'Bit late for that, isn't it?' Dave murmured, buckling his

belt. Every so often, he opened his mouth to speak, but held out until they were on the ring road before breaking the silence. 'Come on, boss, you're bigger than this.' Even then his voice was softer than usual. 'And you're a better cop than he'll ever be.'

'Am I?' Sarah swallowed, blinked hard, for the first time in years felt tears prick her eyes. 'Try telling Starr that.'

'Starr?'

Frowning, she cut him a glance. 'Who else?'

'I thought you meant Brody.' The DI had been bragging all over the shop apparently about a break a mile wide in the Panther inquiry, bigging it up like there was no tomorrow.

Was that why Starr had banged on about Brody's priorities? Sarah turned her mouth down. She'd kept up to date on the state of play, read the overnight reports, caught most of the incoming stuff, couldn't recall anything major. 'What's he got then?'

'A witness. Walked in off the street. Not long after the brief.'

'To?'

'A man hanging round Zoe Darby's place the night she was attacked.'

TWENTY-SEVEN

William Lomas sat under a 'No Smoking' sign in IR1 puffing on an e-cigarette. Uptight wasn't in it. The old boy looked like a one-legged rabbit caught in the headlights balancing on a cheese wire. Brody had given him special dispensation to indulge the habit, hoping the emotional prop would calm the nerves. He'd drawn the line at the real thing: Lomas' pack of Embassy poked from the top pocket of his shiny blue blazer.

'I'd have come forward earlier had I known, Inspector.' He stroked thumb and forefinger along an off-white pencil moustache. A still full head of hair, probably once dark blond, was now the colour of weak tea.

'You're here now, sir. And it's been a great help.' Brody realized that Lomas wouldn't have seen anything had he not wandered into the garden for a sneaky fag on the night in question. The DI had a certain amount of sympathy, his missus wouldn't let him smoke in the house either. Whatever. The significance hadn't dawned on the old boy until he caught Michael Darby's appeal on TV. 'Cause wouldn't you know it? Mr and Mrs L had taken off – literally – the morning after Zoe's attack to stay with their daughter in Edinburgh. Ten o'clock flight from Birmingham Airport. Who knows? If Quinn had pulled her finger out getting the house-to-house underway, they might have got an earlier steer. Still, better late . . .

Lomas made as if to get up. 'Well, gentlemen, if that's all?'

'Actually,' Brody said, 'if you wouldn't mind, I'd like to take it once more from the top. Try and picture everything from the moment you stepped out the door.' Hunt had a written statement in front of him but a second recital often flushed out more detail, no witness had total recall first off. 'Give it your best shot.' Brody smiled. 'No rush.'

Just make it snappy. Sooner they issued the description and a release the better. He watched Lomas' long tapering fingers flutter like paper twigs as he took another deep drag. His sallow cheeks sank in so far Brody reckoned the guy had to be missing a few teeth. Not that the DI cared when the marbles appeared intact.

'Any chance of a cuppa?' The smile proved Brody right. Even the teeth that remained looked as if they were on the way out.

Brody stifled a sigh. 'Sergeant? Can you sort it?'

Hunt lay down his pen, scraped back the chair. 'Tea, OK, Mr Lomas?'

'Excellent, officer. Excellent.' He looked to be enjoying himself a little more now, darting eager glances round the room like a kid at a fun fair. Brody reached for the statement, aware of Lomas' sudden scrutiny. 'Your face looks familiar, Inspector. Have I seen you somewhere before?'

'Doubt it, sir.' He lifted a corner of his mouth. 'Unless I pulled you in for something?'

Lomas ignored the quip, didn't even appear to have heard. '*Crimewatch*, maybe?'

He rolled mental eyes. 'Not guilty.'

'I'm sure I know you from somewhere.' Wagging a finger.

'Yeah, well they reckon we've all got a double.' Sniffing, he picked up the statement signalling an end to the cosy little chat.

'You carry on, officer.' He waved his fake fag in the air as if granting permission. 'It'll come to me. I never forget a face.'

Brody forced a lop-sided smile. Shame the old boy couldn't recall the stalker's face in more detail. OK, stalker was pushing it a bit. But what else was a bloke doing in Zoe Darby's back garden in the middle of the night? He'd hardly have been there for a spot of weeding. Not wearing a leather jacket with a skull and cross bones across the back. Pensive, the DI chewed his bottom lip. The physical description might not be great but the distinctive clothing could be enough to get a result. The serial rapist had to have the biggest collar in town.

He tried not to smirk as he imagined nailing the bastard, watching him in court, gloating as he got sent down. Talk about feather in a professional cap? Not to mention a nail in Quinn's professional coffin. Under her watch the case had barely moved. A slug on slow pills had more get up and go.

Brody glanced at his watch. Huntie was taking his time, too. Talk of the devil. He watched the Sergeant reverse in carrying a tray of mugs. 'Where'd you get to? China?'

'What a comedian.' Hunt's laugh was faker than the e-fag. 'Boss been keeping you entertained, Mr Lomas?'

'Indeed, indeed. I've been trying to think—'

'Let's just get on with it, shall we?' Brody snarled, rising to get the door. Some people had no sense of urgency. 'When you're ready, Mr Lomas.'

Lomas stirred in more sugar then took another noisy slurp. 'Lovely cuppa, Sergeant. Right, where were we?'

'Talk us through it again would you, Mr Lomas?' Brody sat back, hands crossed behind his head, hawk-like gaze fixed on the witness. It took less than five minutes. The account wasn't verbatim and nothing new emerged but at least there were no discrepancies, backtracks or contradictions. The old boy had slipped out the back about one a.m. in dressing gown and pyjamas. He'd already been in bed a couple of hours but with the excitement of the trip he couldn't sleep, needed a pee, thought as he was up he might as well have a smoke. He didn't hear anything and at first it was pitch black and brass monkeys. As his eyes adjusted to the light, he clocked what he thought was a dark shape hunkered down in the shadow of next door's shed. Lomas deliberately tripped the security light and for a split second his eyes locked on a face: white male, beanie hat, stubble. Lomas shouted, he couldn't remember what, and the intruder turned tail and fled, it was then he saw the skull picked out in what he thought were brass studs.

Brody pushed again on age and build. Lomas took a pensive puff on the fag. 'As I say: late twenties, early thirties, five-ten-ish, not thin, not fat.'

'And you'd definitely not seen the guy hanging round before?'

Lomas shook his head. 'Nor since. I'm pretty sure I'd recognize him again.'

Brody traced a finger along his eyebrow. 'You didn't think to call the police?' It was the wrong thing to say, he'd clearly hit a nerve.

'No I didn't,' he snapped. 'Far as I was concerned, I'd seen him off. How was I to know—?'

'I'm not blaming you, Mr Lomas.'

'Aren't you? That's what it sounds like.' The old boy sat up ramrod straight. 'And what would your lot have done? You take your time coming out when there's a real break-in never mind some bloke hanging round in the dark. I didn't even realize a young girl lived next door, let alone lived alone.'

So much for Neighbourhood Watch.

The fight went out of Lomas then. He slumped back in the chair, rheumy eyes tearing up. 'If I'd known then what I know now . . .'

'As I say, Mr Lomas, I'm not blaming *you*. With what you've given us, there's a good chance we'll track the man down. I'll get Sergeant Hunt here to sort a news release then we can—'

'It's underway. I called the details in to the news bureau while I in was in the canteen. Queuing.' Hunt slipped the statement across the desk to Lomas. 'If you could just read this through and sign here, sir.'

Presumptuous sod. Brody bit back a barb. 'Well done, Sergeant. Anything to make up for lost time. But what if—?'

'I said if there were any new lines, you'd give them a bell.' He cut Brody a glance. 'But there aren't, are there?'

'All present and correct.' Lomas handed back the statement then smiling from ear to ear pointed at Brody. 'I've got it now. The cop in *Life on Mars*. Dead funny he was. You're a dead ringer.'

Brody was at a loss. 'Sorry?'

'Gene Hunt.' Huntie helped out, deadpan. 'Nearly as bad as the villains.'

'That's the one.' The old boy chuckled. 'He didn't half make me laugh.'

'Thank you, Mr Lomas.' Unsmiling, Brody rose and stretched out a hand. 'You've been a great help. The Sergeant here will see—'

'Actually, Mr Lomas,' Hunt started gathering the paperwork, 'before you go can I show you to a viewing room, I'd like you to cast your eye over a few visuals.' He told Brody he'd called the squad room, tasked a DC with downloading images of skull and cross bones-encrusted leather jackets.

Lomas looked up from polishing his specs with the end of a knotted tie. 'If you think it'll do any good. Certainly, Sergeant.'

'It's what we call a long shot, sir, but if you spot something similar, the boys in the press office can scan it and add it to the release. It might help narrow things down.' He cut Brody a glance as he ushered Lomas towards the door. 'Wouldn't you say, Inspector?'

'I would indeed, Sergeant. Anything to speed things along.' Mouth tight, Brody watched them leave. He didn't take kindly to being upstaged or put down by a junior officer. Especially one with a foot so firmly entrenched in Quinn's camp.

TWENTY-EIGHT

Emma Vane lived with her mother in a tatty pebbledash semi on a council estate in Aston. Sarah hesitated to call it a stone's throw from Drake's house, but the fact remained it wasn't a million miles away. Unlike Emma's father who hadn't been around for years. Since the detectives' arrival, other facts had been in short supply. On the plus side, given their cards-close-to-chest interview strategy, it worked both ways.

Sarah currently perched alongside Harries on the edge of a cracked fake leather two-seater. The room's lurid green and brown flecked wallpaper was probably an acquired taste. Chocolate mint ice cream sprang to Sarah's mind, which was probably fine in small doses. An ill-fitting, grubby jade carpet was so rucked it looked as if epileptic moles had been break-dancing under it. The heady odour of cheesy feet and unwashed flesh lingered in the air. It was the sort of place where even Harries would've turned down a hot drink. Had one been on offer.

Emma and Bridic Vane had barely torn their gaze from a wall-mounted plasma TV currently screening the Jeremy Kyle show. Wearing clashing animal-print onesies, the women slumped on the sofa opposite, dipping desultorily every now and again into a family bag of popcorn nestling on Bridie's more than generous lap. Sarah reckoned that so far Kyle's hit rate for extracting information had been higher than hers. The women had skirted just about every question. Doubtless a technique they'd picked up from watching too many cop shows.

Time to get real. Sarah reached for the remote. The dynamic duo now looked as blank as the screen.

'Hey. You can't do that,' Emma whined.

Sarah smiled. 'Watch me.'

Scowling, the girl scraped lank mousy hair into an eye-wateringly tight topknot. Her features were sharp enough

without the facelift. Croydon or otherwise. As for her raw
pastry complexion and a crop of angry looking pimples at the
side of her mouth, the stick-thin teenager put Sarah in mind
of a Poundland Kate Moss.

'Yeah, what right you got?' Mrs Vane carried a lot more
weight. In every sense of the word. Reaching for a can of
full-fat Coke, she shifted some of the flab now, her small
feline eyes fixed all the while on Sarah. 'I let you in here in
good faith.'

Not quite. The main reason behind the visit had been
withheld. She'd spun a line about looking into further allegations made against Lawrence Drake. Hoped Emma and her
mother might be able to help with inquiries. They hadn't.
Sarah held the woman's gaze, let the silence ride.

Bridie jumped in to the vacuum. 'I mean what more do you
want? We've answered you best we can.'

Bullshit. Apart from shovelling in popcorn, until just
now the women had barely opened their mouths. The few
words uttered had been just about enough though. 'One or
two more questions then we'll leave you to it,' Sarah said.
When Dave nudged her elbow, she glanced at his notebook.
Heard the lisp? She masked a smile: they were on the same
page.

'What's the point?' Mrs Vane sniffed. 'Drake's dead, isn't he?'

'Larry Drake?' The gormless expression did Emma no
favours. 'That right?' She turned the slack-jawed gawp to Sarah.

'Looks like suicide. But we still have to investigate. As I
say, we believe he was responsible for a string of recent attacks
on young women.'

'Good riddance to bad rubbish if you ask me,' Mrs Vane
muttered.

Sarah cut the woman a glance. 'Anyway, Emma, a victim
left his name on our hotline and we're extremely keen to talk
to her. Any ideas?'

'Why ask me?' She sat up straight, hugged her knees. 'What
the hell's it got to do with me?'

'You tell me.'

'I didn't even know he lived round here.'

'Your mother didn't think to mention it?'

'Didn't want to upset her did I? That man done enough damage to my daughter.'

'So you definitely didn't ring our special number?'

The girl gave a theatrical sigh. 'How many times I got to tell you? I definitely didn't ring no—'

'Fair enough.' Sarah flapped a hand. 'We thought you were trying to help. Bring a man to justice and all that. Shame though.'

'Shame? How come?'

She brushed a hair off her skirt. 'I heard there could be a reward in it.' She'd also heard enough to quash any doubt.

'What, like cash?' The girl sat up straight.

'For information received. But if you didn't leave a message – no matter.'

'How much like?'

'Can you remember?' She turned to Dave. 'Few hundred quid wasn't it?'

'Usually a couple a grand.'

'Look, I'm not saying I did, but what if it *was* me?'

Sarah nodded at Dave then got to her feet 'You've said enough, Emma. I'm taking you in.'

'Leave her out of it,' Mrs Vane snapped. 'She knows sod all. I made the call. I wanted you lot to give him a hard time. Make him suffer. I never thought he'd top himself. Never in a million years.'

'What if she'd not put her hand up to it, boss?' Dave cut Sarah a glance as he turned the motor into Foundry Road. She'd just been on the phone to Starr, filling him in like a good girl. As for Bridie Vane, every time she opened her mouth, she'd damned herself further. She and Emma were verbal peas in a pod, the voices so alike if you closed your eyes, you'd struggle to know who was talking. Except for Bridie's slight lisp on the 's' sound – totally absent from Emma's speech.

Sarah had counted on Bridie not letting her daughter take the blame. 'I took what you might call a calculated risk, Dave.'

He gave a low whistle. 'DI Quinn. Shock horror. That's not like you.'

You can say that again. She knew they'd been skating on anorexic ice throughout the interview. Omissions, half-truths, vague suggestions. That Emma would grab the cash bait with both hands had been a gamble. Win-win as it turned out. The tactic had paid off for Sarah and – albeit not financially – for Emma, in as far as Bridie did the decent thing and leapt to her daughter's defence. The last-minute confession saved the cops time and effort. On the other hand, Bridie's belief that Drake had taken his own life suggested she was ignorant of how he'd died. If Sarah hadn't been pretty convinced of that, she'd have run the woman in rather than leave her to stew in her own toxic juices with the threat of police charges hanging over her. On the downside, as far as the inquiry went it looked as if they were back to square one. She'd left her numbers on the off-chance either had anything to add. Like the good citizens they weren't.

'Oh joy.' Sarah narrowed her eyes. 'Is that who I think it is?'

Dave followed her gaze. He'd parked two doors down from Drake's place. 'Why the hell didn't he tell you he was here?'

Starr knew where they were heading, she'd mentioned it on the phone. 'He's keeping us on our toes, isn't he?' She had no doubt how much Starr would love to see her put a foot wrong.

Not that he'd spotted them yet. The DCS had his back to them, chatting to a couple of DCs she'd tasked with knocking doors.

'We could always drive round the block.' Dave sounded dead hopeful.

'Nah.' She'd only get it in the neck for being late. Besides Starr had heard the car.

He turned, watched their approach, hands clasped behind his back. 'There you are DI Quinn.'

Shit-hot detecting skills. 'Sir.'

'Good work, chaps. Stick with it, eh? I'll let you get on now.' He waved the men off then held Sarah's gaze tightening his black leather gloves. 'I like to rally the troops, Inspector. I find they appreciate a few words out in the field.'

'That they do.' She always went out of her way to boost morale. Far as she knew this was Starr's first foray anywhere near a crime scene since he took up the post. She nodded towards number thirteen. 'Have you been inside?' *Taken a look with that fresh pair of eyes?*

'Briefly. Cooks and broth though, DI Quinn. Doesn't do to get under people's feet.'

As opposed to under people's skin. She nodded. The cliché-speak went without saying. She knew the forensic team was still hard at it, could see one of the guys through the window talking to someone else in the room.

'Can I help you with anything, sir?' She considered pointing out how perilously close his shiny black brogue was to a dog turd.

'No, no. I'm just taking stock, getting a feel for the locale.' Semis and satellite dishes; bus shelters and bin liners. Wouldn't take long. 'Pity the Vane lead didn't go anywhere. I'm still not convinced you shouldn't have charged the woman.'

She'd no intention of repeating herself. She'd spelled out her thinking on the phone: the threat could give them leverage down the line. As far as she was concerned, the Vane women were neither exempt nor eliminated from further inquiries. She'd closely questioned them about the vendetta against Drake, cited incidents from the journal. They denied all know-ledge let alone involvement. Sarah found it difficult to believe. It wasn't like either of them was a bastion of the truth. She'd already asked a DC to do some digging.

'Still,' Starr said, 'I'm sure you know best. Righto. I'll leave you to it, Inspector.' *Whoops.* Oblivious of the hazard, he'd stepped right in it and strode off. They watched him leave a trail of dog shit along the pavement.

'Good to see he's left his mark. Shame about the shoes though,' Harries murmured. 'Anyway, what was all that about, boss? I can't see why he bothered coming out.' He cut her a glance. 'What's so funny?'

'Just a thought. Come on.' Still smiling, she tightened the belt on her coat. 'What number are we looking for?'

'Seventeen. Are we going to share?'

She shook her head. 'It'll get lost in translation, Dave.' But in the putting-a-foot-wrong-stakes, Starr would take some beating.

TWENTY-NINE

'If you think that hurt, you've seen nothing yet.' Ian Webb massaged the knuckles of his right hand, the skin was still unbroken. Just. 'Man up, big boy.'

Zach Fraser was finding it difficult to open one of his eyes, let alone see through the swollen lid.

'I don't want to hit you again, but believe me I will.' Fraser was already shit scared, the reek coming off him made that obvious. Webb would happily beat another seven shades if the toe rag didn't fess up.

'Please . . . I've told you everything.'

Webb looked down, arms folded, fake smile in situ. 'Oh I don't think so, sonny.' The guy who'd phoned the landline that morning had given Webb more gen than the snivelling git cowering in the corner. The cosy scene in The Dark Horse, Fraser following Lisa out, boarding the same bus. Webb hadn't a clue and couldn't care less who'd snitched, the guy had done him a damn sight bigger favour than the cops ever had. The boys in blue hadn't even had the decency to inform him they'd pulled a suspect in for questioning. Or that they'd had to let him go for lack of evidence. Yeah, well, Webb wasn't bound by the same rules of etiquette. He could afford to play the heavy, go in hard. If they couldn't do the job properly it was time somebody did.

'Fetch me a drink will you, son?'

Anthony kicked Fraser's foot out the way. 'Shift it, shit-for-brains.'

Webb watched Ant saunter off, hands in pockets. Maybe he shouldn't have brought the boy along, but he'd overheard the call, knew something was brewing, pleaded to be in on the action. If anything, Ant's presence was acting as a brake on Webb. Instead of sitting there wallowing in self-pity, the bastard should think himself bloody lucky he still had breath in his body.

'Quit snivelling.' He toed Fraser in the ribs. 'Unless you really want something to blart about.' The scumbag had known it wasn't a social call the second he opened the door, he'd tried slamming it sharpish, but with a size twelve parked in the jamb it wasn't going to happen. They'd obviously caught him just before he sloped off to the gym. The holdall slung over a shoulder gave the game away, plus the hi-tech trainers and designer tracksuit. The design had a fault now. Tough. A boil wash should have no trouble getting rid of the stains.

'Why not come clean? Make it easier on yourself? Have a think, see what you come up with, eh?' Webb swept his gaze round the small back room. Bland neutral shades, pale woods, furniture that looked like a job lot from Ikea. Cheap-chic. He wandered off to one of the wall units, rifled through paperbacks and CDs, opened a drawer full of junk and fast food flyers. God knew what he expected to find. Either way he'd drawn a blank.

Punching a fist into his palm, he headed back to Fraser's corner. 'Right. I'm all ears.'

Jammed against the wall, Fraser had no space left to squirm. 'Mr Webb, you have to believe me. I didn't touch her.'

'Lisa. Her name's Lisa, asshole.'

'Lisa.' He brushed a tear off his cheek. 'I swear I never laid a fing—'

'Lying won't save your neck.' If he had nothing to hide, why hadn't he come forward? For crying out loud he'd hit on her the night she died; at the very least he had to know something. Besides, Webb didn't do coincidence. Looking back, he almost blamed himself. He should've realized something was going on when he'd hired the bastard to do that job. Ant, too. Apparently he'd caught Fraser ogling Lisa more than once. She'd not said anything of course, but he knew his daughter. Wasn't like her to be moody, withdrawn. It happened every time Pretty Boy had been around.

Webb snarled. 'To think I let you in to my house.'

'I swear nothing happened.' Fraser wiped the back of his hand across his mouth, smeared snot into the mix now. 'Lisa . . .'

'Lisa, what?' Webb yelled, yanked Fraser's head up by the hair. 'What were you going to say?'

'Dad.' Ant walked back carrying a lager. 'Let him finish. Lisa what?' Webb released his grip, Fraser's head lolled onto his chest.

'Hey, douche bag,' Webb Junior sneered. 'We asked you a question.'

'She . . . Lisa . . .'

'Look at me when you're talking.'

Fraser lifted his head. 'Nothing. Lisa didn't do anything.'

'Sure about that?' Webb Senior weighed in again. ''Cause it sounded to me like you were about to slag her off.'

'Yes. No. Look . . . I'm sure.'

Webb pulled the ring can. 'What happened when you got off the bus?'

'I told you. I didn't get on any bus. I chatted to Lisa and her friend in the bar. They left. I stayed on.'

'See that's where we part company. You were seen following her.'

'They're mistaken, I couldn't have been. Why won't you believe me? The police do or they wouldn't have let me go.'

'Doh. Silly me.' Webb slapped his own forehead. 'Why didn't you say so before?'

'It's true. They turned this place over trying to find—'

'Yeah right.' Webb curled a lip. 'Cops I know couldn't find a turd in a sewer.'

'I'll tell you one thing.' Ant reached into his back pocket. 'They sure didn't find this.'

'Where was it?' Eyes narrowed, Webb took hold of a photo that had been folded into squares.

'Gym bag.' Ant jabbed a thumb over his shoulder. 'In the hall.'

As he unfolded it, Webb felt the colour drain from his face, tears prick his eyes. Lisa, semi-naked, pouting, cupping her breast. 'This is my daughter, Fraser.' He could barely get the words out.

'She . . .'

'Shut the fuck up.'

'Please, Mr Webb . . . let me explain.'

'No.'

'I'll do anything . . .'

'Damn right you will. And I'll tell you exactly what.' He glanced at Ant. 'See if you can find a pen and paper will you, son?'

THIRTY

'Thanks, Twig. Appreciate it.' Dave ended the call, slipped the phone in his pocket and pulled out a Mars bar that looked like it had been squatting there for days.

Sarah cut him an exasperated glance from the driving seat. 'Come on – give.' She'd asked him to try and ferret out the latest on Natalie Hinds. Damned if she'd go metaphorical cap in hand to ask Brody direct.

'Want some?' He was picking at bits of wrapper stuck in the chocolate.

Do me a favour. 'Get on with it, Dave.' Stifling a sigh she pulled up at a red on Bristol Road and watched him bite off a chunk.

'Brody sent Beth Lally first thing to the Hinds' place in Stirchley.'

'Lally's back in action?' Sarah raised an eyebrow, hoped the voice hadn't betrayed her thinking. Fact was even when the young DC wasn't on sick leave, she'd hare off at the end of every shift, performed the barest minimum to cling on to a coveted CID post she'd not held that long. Being a new mum couldn't help, but . . .

'Beth's not that bad, boss.'

Says you, DC Telepathic. Mind, most of the blokes at the nick would agree. The blonde, blue-eyed, legs up-to-her-armpits Lally had them eating out of her hand. Sarah had never played the female card, had a problem with women who flaunted it. 'So what did she come back with? And watch that bloody chocolate.'

'OK, OK. Keep your hair on.' He licked a finger to scoop up the crumbly bits flecking his trousers. 'Not a lot. No one was in. She had to push a note through the letterbox.'

In other words a big fat zero. 'As much as that?' Lips pursed, Sarah glanced at the clock on the dash, did a quick calculation. 'You've been to the house, haven't you?'

About to take another bite, he paused. 'And?'

'It'd only take a few minutes.' Drake's neighbour hadn't exactly given them much to go on. Maybe Tracey Hinds would have more to offer. He was mid-chew, but a mouth full of Mars bar hadn't prevented him answering her before. 'Come on, Dave. What do you reckon?'

She glared in the mirror. 'If he paps that bloody horn again, I'll book him.'

'They're on green boss.'

'I can see that,' she snapped. And the old dear who'd not finished crossing the road. She let silence ride till they were in second gear. 'And the answer to my question is?'

'I can't see the point, boss. It looks as if the girl's OK.'

She tapped the wheel. 'You can't *know* that, Dave.'

'Brody reckons she probably took off with some bloke. Could be she's too scared to come home, face the music.'

Probable's and could's. Besides she was only fifteen. More than that: 'For crying out loud, she could hold the key to Lisa Webb's murder.'

'Brody doesn't seem to think so.'

'What's the fucking address?' The wheel took a whack this time.

Wordlessly, he tapped the details into the satnav. It was lucky he'd finished the Mars bar, he didn't open his mouth for at least a mile.

'OK, then boss.' He turned in the seat to face her. 'What if Brody founds out we poked our nose in?'

'If you want to bail out Dave, just say so.'

'All I'm saying's – it's not your case.'

'Damn right.' But it had been.

Tracey Hinds wore a black suede coat and a sullen expression when she opened the door of the scruffy mid-terrace. Flecks of dandruff across her shoulders looked like a light scattering of snow. Her brisk nod acknowledging Dave meant she knew this was neither cold call nor social visit.

'Actually I was just nipping out.' *Not jumping for joy? Weird.* And not the warmest of welcomes.

'Good job we caught you then Mrs Hinds.' Sarah's smile wasn't effusive either. 'I'm Detective Inspector Quinn.'

She dragged a hand down a cheek. 'Will this take long?'

'Why?' Eyebrow raised. 'Are you in a hurry?'

With what sounded like a resigned sigh, she stepped to one side and indicated a door on the right. 'Go in.'

The small room was twee and could've been snug, apart from smelling like a wine bar, or how wine bars used to before the smoking ban. Sarah's glance took in blowsy lilac roses on the wallpaper, chintzy wing chairs either side of a fake log fire. A low coffee table patterned with ring stains held one wine glass, two empty bottles of Chardonnay, an ashtray overflowing with butts, some of them partially burying Beth Lally's business card. *That much of a priority, huh?* From the settee, Cheryl whatever-her-name-is-this-month beamed up from the cover of *Heat* magazine.

Sarah turned to find Mrs Hinds still wearing the coat and this time wringing her hands.

'Where were you off to?' Despite the tepid smile, the DI's question wasn't an ice breaker and nowhere near as casual as it sounded. She was curious why a suitcase stood in the hall.

'Just nipping to the shop.' Her fingers trembled as she swept back a flimsy curtain of fine mousy hair. If she'd said she was going to the doctor's it wouldn't have surprised Sarah. Ashen-face, mocha shading round dull eyes, stress lines etched into dry, sallow skin. The woman looked sick and knackered. *Unless she was nursing an industrial hangover?* Impassive, Sarah left the conversation ball in Mrs Hinds' court.

'Now you're here I suppose you may as well . . .' Like her words she drifted off, perched on the edge of one of the wing chairs, leaving the settee free for Sarah and Dave who exchanged bemused glances. Surely the woman had to know why they were here, what they were after.

Again, Sarah let the near-silence ride, interested to know where Tracey would take it. A ticking wall clock wasn't getting them anywhere, and they didn't have all day.

'So, Mrs Hinds,' Sarah said. 'You must be mightily relieved?'

She nodded, glanced at her watch. 'Goes without saying, doesn't it?' Without eye contact and without the hint of a smile. For a woman whose daughter had surfaced after vanishing without trace, Tracey Hinds had a funny way of showing unalloyed joy.

'Do shops close early round these parts, Mrs Hinds?'

'No.' Sulky tone.

'Why not take off your coat then? Relax.' Sarah sat back, crossed her legs, steepled her fingers.

Unsmiling, Mrs Hinds shed the coat. Relaxing was clearly a bigger ask. 'What do you want to know?' Still waiting for eye contact, Sarah watched the woman play a strand of her hair through her fingers.

'The same as the officer who left her card earlier.'

Mrs Hinds' glance darted unwittingly to the ashtray. 'Yeah, well I would've called.'

'No worries. We're here now. I'd like to know what Natalie said last night, and I'm amazed you need me to tell you that, Mrs Hinds.'

'Why? I spoke to your lot. I rang soon as I heard from her. Gave them phone numbers and everything.'

'Good.' Smiling she made a mental note to find out who'd been tasked with getting a trace on the call. 'So it shouldn't take long to go through it again.'

The woman snatched a cigarette from a pack of Mayfair but shook so much that lighting it was beyond her. Cursing, she chucked fag and lighter back on the table.

'Is something wrong, Mrs Hinds? You seem on edge.' As understatements go, it disappeared into the sunset holding hands with the bleeding obvious. She looked as nervous as a kitten at Crufts. Sarah recalled Shona's verdict the first time she met the woman. Shona had sensed she knew more than she was letting on.

Biting her lip, Mrs Hinds held Sarah's gaze for the first time. 'Look, I'm sorry. It's been such a . . . strain. I've been at the end of my tether.' Eyes wide, she jumped to her feet. 'What must you think of me?' It was like invisible strings had been jerked. 'I'll make us a cup of tea or something. I can do coffee if you prefer.' *And get yourself a sneaky top up?*

'Nothing, thank you. Please, sit down.' A 'hostess with the mostest' badge wasn't going to get her off the hook. Sarah watched the woman dither for a few seconds before sinking back into the chair, clasping her hands in her lap. 'So,' Sarah said, 'what time did Natalie call and what did she say? Exactly.'

The sigh blew her cheeks out and the stale booze on her breath. 'It must've been just after ten, the news hadn't long started. Tell you the truth I didn't catch every word. I'd been . . . dozing and the line was rubbish. She just said she was OK and I wasn't to worry.'

'Where was she calling from?'

'She didn't say.'

'Didn't you ask?'

She circled a wedding ring that looked loose on the finger. 'I was so . . . shocked . . . and . . . thrilled to hear her voice I didn't think to. I mean the call came out of the blue. I could almost have imagined it except I had the phone in my hand.' The laugh was spun sugar brittle.

How frigging dense was she? Her fifteen-year-old daughter legs it, sparking off a massive police hunt and she didn't think to ask where she was staying, what the hell the girl thought she was playing at?

'How did she sound?'

'How'd you mean?'

Sarah took a calming breath, then said, 'Think about it, Mrs Hinds. She's not on a skiing holiday, is she?'

'No need to be sarky.' She sniffed. 'As I say it wasn't the best of lines but she sounded pretty normal till we got cut off.'

'Normal.' The word dripped with incredulity.

'I'm sorry if you don't believe me. Nats sounded fine.' She smoothed a crease in her faded denim skirt. 'She knew I'd be . . . concerned . . . just wanted to put my mind at rest that she'd come to no harm.'

Sarah paused a beat or two then, 'Shame we can't say the same about her best friend.'

The intake of breath was audible. 'That is well out of order.' Her eyes welled with tears. Tough. The woman's pig ignorant complacency was getting to Sarah.

'Did you think to ask Natalie about Lisa?'

'I didn't have time. I told you we—'

'Got cut off. Yes, you said.'

'I don't know why you're having a go at me.' She snatched the cigarette from the table where she'd slung it. Dave stood to get the lighter and helped her spark up. 'Thanks, love.' She took a deep drag, released the smoke through her nostrils.

Sarah hid her distaste. If the nicotine hit kick-started the bloody woman's addled brain, so be it.

'Actually, Mrs Hinds,' – he still hadn't sat down – 'I'm desperate for the loo?'

Sarah tapped her thigh while directions were issued. Waited while the woman released another lungful of smoke.

'So did Natalie tell you why she took off?'

'She didn't.' And, of course, she'd not had time to ask. The woman sounded like a stuck record.

'Did she say who she was with?'

'She's on her own.' The quickest, sharpest response so far.

'You managed to ask that, did you? Before getting so suddenly cut off?'

'I don't like your attitude.' She took another puff, eyes creased against the smoke. 'Besides what does it matter? She's safe and well. Surely that's all you need to know.'

'Do you think?' Sarah glanced up as Dave came back then pushed the woman on several more fronts: did Natalie have a boyfriend? Had she mentioned problems at school? Had there been a falling out at home?

The negatives came thick and fast.

'Look, Inspector.' She stubbed out the butt. 'I've told you everything, I know.' *Yeah, and I'm the next Dalai Lama.* 'I want you to go now.'

Sarah stifled a sigh. Reality was, if people refused to cooperate or withheld information there was very little the cops could do to force issues. 'Bear in mind we're still investigating a murder, Mrs Hinds.' Standing, she took a card from her pocket. 'When Natalie gets in touch again, please ask her to call.' She could only hope the numbers didn't end up with Beth's.

The woman led the way out, held the door open. Dave paused on the threshold. 'Have you spoken to Natalie's dad recently? Any idea where we might find him?' His questions took Sarah by surprise, but nowhere near as much as they threw Tracey Hinds. It wasn't so much what she said, for several seconds her mouth moved in much the same way a fish's did, it was the look that flashed in her eye that spoke volumes. Problem was Sarah didn't recognize the language.

Kaz's Kozy Kaff wasn't the DI's favourite pit stop. Apart from the owner's tenuous grasp on English, he was heavy-handed with the lard. Everything in the place – and not just the food on the menu – came with a film of grease. Not that it put Dave off his stride. Sarah had just watched him scarf down sausage, chips, eggs and fried bread times two. The only seconds she'd plumped for was another black coffee.

She nodded at the sugar. 'When you're done.'

He dropped two more spoonfuls into his mug of tea then slid the bowl across the red Formica. Like he so needed the calories. Smiling he sat back, patted his stomach. Still washboard, she noticed. Where the hell did he put it?

'She's hiding something, y'know Dave.' Sarah stirred her liquid lunch. She'd had time to mull over the visit to Tracey Hinds during his refuelling. Still didn't have a clue what the woman was keeping super-glued to her chest. Or why.

'She was well jumpy, I'll give you that. Regular Mrs Skippy in fact.'

'Nothing regular back there.' Not much in the way of facts either. Surely Tracey should've been leaping for joy after her daughter made contact. As for being cut off before voicing a bunch of questions, it struck Sarah as too damn convenient. She reckoned the only rubbish line was the one Tracey Hinds had almost certainly been spinning. Either the woman wasn't all there, or was way ahead. Mind, recalling the empties and

the boozy breath, another possibility sprang to mind – the
woman could've been off her face last night.

'Course,' – Dave turned his mouth down – 'there's no
guarantee she was even sober when she took the call.' Sarah
nodded. Should've known he'd clocked the drinking too.
'Could be her way of coping I guess, boss. Whatever gets you
through and all that? As I say, when I first spoke to her – she
was in bits.' He glanced at Sarah over the rim of his mug.
'You're not convinced?'

She shrugged a 'who knows?' The woman's heightened
state could be down to withdrawal symptoms, but why the
shifty eyes and evasions? She'd skirted more questions than
a shady politician.

'She'll maybe relax once the girl's home?'

Sarah snorted. 'Trusting all of a sudden, aren't you? Christ,
Dave, we've only got her word for it that Natalie actually
phoned.'

'Why'd she make it up, boss?'

Good question. Unless? She narrowed her eyes. 'What if
she wants us to stop looking?'

His frown deepened. 'Again, why'd she want that unless
she was a hundred per cent sure Natalie was OK?'

Had he slowed down all of a sudden, or was he playing
devil's advocate? 'She can't *know* that, Dave?' To all intents
and purposes, her daughter had taken off on a whim during
a night out. 'The girl's fifteen. Where's she sleeping? How's
she feeding herself?' Tracey Hinds had told Shona and Jed
Holmes that when Natalie went missing she had no more than
a few quid on her, no change of clothes, not so much as a
toothbrush. Sarah held his gaze. 'She can't cope out there on
her own. So . . .?'

'She must be staying with someone.'

'And I bet Tracey has an idea who. You done here?' In sync
they scraped back their chairs across the tacky tiles. 'What's
more, I know who gets my vote.' The woman's reaction to
Dave's question about her old man's whereabouts was beginning to make sense now.

Glad of the slightly fresher air, Sarah waited outside while
he settled up. Well, the traffic fumes from Stirchley's main

drag made a change. There was a chill in it though. Hugging her coat closer, she stamped her feet. *Come on, Dave, get a move on.*

'OK. Say she's with her dad.' Mentally he hit the ground running as they walked in step. 'Apart from the pair of them wasting a hell of a lot of police time, what's the problem? At least it means we know she's safe.'

Did they? He must be back on the gullible pills. Even if Natalie was unharmed, it didn't make Lisa Webb any less dead. Problem was Sarah still couldn't see if there was a connection. She still hadn't come up with anything by the time she pulled the Audi into a parking bay back at the nick. Cutting the engine, she glanced at Dave who'd been staring down at his lap. 'What's up?'

'You know when you said I was trusting . . .?'

'Go on.'

'Remember I went for a leak?' He met her gaze. 'I took a peep in the suitcase.'

She widened her eyes. *What!* 'You took a bloody risk. That's what you took.' No wonder he'd kept it quiet. So why open up now? 'Well?'

'It was full of clothes.'

Her hand stilled as she reached for the keys. 'So when Tracey said she was popping out' – she ran her gaze over his face – 'unless she'd a charity shop in mind?'

'Good thinking, boss. But if it was just a trip to Oxfam – why'd she need Natalie's passport?'

'Shoot, Dave, search me, unless . . .' She caught the glint in his eye. 'Don't even think about it, detective.' He'd done enough rifling for one day.

'Unless what, boss?'

Unless Natalie intended skipping more than school. 'Tracey needs keeping tabs on, Dave.' But they'd been poking their noses into Brody's case. How the hell could Sarah sanction surveillance?

He held her gaze. 'I've got some time owing, boss.'

THIRTY-ONE

Sarah tapped a pen against her teeth, still trying to process what Paul Wood had just told her. The news held a damn sight more interest than the reports she'd been reading.

'You're saying Zach Fraser phoned and confessed to killing Lisa Webb?'

'I know. Frigging amazing, isn't it?' Twig scratched his neck. 'Anyway, Brody gets uniform to despatch a car pronto, bring the guy in. Except it's already too late. Fraser's a goner.' A couple of patrol officers had found the front door open, a suicide note in the hall and Zach Fraser's body slumped against a wall in the kitchen, syringe still in his arm.

Wondering why the development hadn't trickled down to her before now, she gestured vaguely to a chair. 'Sit down, Twig.'

'Best not, ma'am. All hell's breaking loose and Brody wants me to hook up with the pathologist down there.'

'Are we really that short-staffed? Whoops.' She smiled. 'No offence Twig. I didn't mean it like that.'

'None taken.' Mind, if the office manager had been called on to leave his post, it showed how thin the squad was spread.

'Brody's already there I take it?'

'No, he's tied up.'

She raised an eyebrow. A suspect commits suicide after confessing to a high-profile murder and the SIO can't drag himself away to take a look at the death scene? She struggled to see what could take precedence. Twig glanced at his watch, clearly keen to get going.

'Mind if I walk you to the car?' Sarah was already on her feet, had a bunch of other questions in mind. Hated feeling she was on the periphery of an operation that had once been her baby.

Twig gave a knowing smile as he held the door for her. 'Fire away, ma'am.'

Transparent? Moi? Dead right. 'This confession then? Who did he speak to?' And where did it leave the inquiry as far as the sex attacks went?

Twig had mostly heard everything third-hand and didn't know the exact content. 'The call was put through to the incident room. Doug Spencer picked up.' *Brody's blue-eyed boy.*

'Did he think to record it?'

'No, and he got a right bollocking. But how was he to know? It's the luck of the draw every time you pick up a phone, isn't it?'

'I'd have thought DI Brody would be cracking open the champagne.' She shivered, hugged her waist, it was cold out here even huddled in the doorway.

'Not so much.' Twig sniffed. 'He's always reckoned it was only a question of time before Fraser coughed. If anything, I think he regrets letting the guy walk. There'll be no big day in court now.' She nodded aware of his gaze on her. 'You don't look like you're bubbling over with joy yourself, ma'am.'

'I'm fine, Twig. Let me know how it goes, eh?' Fine but well curious. Brody had released Fraser because he'd no real evidence to hold him. Yet less than twenty-four hours later, Fraser tops himself. How did that work?

Frowning, she watched Twig walk towards the car pool. 'Hey, Twig, what is it the DI's so tied up with?'

He glanced back. 'Would you believe another suspect?'

Pensive, Sarah made her way back to the office. What did they say about buses? You wait for one . . .

They say something about curiosity, too. Sarah pursed her lips. It only applied to cats. Besides, the incident room was on the way and her office wasn't going anywhere. She popped her head round the door, spotted Blue-Eyes, head down, with his feet up on the desk. Glancing round, she saw the reason why. The big cats were clearly away and apart from a couple of civilian support staff, it seemed Spencer had been left to play. *Angry Birds* by the look of it.

'DC Spencer?' she tapped his shoulder.

He spun round so sharply, he almost lost his balance. 'Inspector. Sorry, I—'

'Can you spare a minute?' Like the question wasn't rhetorical. Clearly he was rushed off his feet.

'For sure.' Standing now he smoothed his hair, straightened the tie. 'How can I help?'

She'd have preferred a chat in the privacy of her own office but as he was holding the CID citadel, she could hardly drag him away. 'You took the call from Zach Fraser?'

His flush deepened. 'That's right. He gave his name but I didn't know who he was. I made a few notes—'

'Where are they?' DI Brody had them, he said. And Spencer's small intestine for garters no doubt. Fair enough. It was incumbent on every officer, however newbie, to keep up with developments. Fraser's identity might not have been out in the public domain but it sure featured in police reports.

'So what did the guy say?' she asked. Sorry, apparently. Over and over again. Kept on and on about not meaning any harm, it had been an accident, all a terrible mistake. Didn't explain what the apology was for until Spencer finally asked. Even when Fraser came out with it, Spencer had taken some convincing.

'To be honest, DI Quinn, I thought he was a time-waster.' His eyes searched her gaze probably seeking a spark of sympathy, fellow-feeling. She shrugged, non-committal. It wouldn't have been the first call of its kind, every major incident attracted loopy attention-seekers. Sarah had lost count of the number of Jack the Rippers and so-called psychics who rang cops.

But Fraser had been Brody's prime suspect.

That Spencer had failed to grasp the import of the call had led to potentially life-saving minutes being lost. Or was that unfair? Should the young detective have been able to divine Fraser's depths of despair? Realize how narrow an emotional knife edge he'd been teetering on? Could anyone *know* when someone was suicidal?

'How did he sound?'

'I thought he was pissed.' Spencer dropped his gaze, toed the carpet. 'He sounded pretty out of it to me.' Even so, he said he'd told Fraser they'd get someone round and the second the call ended he alerted Brody.

'How'd you know where he was calling from?'

He glanced up, frowning. 'I . . . just . . . assumed. He didn't correct me or anything.'

'I take it he didn't mention Zoe Darby or any of the other victims?'

'No, and—' Eyes wide, he clammed up. Whatever he'd spotted over her shoulder, she guessed it wasn't the Loch Ness monster.

'I'm surprised you have time to stand round chatting, Inspector.' *Close.* The stealth bomber had struck again.

Inwardly bridling she managed to keep a straight face. 'DI Brody.'

'Unless congratulations are in order? No, they can't be, can they? I hear Drake's killer's still at large.' *Unlike Lisa Webb's.* The smile didn't reach his eyes, barely troubled a lip.

'Oh, and to answer your question, Fraser wouldn't have mentioned Zoe Darby. How could he? I'm holding a guy on suspicion of rape. Anyway must get back, I'm up to my neck. You know how it is, I'm sure.'

He turned before reaching the door. 'If you're at a loose end, Inspector . . .?' *Cheeky sod.* 'You could drop by the Webbs' place when you knock off. Let them know about Fraser's confession. Far as I'm concerned the inquiry's done. I prefer sticking with live cases any day.'

THIRTY-TWO

The first thing Hunt saw when he walked in was the skull and cross bones grinning at him from across the back of the suspect's jacket. The second was Brody's barely concealed smirk. The clothing hadn't given Joel Price away apparently. Brody was keeping the detail up his sleeve but Hunt had heard rumour round the nick that a relative had grassed.

The DI sat across the metal desk from Price, hands loosely folded across his paunch, legs taking up more than their fair share of floor space. He cut Hunt a nod that said 'chop-chop'.

'Sir.' Hunt slid a few files on the desk before taking a seat. *We can't go on meeting like this* wasn't a line he'd be voicing any time soon – however much the thought appealed. He'd been summoned at short notice yet again to sit in on a Brody-led interrogation. There'd been no time for Hunt to digest Price's past record let alone discuss interview strategies. Acting as the DI's sidekick was getting to be a habit and not one Hunt was keen to keep up. Last thing he needed was to be regularly partnered with a guy he viewed as Starr's right-hand man.

'Sergeant Hunt,' Brody said. 'Mr Price has something he'd like to get off his chest. Isn't that right?'

Glancing over at the guy, Hunt reckoned lifting his head from his chest wouldn't be a bad start. Apart from the slack posture concealing his face, the ceiling light bounced off a bald spot the size of a planet. Like a lot of youngish follically-challenged blokes, he'd let the remaining hair grow longer than it should and limp, greasy strands were tethered in an elastic band at the nape. Not so much a ponytail, more a gathering of dead rats tails.

Hunt tore the cellophane from the first of two cassette tapes. 'I'll just get the equipment set up and we'll be good to go, Mr Price.' Head still down, hands nestled in his crotch, Price twiddled his thumbs. The fingers held enough rings to hang curtains and ingrained nicotine stains explained one of the smells wafting off the guy. The other could be down to trapped wind.

'Did you hear, Mr Price?' *Maybe he'd dropped off.* Hunt sniffed. Clocked a skull printed on the grubby white T-shirt and the brass skull-shaped buckle on his thick leather belt. Damien Hirst had a lot to answer for. Or not. According to the crime sheet, Price's art education – like the rest of his curriculum – had been curtailed when, at fifteen, he'd torched a classroom at his school. There'd been no one around or the arson attack would have led to more than nine months in a young offenders' institute. Over the next decade and a half,

Price had done more porridge than Goldilocks. Drug dealing, sex assaults, GBH. Regular nice guy.

Hunt glanced at Brody and mouthed a one-word query: 'brief?'

'No.' He straightened, tidied the papers in front of him. 'Mr Price says he doesn't feel the need for legal representation. Tell the Sergeant why, Mr Price.'

Finally he raised his head, flicked a glance at Brody. Hunt glimpsed the palest blue eyes he'd ever seen, but it was the tattoos that caught his gaze. Tiny skulls were inked across the forehead like some sort of sporty sweatband. Hunt had a sudden vision of the young McEnroe yelling, 'You cannot be serious.'

Price certainly looked to be having a laugh. He gave Brody a wide-mouth grin. 'Say, please.' The guy had clearly taken a file to his teeth – they could play a bit part in *Jaws*.

What sort of nutter ruined their looks like that? Struggling not to show any reaction, Hunt started the recording then ran through the spiel – time, date, people present.

'Right, Mr Price,' Brody said. 'Can you repeat for the tape what you told the officers who brought you in, please?'

'Which bit?' He flashed the inane grin again. 'It's a fair cop?'

Was the weirdo on something? Hunt picked up a pen to make notes, but it soon became clear there'd not be a lot to get down on paper. Price admitted raping Zoe Darby, said she'd been gagging for it. That he'd plead guilty when it came to court and that was it. The guy sat back, arms crossed, lips buttoned.

Hunt cast Brody a glance, but the DI was jotting something on a notepad. Hunt looked back at Price who was chewing an already ragged fingernail. Momentarily the Sergeant was struck dumb. As a veteran cop, he'd thought he'd seen just about everything, knew it took all sorts blah-blah, but Price's incomprehensible behaviour took a packet of Garibaldi. Hunt cleared his throat. Brody was still otherwise occupied. OK, someone had to break the silence. 'It doesn't work like that, Mr Price.'

The guy leaned over to lift a butt cheek. 'Do I look like I give a flying fuck?' Hunt reckoned he looked like a sleaze ball with flatulence and a skull fetish, but it was hardly the point.

'We have to have—'

'I've told you I did her. What more do you want, cop?'

'Detail?' Hunt raised an eyebrow. Chapter and verse. Easiest thing in the world to retract a confession once a defendant stood in the dock. Every word had to be backed by hard evidence. Brody nudged his arm and showed what he'd written. *Stupid sod filmed it on his phone. His ma's down the corridor singing like a canary.*

Hunt tightened his mouth. *Thanks for sharing.*

'OK, Mr Price,' Brody said 'You've had your bit of fun. Now let's hear about the other victims.'

The skull tattoos collided as the guy creased his forehead. 'What other victims?'

Brody sighed, reached for a file. 'How about I give you an aide-memoire.'

'Aide what?'

'Never mind.' He slid two photographs across the desk: Hannah Winter and Jessica Silk.

The casual glance Price cast bordered on cursory. The tongue he darted across his top lip told a different story. Hunt caught a whiff of something else: fear.

Brody sniffed. 'In your own time, Mr Price.'

'No way, cop.' He held up both palms, swore he'd never set eyes let alone anything else on either woman. 'I put my hand up to the other bird but you ain't doing this.'

Brody sighed, traced a finger along an arched eyebrow. 'Why not save everyone a lot of time and trouble, Mr Price? You never know the courts might go easier on you.'

'Are you out of your mind, dude?' Glaring at Brody he bit his bottom lip. Hunt watched beads of blood appear where the razor sharp teeth had punctured the skin. The only sound in the room was Price's foot tapping a beat on the tiles. Fifteen, twenty seconds passed, then: 'I ain't coughing if that's what you're waiting for.'

'I'm waiting for you to see sense—'

Red's what Price saw. Lightning fast, roaring like a wounded animal he sprang out of the chair lamped Brody before Hunt could jump to the DI's defence. The second blow probably did most damage. It smashed Brody's head into the wall.

THIRTY-THREE

'I'm glad the bastard's dead.' Angela Webb had shredded a tissue into what looked like grey rice grains scattered in her lap. 'Nothing's going to bring her back though, is it?' Her dull eyes searched Sarah's face, but she knew the answer anyway.

Sitting next to her in the lounge, Sarah simply shook her head. If she'd not found the woman home alone, she'd have been on her way by now, but it seemed pretty heartless to tell her Lisa's killer had topped himself then immediately bow out. Mrs Webb had been in the middle of a pile of ironing, the board still set up near the TV. The smell of warm linen mingled with furniture polish, failed to mask the woman's body odour. Maybe it hadn't always been the way, but a clean house currently took precedence over personal hygiene.

Leaning forward she snatched another tissue from the box. 'Why do people bang on about closure eh, Inspector? Totally bloody meaningless. I've never understood it. Nor Karma. What did Lisa ever do to deserve dying like that? I keep imagining her final . . .'

'Don't, Mrs Webb.' Reluctant, Sarah reached out but the woman batted away her hand.

'Only sodding closure I'll get is when I'm six feet under.'

Sarah stifled a sigh. Almost wished the touchy-feely Dave was here rather than moonlighting on what looked like an increasingly wild goose chase. Even more so with Fraser's confession in the bag. On the other hand, Natalie had been around when Fraser chatted up Lisa in the wine bar. Detectives still needed to talk to the girl, once she'd been found.

Shona was good at the empathy stuff too. Not that she'd been in the station much today. She'd been out doing her Spielberg impersonation again, this time with Jessica Silk and her parents. Brody might have a suspect in custody, but another appeal could flush out more witnesses. As for Mrs Webb, Sarah could have brought the Pope in tow, nothing anyone said could change the woman's reality. And she wasn't listening anyway.

'It would have been her birthday tomorrow.' A quick flick sent the tissue flying over the carpet. 'Makes it worse somehow.'

'Look, can I get you a cup of tea or something?' Keg of brandy, maybe.

'Sweet sixteen she'd have been.' Smiling, the woman nodded towards a framed photograph on the wall. Lisa looked back with a cheeky grin. 'I bought all her pressies ages ago. Had to hide them. The little madam would have found them else.' The smile faded. 'Why did she have to die, Inspector? I miss her so much.'

'Where's your husband, Mrs Webb?' Sarah glanced round willing him to show up.

'I dunno.' She shrugged 'Gone for a drive probably. He does a lot of that these days. We don't really . . .' *What? Talk? Get on?* The woman shook her head then blew her nose.

Sarah glanced at the mute TV screen. The local news programme was partway through. She wondered if the Silk piece had aired.

'What's he like, Inspector?'

'Sorry?'

'The killer? What's he like? Did he say why he did it?'

Sarah recalled Fraser telling Spencer it had been an accident. That was bollocks, given what she'd seen in the park, and hardly what a heartbroken mother would want to hear. The suicide note might be more specific, but no one had got back with any detail yet. 'I'm sorry, Mrs Webb. I can't really help you. I never met him. Were you not in when he came to the house?'

'I wish. I might've sensed something.' Mouth twisted in a grimace, she shuddered.

Done with what felt like baby-sitting, Sarah itched to get away now. She took a covert glance at her watch. 18.45. 'Actually, Mrs Webb is there anyone I can call to—'

'Makes my skin creep. The thought that he was here. Ian hired the bastard. God knows what he'll say when he finds out.'

'Finds out what, love?'

Sarah breathed a mental sigh of relief, turned her head to see Webb standing in the doorway still wearing his coat. His glance darted between the two women before he strolled in and perched on the arm of a chair.

'Come on, Inspector. Finds out what?' He held her gaze throughout as Sarah repeated the same bare bones she'd related to his wife. Maybe it sank in on the second telling, by the time she'd finished, Mrs Webb was in pieces, sobbing, shaking. Webb just looked shell-shocked.

'I can't get my head round it.' He stared down at his hands. 'I invited my daughter's killer into my own home. Christ, I'll never forgive myself.'

Going by the look on Angela's face, neither would she.

'I'm sure you have things to talk about.' Sarah reached down for her bag, couldn't get away fast enough. 'I'll say goodbye for now.' A colleague could get in touch about details for releasing Lisa's body. Mrs Webb was in no state to take anything else in.

As Sarah walked past, the woman made a grab for her arm. 'Please, please,' she wailed, 'if you find out why he did it . . .?'

'Leave her be, Angela.' Webb rose. 'Surely it said in the note?'

Sarah snatched her arm away, could barely hear herself think over the racket. 'I don't know.'

'Hey, love, shush.' He nodded towards the door. 'I'll see you out.'

'Your wife needs you, Mr Webb. Stay where you are.' Something caught his eye and he turned his head, didn't even appear to have heard her 'goodbye'. As she left the room, Sarah glanced back. He'd not moved an inch, just stood staring into space, a haunted look on his face.

The phrase 'seen a ghost' sprang to Sarah's mind.

Even after the face on the screen was replaced by some bland boy presenter's, Ian Webb remained rooted in front of the TV, haunted gaze transfixed. He told himself he'd imagined it, that he'd been seeing things, a million thoughts darted through his already throbbing head. The incessant wailing didn't help. Fists balled, he spun on his heel.

'Fuck's sake, shut up woman.'

The noise level went through the roof then faded as his wife fled the room. He heard her stomp upstairs, doubtless intending to shut herself off in Lisa's room again.

He knew he should go after her, offer comfort, but right now he needed reassurance himself. With thoughts still racing, he flopped back into the depths of the armchair trying to make sense of what he'd seen. The name on the screen – Jonathan Silk – meant nothing to him, but Webb was almost sure he'd come across the man before. *Like the guy on the telly the other day.* Darby, was it? Again the name hadn't registered, but in itself that meant nothing, everyone knew it was easy enough to change a name. So Darby and Silk? Two middle-aged blokes whose daughters had been sexually attacked. Webb narrowed his eyes. Seemed to remember there'd been another girl. All victims of, what did it say in the press? The Ski Mask Killer. He was sure he'd seen that line in the local rag.

Rising quickly, he shucked off the coat. Angela recycled papers like there was no tomorrow, but there was bound to be something on the net. His glance fell on the laptop. He tucked it under an elbow and strode into the kitchen. Beer first. He grabbed a bottle from the side, gulped half of it down, then dragged a chair out and nudged the mouse.

The pain at seeing Lisa's pic every time he logged on was almost physical, but they'd chosen the background together, he was damned if he'd change it. He'd had to ask Ant to get rid of the photos they'd found at Fraser's, all bar one which he'd left for the old bill to find. Even though the pics sickened Webb, they showed his daughter and he couldn't bring himself to destroy her image. Not that he could eradicate the filthy things from his head, they'd be stuck there until the day he died. If Ant hadn't found them – would Fraser still be alive? Webb had asked himself the question several times. The answer was yes, probably. He'd gone to the house to force the shyster to come clean, do the bloody cops' job for them. But whether Fraser had killed Lisa or not, once Webb had seen her posing for Fraser's sleazy shots, as far as he was concerned the fuckwit would pay for corrupting her innocence. No one messed with Webb's flesh and blood.

Wincing, he unfurled a fist then realized why the palm stung. Blood oozed where the nails had pierced the skin. Fraser's fucking fault again. Focus, man, focus. Fraser was dead and metaphorically buried. It was the living Webb needed to attend to. Squaring his shoulders, he clicked the mouse. Another click brought up a link to the *Birmingham News* website. He entered a search for 'Ski Mask Killer', ran his gaze down the page. As he read, light from the screen flickered in his dark eyes, cast shadows over the planes of his face.

He'd recalled right. There was a third victim: Hannah Winter. Webb stroked his jaw-line as he studied her face. It didn't bring anyone to mind and, again, the name meant nothing. The visuals of all three girls were pretty decent, the head-and-shoulders of Michael Darby a tad fuzzy and there was no shot of Daddy Silk. Webb sat back in the chair, sank the rest of the beer, then raked his fingers through his hair. He'd caught little more than a fleeting glimpse of the guy on the box, but still he'd pay good money their paths had crossed. Jessica's features certainly favoured her father's, especially the snub nose. The real clincher would be finding out what Hannah Winter's old man looked like. That and trying to get hold of Darby's phone number and arrange a meet.

He snorted. Should've asked Quinn while she was here lording it. Was there an Oscar for keeping a straight face while a clueless detective tells you things you already know? Webb reckoned he'd be a shoo-in, given he'd force-fed Fraser every line during his call to the cop shop. Despite what Quinn believed, the little shit hadn't actually fessed up: Webb had couched the speech carefully. The idea had been to keep Fraser in the picture so the law didn't let him out of its sights. Like the first thing the plod would've clocked when they entered the guy's pad was the note. Of course, they'd jumped to the wrong conclusion – suicide hadn't been spelled out.

Webb should know, he'd dictated it.

I'd be better off dead.

Short and – given the needle in his arm – to the point. But the heroin wasn't meant to be fatal. It was supposed to look like an accidental overdose – the flake couldn't even get that right. Webb scowled. Fraser's death had freaked out Ant though; he'd gone straight upstairs soon as they got back. Better that than come face-to-face with Quinn. Webb doubted his son could've brazened it out in the same way.

Sighing, he reached for another beer. To Webb's way of thinking the Fraser scenario was a distraction, water under the proverbial. Priority was to find out if his suspicions about Darby and Silk were well-founded. Until he was a hundred per cent, he didn't fancy just turning up on the doorstep. By the look of them, they'd done OK for themselves. Webb raised a mock toast to the now blank screen.

Sombre again, he swallowed a mouthful of beer. Then another. He was still pretty sure Hannah Winter's old man held the key. If it turned out he was the guy Webb thought he knew, it would knock any doubt on the head. He'd have no option but to break cover, make himself known to the men. Not that he could see any of them welcoming a blast from the past with welcome arms. On the other hand, if Webb was on the money, none of them could afford to ignore what was going on. Nor afford to let it happen again.

'Dad?'

'Fuck's sake, Ant. You nearly gave me a heart attack.' The lad didn't look too hot himself. 'You OK, son?'

'What do you think?' Strolling into the kitchen, he slung a white envelope on the table. 'I need a beer.'

'You know where it is.' Frowning, Webb picked up the envelope. 'Where'd this come from?' No address, no stamp, just his name in type.

'Dunno. It was on the mat when I came down.'

Webb's frown deepened as he unfolded the single sheet of paper inside. The words had been cut out of newspapers stuck on with glue.

I know what you are. How do you live with yourself? Call yourself a father?

Ant was about to take a drink, but the bottle stilled in his hand. 'What's wrong, Dad?'

'Nothing.'

Or there wouldn't be. When he'd tracked down the bastard threatening him and his family.

THIRTY-FOUR

S arah paused as she opened the driver's door, looked back at the house. Through the window it was clear Webb still hadn't budged. Something about the stance bugged her. He'd made no move to comfort his wife whose crying was audible even out here. It was enough to melt the heart of a statue. What was wrong with the guy?

'Slumming it are we, DI Quinn?'

Sarah recognized the voice and registered the tongue-in-cheek tone.

'Caroline,' she said, deliberately keeping her gaze averted. 'Long time no . . .'

Eyes wide and jaw slack, her voice petered out as she turned to find King jogging across the road towards her. Literally. The Lycra was a revelation too. Again, literally. The short shorts and skimpy vest showcased body parts normally under wrap in sharp suits and cost-a-fortune couture frocks. The running gear was in her signature colour combo though – red and black.

'So what are you doing here?'

'You're the detective. What does it look like?'

Still open-mouthed, she couldn't say.

'Christ, Sarah, are you having a turn,' – pant, pant, – 'or have you swallowed a bus?' Puce-faced, Caroline bent forward from the waist, hands on knees. Sounded suspiciously to Sarah like she was trying to catch her breath.

You can talk love. Or maybe not right now. Sarah masked a smile. 'Me? No. I'm fine. How about you?'

Caroline glanced up through her fringe. 'Are you taking the piss?'

'Would I?' She curved a lip. 'I just never saw you as a . . . jogger.' All hot and sweaty. Mind, even now the reporter's make-up was immaculate and the glossy black bob barely had a hair out of place. As for pounding the pavements,

it seemed too much like hard work for a woman like Caroline.
Normally she got other people to do the running round for
her.

'Yeah, well.' She straightened. 'Book. Cover. Judge. There's
more to most people than meets the eye, you know.'

'Indeed there is.' And quite a bit of Caroline's goose-bumped
flesh was on show.

'You need to work on the sarcasm.' She sniffed. 'I've been
running for years. Off and on.'

Sarah cocked her head. 'Mostly off, I take it.'

'Ho, ho. Nothing like a bit of fresh air and feeling the
burn. You should try it sometime. It's good for you. You might
catch more bad guys.'

'Thanks.' Smiling sweetly, she slung her bag onto the
passenger seat. 'Don't let me keep you—'

'Hey, do you have to rush off?' She reached out a tentative
hand. 'I'm only round the corner. And you're right, it has been
too long.'

She must be after something, or on something. It wasn't
like they were best buddies. Sarah narrowed her eyes. 'What's
in it for you?'

'I finished a book today.'

'Reading it?'

'Missed your vocation, you. And you know what I mean.
It'd be nice to celebrate. I've got a bottle of bubbly in the
fridge. We can catch-up over a quick drink.'

Tempting though the offer was, Sarah said thanks but no
thanks. Caroline gave a suit-yourself shrug but hung round
while Sarah got in the car. Knowing the reporter, she'd already
have a big story in mind and wanted to pump Sarah for gen.
Not that it wouldn't be novel for once to socialize with someone
who wasn't a cop. With the engine running, she lowered the
window. 'Some other time maybe.'

'Sure.' She looked genuinely forlorn, fluttered half-hearted
fingers. 'See you around.'

The DI was half way down the road before she glanced in the
driving mirror. Just in time to see Caroline take an almighty
dive. *Ee-ouch.* Wincing in sympathy she jammed the anchors

on and put the Audi into reverse. The reporter was still sprawled on the pavement when Sarah reached her. 'Are you OK?'

'Never felt better.'

Her lip wasn't damaged then. Biting back a barb Sarah squatted down, helped her to sit. 'Where does it hurt?'

'Ankle, mostly. I went over on it.' Gingerly she stroked her fingers over what already looked like a swelling. 'Think it's a sprain.' The scratched bleeding knees didn't look too good either.

'Can you stand?' Just. With a supportive arm round her waist. 'Come on, I'd better get you home, hadn't I?'

Through teary eyes, she smiled. 'Thought you'd never ask.'

THIRTY-FIVE

'You didn't do it on purpose, did you?' Laid-back, if not supine, on an ivory velvet Chesterfield, Sarah cast a semi-suspicious glower at her drinking partner seated alongside.

'Inspector Quinn! What a thing to suggest.' Caroline had just leaned over to top up Sarah's glass and now tipped the dregs into her own. 'As if I'd stoop that low.'

Sarah raised a sceptical eyebrow and tacit toast. She'd not have put such a ruse past the reporter a few years back, but maybe they were both mellower now. And merry – given the champagne.

'OK. I'll let you off, just this once.' Smiling she cast her gaze round the living room. The place had changed a good bit since her only other visit. It was all soft lighting, clean lines and classy fabrics: more Heal's than Homebase.

'Besides,' Caroline said. 'What if I'd fallen flat on my face? Risk the assets? I don't think so.'

'Can't argue with that.' She waved an airy glass. Come the cold light of Saturday, she might regret the booze, but an hour or so spent in Caroline's company had lifted her mood. Well it had after she'd played doctor and strapped the ankle, helped the patient into slouching gear, dragged a footstool over, opened the champagne, put some music on – Coldplay – and sat down. Then she'd finally started to chill.

She'd also steered clear of shop talk: cops mixing with journos was a no-no these days. Even more than that, the DI just wanted to forget the job for a while. Caroline guessed what – or who – had brought Sarah to Selly Oak, but she'd not pressed for details. In the reporter's book, it was a bog standard murder and she could live without stories like that. For the most part Sarah had listened to Caroline babble on about her writing. How the hell she'd inveigled Baker into doing research work, Sarah would never know. She'd made a mental note to give him a bell tomorrow. If the old boy was back in the police fold, conflict of interest sprang to mind. Never mind sticky wicket.

'Course if my lodger was around he'd be over you like a rash.'

'Painful.'

'Nah. Mark's a softie.' But dead keen on covering crime according to Caroline and obviously the current biggie was the serial rapist story. Prompted by her next book idea, Mark was now apparently immersed in the whole rape issue, unearthing case histories, back stories, victims to interview. Caroline suspected his willingness to take on the extra work was partly a distraction. His mother was terminally ill and getting his head down meant something else to occupy his mind.

'Not exactly light relief, is it?' Sarah said.

'Maybe not. Still he could be working in tandem with your old boss soon. Fred's always game for a laugh.'

Sarah turned her mouth down. Baker working in tandem with anyone was a joke – but a hack?

'Not convinced?'

She shrugged. 'We'll see.'

'Too right. Even if Baker backs out, Mark's got the bit between his teeth now so he'll plough on either way.'

'You'll be telling me next he's got a bee in his bonnet.' Sarah cocked an eyebrow.

'OK, OK. Cliché-alert.' She lobbed a playful cushion, but at least had the grace to look sheepish. 'Seriously though, he's really on board, reckons sex attacks are on the increase, not enough cases go to court and when they do sentences are too light. He keeps chucking stats at me.'

Tell me something I don't know. The figures in Sarah's in-tray showed a thirteen per cent increase in sexual offences on her patch, and in England and Wales rape at knifepoint had shot up a whopping fifty per cent. That was reported attacks. As for sentences, average was five years. 'If he's so bothered, tell him to join the law.'

'God, you're all heart. I know one thing, he'd love to shadow an inquiry, gain a proper police perspective.'

She gave a laboured sigh. 'Look, Caro—'

'Sorry. I'll back off, shouldn't even have mentioned it. And we're getting heavy here. Let's change the subject, lighten up.' It didn't take long to get back to her favourite topic.

'Hey, want to know what I hate most about being a writer?'

'Enlighten me.'

'WB.'

She frowned. 'Writer's block?'

'Writer's bum. Wobbly bits.'

Sarah gave a lop-sided smile. It explained a lot. Only something as drastic as a droopy derriere would get Caroline off her backside and into running gear. The DI was even toying with the idea herself. Tomorrow was a rest day and she'd have a bit of precious free time on her hands. She'd maybe jog along the towpath, check her fitness levels were still up to scratch. Once she'd picked up the motor. She glanced at her watch. Yeah, it was probably time to call it a night, and a cab.

'Don't even think about it.' Caroline wagged a school-ma'am finger. 'Why don't we eat? I could murder a curry.'

'Murder? I'd have to run you in then.' *Run.* 'Get it?'

She tilted her glass. 'If I didn't know better I'd say you were tipsy, DI Quinn. Mind, it suits you, makes a change to hear you laugh.'

'Yeah, well.' Boundless mirth was in short supply these days.

'Go on.' She'd picked up on the flat delivery.

'Nah. Forget it.' Sarah wasn't *that* pissed; pissed off more like – the nick's macho mafia had got to her more than she'd care to admit. Probably one of the reasons she was still here. For the first time in a while she'd actually blanked out the niggling thoughts, latent fears.

'Fair enough. But you know what they say about all work . . . I reckon you should let your hair down more often.'

'What, this?' Pointing to the crop, she forced a smile. 'Won't get me very far, will it?'

'Reckon you could stagger to the kitchen?' There was wine in the fridge, Caroline said, and a drawer full of takeout menus. 'I'd go myself, but . . .' She sighed, gazed pointedly at the gammy ankle. 'Go on, Sarah, a feast is only a phone call away.'

'Yeah, OK.' *Sod it. Why not? In for a penny in for a prawn tikka masala.* It'd save having to pick up something on the way home or – God forbid – cook. Her non-resident chef had other things on his plate tonight. Staking out the Hinds' house was a hell of a long shot, but Dave's reasoning was that if Tracey was going to make a move, she'd not hang about. His latest text said she was still in residence, the car parked outside.

'Get what you want,' Caroline called after her. 'I'll have the lamb madras.'

'That's big of you,' she murmured. Rolling her eyes, she opened the kitchen door and pulled up pronto. *If he was around,* Caroline had said. Mark was well and truly in-house, sitting at the breakfast bar, a laptop in front of him. He glanced up, smiled.

'Hi there, I thought I recognized the voice. I was about to pop in, say hello. Honest.'

'Hi. No worries. I'm looking for—'

'Third drawer down.' Pointing a pen. 'I needed to check a few things first. Afraid I got a bit carried away.' On a sea of papers and press cuttings, by the look of it.

'As I say, no worries.' Head down, she rifled through a stack of restaurant flyers.

'Oh and she prefers Spice Avenue. They chuck in free poppadoms.'

'Hey, you, I'm not the cat's mother.' Well, well, well. The invalid had dragged herself from her sick stool. Clutching the frame with both hands, Caroline balanced on one foot in the doorway. 'He's right about the poppadoms though.' There was a smile in her voice and a knowing look in her eye directed solely at Slater.

'Caro, you're hurt. What happened?' He slid off the barstool and hurried towards her. Sarah reckoned the guy couldn't sound more in bits if she'd had a leg amputated. 'Come on, take my arm.'

'I'm fine, Mark. It's no big deal. Besides we . . . I have a guest – she's been spoiling me rotten.'

We? And not the royal kind. Lips tight, Sarah turned and popped the menu back in the drawer.

'Decided?' Caroline gushed. 'What are you having?'

Certainly not gooseberry. 'Actually, Caroline. I'm gonna leave you to it. I've got a few calls to make.' She cut a glance at Mark. 'And I can see you're in safe hands.'

Lucky her fists were balled, Sarah still felt like throttling the bloody woman. Talk about a tissue of lies, Caroline had spun a box of Kleenex. And she, the ace detective had fallen for it. Fallen for it? Nice one. Even if she'd tried she wouldn't have been able to stifle the snort.

'OK back there, love?'

Sarah's eyes met the cabbie's in the driving mirror. 'Fine thanks.' Apart from the splitting headache and feeling like a frigging numpty. Mind, she doubted Brody was feeling too hot at the moment. Huntie's text hadn't gone into detail apart from the fact Brody had been knocked out cold by a suspect. She was dying to find out the juicy bits, but hadn't been able to raise Huntie on the phone. The text's only other snippet told her charges were about to be laid.

'Yeah, loadsa colds about at the moment, love. Tell you what I swear by—' Her ringtone went off. Thank God. She lifted a restraining finger while scrabbling in her bag with the other hand. The phone was at the bottom of course. Under the fish and chips. Yeah, the healthy option. But she was starving and the chippie was on the same road where she'd met the cab. Who cared anyway? The exercise would cancel out the calories and, boy, had she needed a brisk walk to calm down. A quick glance at caller ID and she almost shoved the damn thing back in the depths.

'What do you want?' Sarah curled a lip. So glad the walking theory worked.

'You left before I could say thanks. I really enjoyed your company, Sarah, and I'd love—'

'It may have escaped your notice, but you already had company. You got me there under false pretences for the benefit of your reporter *buddy*.'

'Bollocks. I'd no idea Mark would be in. He was supposed to be visiting his ma. He got back early is all.'

Sarah let her silence do the talking.

'Come on. What do you take me for?' *Don't tempt me.*

'Let's leave it, eh?' The DI was sick and tired of arguing with people. She had enough of it at work. Truth was she'd enjoyed the evening too, just hated the feeling of being duped.

'Look, I swear I was on the level.'

'Fine. OK.' She could just about credit Caroline hadn't engineered the encounter, but why not mention Slater was more than a lodger?

'Mark's a mate but—'

'You don't say?'

'I can't see the problem. We're consenting adults. And you have to admit he's . . . tasty.'

Sarah twitched a lip. Caroline had more cheek than a sumo wrestling tournament, but Slater was definitely hot.

'Yeah, OK, he's fit.' And the evening had been fun.

'So I'm forgiven? Great. And, Sarah, I meant it – let's do it again sometime. Ciao.'

Glaring at the phone, she slung it in her bag. How come the bloody reporter always had to have the last word?

THIRTY-SIX

Bleary-eyed, propped up on one elbow, Sarah fumbled for the phone and groaned. The one time she was looking forward to a lie-in and she gets an early call. Not just early. The digital display read 01.29. Cracking hadn't even crossed dawn's mind yet.

'Morning all. Have I got news for you.'

Wide awake now she kicked off the duvet, swung her legs out of bed. 'What's happening? Where are you, Dave?' Sitting in his car, he said, at a motorway service station near Hereford.

'Sounds dead exciting.' There was a smile in her voice; his had told her there was more to come.

'You're right. The view's stunning. Lorries, vans, coaches, bikes, trees swaying in the—'

'Come on, Dave, don't milk it.'

'OK. I'll tell you about the touching reunion going on inside. Tracey and Natalie are sitting opposite each other at a table by the window. Have to say the conversation doesn't look to be flowing. Pete Hinds is buying drinks at the counter casting not so loving looks at his missus.'

If Dave could see what was going on . . . 'Can they spot you?'

'Yeah, course they can. Christ, Sarah, think I'm thick or something? I've just tailed the bloody woman from Stirchley.' Tracey had left the house around half-twelve, he said. Clearly not out for a local spin, the suitcase she stowed in the boot had given the game away. There'd still been a fair bit of traffic heading into the city so he'd only come close to losing her once. 'When we hit the motorway it was more of a doddle,' he said. 'Mind, she's a crap driver. Ought to use her mirror more.'

'Kinda lucky, isn't it?'

'Yeah well I'm wearing my trusty baseball cap as well.'

'The right way round?'

'Ha ha. As for Pete Hinds and the prodigal daughter, even if they noticed a tall, dark, handsome stranger killing time sitting in his . . .'

'Yeah, yeah.' They wouldn't know him from Adam. Slipping into her dressing gown, Sarah wandered through to the kitchen. 'You say prodigal, Dave, but Natalie's not home yet.'

'True and I can't see her sticking round here much longer. What do you reckon I should do, boss?'

'Not sure, Dave. Give me a min.' Pensive, she poured milk in a pan then reached to open a cupboard. She wished she'd thought it through more. She hadn't really believed it would get this far. If their off-the-radar operation came to light, Brody would go ballistic. On the other hand, she didn't want to risk losing track of Natalie, not when the girl could hold key information. She pulled a spoon out of the drawer.

'What you doing?' Dave asked.

Making hot chocolate. 'Still trying to decide the best plan. If you make an approach now, Tracey'll know we're onto them. On the other hand . . .'

'Get a move on, boss. Natalie and her dad are on their feet. He's fiddling with his keys. Look, Tracey's not going anywhere and even if she does . . . Shall I follow them?'

'Yeah, but keep me posted and—' *Take care.* Too late, he'd hung up. 'Shit!' She grabbed the pan off the heat. Too late again. Spilt milk stuck to the hob. What's the saying? No use crying.

THIRTY-SEVEN

Six hours later, Sarah really did feel like weeping. After Dave's call she'd not been able to get back to sleep – tossing, turning and cursing till gone four. And now the bloody phone was ringing again. She stretched a reluctant arm out from under the covers. Talk about déjà vu.

'Dave?'

'Sorry to disappoint you, ma'am.'

'Huntie?' Frowning she sat up, leaned back against the pillow. 'Sorry. I was kind of expecting a call.' Come to think of it, why hadn't Dave got back? It was nearly eight now.

'No worries. You'll not be expecting this though. I know you're not in today so I thought I'd give you a head's up. Brody's about to throw the book at Price. Three rape charges.'

'Three?' From what she'd gathered earlier, Joel Price had only admitted to the attack on Zoe Darby. She flung back the covers, strolled to the window, peeped through the curtain. Damn. Not so much as a cloud in the sky. She cast a rueful glance at her running kit laid out over the back of a chair.

'Yeah. What you might call a hat-trick.'

'Right.' She turned her mouth down. Presumably more evidence had come to light. She'd heard about Price's confession and the sick home movie. Imagine finding something like that on your son's phone. No wonder Mrs Price had done the decent thing and grassed on him. Probably couldn't wait to chuck him out and fumigate the house. What was the guy still living at home for anyway?

'Not forgetting assaulting a police officer of course.' Hunt sniffed.

Brody certainly wouldn't forget in a hurry. But then if he'd got a result and Operation Panther was being wound down, doubtless he'd get over it soon enough. From what Sarah knew of him, he'd be dining out on it in a week's time.

'How is DI Brody? Not letting it go to his head, I hope.' Whoops. The Freudian slip did exactly that.

'You mean getting a result or Price's flying fist?'

'You know full well what I mean, Huntie.' Brody getting bopped was no laughing matter. Well, OK, just the teeniest bit between her and the gatepost. But taking the piss was out of order and condoning violence should be the last thing any cop would do.

'Yeah, but I was there and trust me – Price landed a couple of almighty thumps, one of his rings gouged a chunk out of Brody's cheek.' *Bruised his ego too she'd bet.*

'What prompted it, Huntie?' She opened the curtain now. Her gaze followed the progress of a narrow boat drifting by on the canal. The Captain Bird's Eye lookalike at the tiller lifted his cap at a couple of joggers who'd just overtaken an old dear being dragged for a walk by her Border collie. All human life . . .

'The usual.' Price swore blind he was being stitched up, Hunt said. 'Brody's goading didn't help though, ma'am. Anyway, I'd best get off. He wants me in on Price's next grilling.'

'Lucky you. Is Twig around?' He'd have the latest from Zach Fraser's place and she'd more or less promised to let Angela Webb know the score.

'Can't see him. Shall I get him to give you a bell?'

'Ta, Huntie.' She might even pop in to the station later. See how her team on the Larry Drake inquiry was getting on. She'd left a task list, mostly follow-up interviews and chasing outstanding house-to-house inquiries. Saturday often saw more people at home. And, boy, the stalled inquiry could do with a shot in the ass. So could her standing with Starr. Surely if she cracked it, he'd have to let her back in the main game.

As for the Natalie Hinds' side show? She tapped a speed dial button on her phone. The call went straight to Dave's voicemail. She decided against leaving a message, he'd see she'd tried to get through to him soon enough. Weird though. He was pretty good at getting back and the last thing she'd said to him was keep me posted. She frowned. Not quite the last thing. She'd said take care. But, of course, he'd not heard. He'd already ended the call.

Shivering, she moved away from the window; goose bumps raised the tiny hairs on her arms. She told herself it was the draught then, with a wry smile, shook her head. *For crying out loud, Sarah. He's a big boy now.* There'd be any number of reasons why he'd not called. She'd try him again when she got back from the run.

Picking up the shorts, she curled a lip. Maybe she should wait just in case? *Wuss.* Shame it wasn't pissing down though, then she'd really have an excuse.

*   *   *

It was that fine rain. Mizzle? That's what Dave's mum called it. He was never sure whether she'd made the word up or not, she had a habit of doing that, bless. His smile faded. Either way he was soaked through to his increasingly clammy skin. Wherever he stood under the dark canopy, every branch seemed to drip and every drop seemed to hit him square in the face or trickle down the back of his neck. His hair was plastered to his scalp like a skullcap – he'd ditched the scarlet baseball cap. Apart from discovering its waterproof credential was crap, there was no sense getting rumbled at this stage. Not after the close calls getting here.

Pete Hinds' van had been trickier to shadow than his wife's clapped-out Fiesta. Traffic on the A-roads had been sparser for one thing and Hinds was no great shakes behind the wheel. On a couple of occasions there'd been no option but to overtake the van, then turn and execute quick U-ies. Three times, Dave feared the trail had gone cold till he caught the distant tail lights.

The weather sure was bollock-freezing now. Not that he'd been hiding out here all night. He wasn't completely barking, unlike the fox he'd glimpsed slinking through the undergrowth. No, once he'd seen the van take a sharp left down a single-track lane, he realized where they had to be heading. The campsite had been signposted several times. He'd parked off road a few hundred yards further on from the turning, doubled back on foot to do a recce and, as soon as he clocked the van's stationary silhouette, had tootled back to the car for a kip.

He'd kept his eyes peeled for a while just in case the Hinds had it in mind to do a moonlight flit. Moonlight being the operative word. A silver glow over the countryside had stunned even the city boy. When it became pretty clear the Hinds weren't leaving in a hurry, Dave had caught a few zeds. He was sure as eggs are oval that the campsite wasn't their final destination, so at first light he'd returned to his low-profile observation post.

The lie of the land was easier to see now, though glowering clouds worsened the dank, almost claustrophobic atmosphere under the overhang. The smells didn't help: damp earth, rotting vegetation and he knew for sure it wasn't only bears who shat in the wood.

Dave mopped his face with an already moist tissue, then started counting the caravans and chalets dotted round the site. Thirty-two – and not one appealed. Each to their own, but they put him in mind of washed-out shacks on stilts and he was guessing most stood empty. A concrete parking area near the toilet block held only four vehicles – including Hinds' van.

Frowning, he sniffed. He sniffed again. Right first time. Someone was cooking bacon. *Lucky sods.* A fry-up beat his half bar of Galaxy hands down. Nah, on second thoughts he'd opt for a proper bed and breakfast any day. No one in their right mind would play happy campers in this dump. It was like a rundown out-of-season holiday resort: bleak, boring, beige, without even a beach to compensate. Benidorm, it wasn't. He'd be glad to see the back of it. First he needed to know exactly which pleasure dome Natalie and her dad were holed up in.

He stamped his feet a few times. Come what may, he'd have to make a move soon. He still had rations to keep him going: coffee in the flask and another sandwich in the car. No, the fact was the Hinds weren't here for the lavish entertainment or the wildlife. He couldn't see them hanging round long.

The problem being – he couldn't pinpoint them at all right now and he couldn't go round knocking on doors. Currently he held the element of surprise, and he didn't want to risk blowing his cover until the time was right. Sarah might opt for alerting the local cops so they could have a word, rather than Dave making a direct approach.

He glanced at his watch: just gone eight. He curved his lip. Might as well switch his phone on and give Sleeping Beauty another bell.

Shit. Would you Adam and Eve it? He patted the other pocket of his coat. Had he left the bloody thing in the car?

THIRTY-EIGHT

The minute she got back to the apartment, Sarah had checked her mobile. She'd also made a mental note never to don running shorts again. Talk about ritual humiliation. Well, she would've talked if there'd been breath enough in her body. Red-faced and dripping with sweat, she'd taken a shower, rechecking the phone on stepping out. Checked it again in the Audi on the way into town. And now, nursing an Americano in Waterstones, she glanced once more at the screen. In two hours, half a dozen texts had pinged in, eight emails and she'd spoken to Baker. Not a word from Dave.

Killing time, she read the blurb on a book she'd bought. *The Burning Girl.* Fictional cops and bad guys didn't normally do it for her, but Costa was situated just beyond the crime section and, according to the author biog, Mark Billingham was Birmingham-born. Local talent then.

'I imagine it must be my animal attraction, Quinn.' Grinning, the chief loomed over her bearing a laden tray. She'd not noticed his late arrival. 'Just can't keep away from me, can you?'

Masking a smile, she slipped the book back in its bag then glanced up, eyebrow arched. 'If I recall right this was your idea?'

'It's not five minutes since we were on the phone. The Alzheimer's not kicking in, is it?' Five minutes? More like an hour. Either way the joke was hilarious. Not.

He cocked his head. 'Any road, budge up, woman.'

Rolling her eyes she shuffled along to make room on the leather couch. At least Baker's chat would divert her thinking from Dave. Not that she was worried exactly. She knew there had to be a reason he'd not been in touch. Even so, a text would put the odd niggle at rest.

Sipping coffee, she watched Baker lay out the goodies on

the low table: chocolate muffin, chocolate brownie, chocolate teacake, chocolate twist.

She gave an indulgent smile. 'Got a theme going on there, have we?'

'Shoulda been a detective, you. Help yourself.'

Why not? She'd earned it. 'What's this I hear about you coming back, chief?'

'You're listening to the wrong people then, Quinn.' He was undecided, he told her. Not convinced he wanted the hassle of professional standards. 'Too much grief in it, I reckon.'

'Sorry to hear it.' She licked chocolate off her top lip. 'The force can live without bad apples. I reckon you'd be pretty good at spotting them.' As much as anything, she'd quite looked forward to seeing him round the nick again. Unlike a lot of blokes, especially bosses, Baker shot from the lip: everyone – cop and crim – knew where they stood. Even when they didn't like the fact he'd put them there. She stifled a sigh. Shame she'd not appreciated it more when he was calling the shots. Glancing up, she realized he'd had his beady eyes on her.

'So how is Starr?' he asked casually. 'And Brody?'

She'd bet a pound to a penny that hadn't come out of the blue. Forcing a smile, she made light of an undoubtedly loaded question. 'You make it sound like they should be in a Western together.'

'What?' He paused a beat or two. 'As in cowboys?'

Her hand paused on its way to a teacake. 'Where are you going with this, chief?'

'Me? As if. I'm just wondering if you're all playing nicely.'

She shook her head. Great. So much for the man who tells it like it is.

'Actually, Sarah, that's bollocks—'

She broke eye contact when her phone bleeped. Quick glance at the screen showed a message from BT. Probably trying to flog broadband. Wow.

'Jumpy aren't we, Quinn?' The Baker antennae never stopped twitching.

'Must be the caffeine. Anyway, you were talking bollocks.' She curved a lip. 'Before the interruption.'

'Cheeky sod. I know what I was talking.' He lowered his

voice a little. 'The word is Starr's gunning for you. And Brody's giving you a hard time. Not in a good way.'

She dropped the smile. Was that why Baker had been so keen for them to get together? 'Thanks chief, but back off, eh? I'm a big girl now.'

'Carry on stuffing chocolate and you will be.' His wink failed to lighten the charged atmosphere.

'I'm serious chief. I can fight my own battles.'

Another telling pause, then: 'So am I, Quinn.' She saw that in the darkening of his eyes. 'Watch your back.'

'I hear what you're saying, but—'

'Not all cops play it by the book, Quinn.' She ran her gaze over his face, tried reading what he wasn't saying. Given she had a little covert operation of her own going on, she'd be bloody glad when he got off the subject. 'Look, Sarah, I'm telling you for your own good – there's a reason they used to call him Scissors.'

She frowned. 'There is?'

He made snipping motions with his fingers. 'Brody had a reputation for cutting corners. And he's still a ruthless sod.' He told her he'd done a bit of digging, sounded out officers at the detective's former nicks. 'There's not much he won't do to get a result. Why do you think Starr parachuted him onto the patch?'

Reflected glory, presumably. Pensive, she nodded, and thanked him for the tip. He'd not made the subtle enquiries entirely for her benefit. Apparently, when he'd last met John Hunt for a drink, Huntie had expressed guarded reservations about Brody's methods.

'More than that, lass,' – he smiled – 'Huntie doesn't like how they treat you. He doesn't want to stand by and see you edged out. And for what it's worth, neither do I.'

Christ, she'd be in tears in a minute.

'Any road, enough of this.' Baker sniffed. 'How's the boy wonder?'

Good question. The last time she'd seen Dave, he'd been fine.

'Looking for this?'

Dave stiffened. The voice had come from behind, but not far. Turning slowly, he saw Pete Hinds standing a couple of arms' lengths away, an iPhone nestling in the palm of his outstretched hand. The guy looked rough, like he'd barely slept, and certainly hadn't shaved for a day or two, but his flat delivery and blank features held no other clues for Dave to interpret. And he had to think on his feet. He took a step forward, offered a smile: known in the trade as brazening it out. 'Thanks mate, I—'

'Stay where you are. Why are you skulking round?' The phone disappeared in one of the pockets of Hinds' donkey jacket. He couldn't have been watching Dave for long, his hair was barely damp.

'I was out for a walk. And that's my property.'

'Yeah and this is private land. Did you not read the signs?'

He was finding the body language easier to decipher. Apart from clenching his jaw a couple of times, Hinds now stood with his feet planted wide apart, both arms clamped tightly across his chest. The macho posture wasn't a problem. Dave knew how to handle himself and had both height and weight advantage.

'Can I have the phone, mate?'

'Tell me why you're snooping and I'll think about it.'

Bird-watching wasn't going to cut it. Nor hide and seek. Sod it. No point bush beating. He raised both palms. 'I'm a detective, Mr Hinds. I need to talk to your daughter about—'

'I know what you need to talk about. You should've just said.' Unsmiling, he passed the phone over. 'Natalie's inside making a brew.'

Dave opened his mouth to speak, but Hinds had turned and started walking away.

'Come on then, let's get it over with.'

THIRTY-NINE

Baker was leafing through Sarah's book when she arrived back ferrying refills. They needed more coffee to wash down what remained of the cholesterol-fest.

'Be my guest, why don't you?'

'Nah.' He sniffed, slipped it on the table. 'I've read it. The butler did it.'

Not quite the point. Baker had helped himself. Sinking down into the cushion, she glanced at the phone's screen. Still nothing.

'I wouldn't have thought crime fiction was your cup of tea, chief.'

'Yeah, well you don't know everything, smarty pants.'

'Unless it's homework, of course.' She twitched a mischievous lip.

The éclair he was about to scoff didn't quite make it to his mouth. 'Way too clever for me, Quinn. What you going on about?'

'This work you're doing for King?'

He caught on fast and laughed. 'You implying Lois makes it up as she goes along?'

'Your guess is as good as mine.'

'Miaow. You should've got yourself a saucer of milk.' The éclair finally reached its destination. He was going to need a napkin.

Smiling, she glanced round. The place was beginning to fill up. People with trays drifted by looking for spare seats, harassed parents shushed bawling kids, a teenager shouted a blow-by-blow account of her love-life into a mobile. It was way too loud in here. Sarah fancied moving on soon. Besides they'd hogged the table long enough.

Baker was still at the trough. He reached for the last cake and polished it off as they chatted about Caroline's proposal. A factual book exploring genuine rape cases and featuring real victims and perps sounded like a tall order to Sarah. She expressed surprise that Baker had agreed to help. He didn't think there'd be a lot for him to do – Mark Slater was keen to take on the lion's share of the work apparently.

'You've met then?' Sarah cut another glance at the screen.

'You know they say there's no such thing as a free lunch?' He winked. 'Well, Kingie picked up the tab for a little get together dinner. I chatted with the guy then and we've spoken on the phone since. Talk about bit between the teeth. He's like a dog with a bone.' She masked a smile. He might have mixed the metaphors, but he'd made the point: Slater was into serious research.

Baker brushed crumbs off his shirt. 'Well, lass, I'd best be on my way.' He cocked his head, frowning. 'That your ringtone?'

Thank God for that. She snatched up the phone. Shit. Not Dave.

'Twig. How goes it?'

'I've just spoken to Raj Malik, ma'am.' *Raj Malik?* The name rang a bell. 'SIO on the house fire at Edgbaston?'

That's right. 'Man's body found upstairs?'

'They've come up with a suspect, prints all over the place. A name flagged up on the system so they've issued an APW.' An all ports warning?

She still didn't see what Twig was driving at. 'And?'

'The name was Pete Hinds. Malik thinks he could be armed and dangerous. Wants him brought in as a matter of urgency.'

Pete Hinds waited at the open door for Dave to catch up.

'Don't go hard on her. She's had a rough time.'

'Sure. I just need to ask a few questions.'

'What's your name so I can tell her?'

'Dave. Dave Harries. Detective Constable.'

'OK. Go in, take a seat.'

Hinds ran a lingering gaze over the site once more before entering the stuffy chalet. He felt pretty confident by now the cop was solo. He'd spotted no back-up in the woods, no police vehicles out on the road. And he'd been up checking for half the night just in case. In his book that meant the cops couldn't be onto them about the big stuff. The bosses wouldn't send in a lone wolf. Not a cub wet behind the ears anyway. If all the lad wanted was to ask Natalie about the girl who'd got herself killed – then no one need get hurt.

'Slip your coat off if you like,' Hinds said, slinging his jacket over a chair. The stifling heat inside had already brought him out in a cold, clammy sweat. Unless it was being up close and impersonal with the law. Not that the cop would've got anywhere near the place if Hinds hadn't shown restraint earlier. He'd watched the guy sleeping like a baby and had toyed with the idea of torching the car. He would've made damn sure not to cock it up this time. The cop had done a slack job. Hinds had clocked the tail on the van before they'd even left the motorway, then bided his time, decided to play it by ear. As long as Natalie didn't come to any harm, he was in no hurry to get more blood on his hands.

'Where is your daughter, Mr Hinds?' The cop raked his fingers through his hair.

He presumed she'd gone for a lie down. The radio was playing softly in the bedroom. 'I'll go fetch—'

'Don't bother.' Leaning against a doorway, the girl darted a glance at her father. 'What's going on, Dad?' Her clothing was crumpled, bare feet grubby, hair greasy.

'It's fine, love. No worries.'

'Yeah right.' She snorted.

Smiling Dave stood and reached out a hand. 'Hi Natalie. I'm DC Harries. Dave.'

She nodded. 'Thank God, it's all over. Can I just get a drink?'

Hinds frowned. What the hell was that supposed to mean? He watched her drift listlessly towards the kitchen, shoulders slumped like they carried the weight of the world. He'd do anything – anything – to lighten her load.

'Hey, Nat, get another cup down. He just has a few questions then he'll be off. That right, Dave?'

'You got it, Mr Hinds.' Dave turned so he could see the girl. 'Actually don't worry about a drink for me, Natalie. I'm fine. Why not come and sit down?'

'What's the point? I know why you're here.' She sounded drained, looked dead on her feet. When the glass slipped from her grasp and shattered in the sink, she screamed, clapped trembling hands to her gaunt face.

Hinds shot across the room and gently helped her towards a bench seat screwed to the wall. Sitting next to her, he stroked her hair then kissed the top of her head. 'Come on, Natalie, all you have to do is tell him about your mate then—'

'He won't, Dad. He's not going anywhere. It's been on the radio. The fire, the murder. The police want—'

'Shush, babe, look . . .'

'No!' Standing, she backed away. 'I'm sorry, Dad. I can't do this anymore. I just can't. You have to tell him.'

'Tell me what?'

'Tell him, Dad. Tell him everything.'

For four or five seconds he held her gaze. The only sounds were the hiss of the gas fire and three people's breathing. 'You sure?'

'Dead sure.'

FORTY

'**G**ive him an hour or so, lass. Dave won't do anything stupid.'

Baker and Sarah walked in step down New Street. Dodging Primark bags and double buggies, she'd reluctantly related the gist both of Twig's conversation and the fact Dave had been off the radar for a worrying amount of time. She'd not had much choice. Baker had seen the colour drain from her face and witnessed her increasingly desperate efforts to get through to his number. He'd finally persuaded her to share.

'He won't know though, will he?' Like her, Dave had seen Natalie Hinds as a bit player in the Lisa Webb inquiry. They'd no idea when he took off to try and round her up that her father was on the run for what could be the leading role in another murder.

'Give him some credit, Sarah. Dave's a good cop, more than capable of thinking on his feet.'

'Yeah, but fact is, if Hinds killed once, he won't have anything to lose, chief.' Whereas Sarah, she realized with a jolt, did. God forbid anything happen to Dave. To make matters worse, it would be entirely down to her meddling in Brody's case. Her part in it would almost certainly emerge now and she didn't even care. If the unthinkable happened to Dave, she'd throw in the badge without a second thought, assuming an internal inquiry didn't fire her first.

'Here.' Baker nudged her elbow, handed her a hankie. She dabbed her eyes, blew her nose and slipped the hankie in her pocket.

'Means a lot to you, doesn't he, Quinn?'

She still didn't trust herself to speak.

'Maybe tell him sometime, eh?'

She nodded. *Definitely.*

He left her to her thoughts before pulling up near the art gallery. 'This is me, Quinn. I'll love you and leave you.'

'Soaking up some culture, chief?'

'Meeting a mate. Where you heading?'

'I'll probably drop by the nick. See what's what and— Hold on, a tick.' Her ringtone was going off, she snatched the phone from her bag, briefly closed her eyes. 'I told you to keep me posted, detective. Where the fuck have you been?'

Baker tapped a salute and wandered off, murmuring.

'That's one way of telling him.'

Sarah sat on the steps outside the Council House. Oblivious to the butt-freezing concrete, and barely registering what was going on around her, she'd been listening to Dave's account of events taking place fifty-odd miles away. It didn't help that the line was bad or a bunch of youths was clattering up and down on skateboards, but surely she'd misheard.

'You're saying Hinds is handing himself in?'

'The girl begged him to, boss, pleaded on her hands and knees. He's doing it for her sake.' Like everything else, from what Sarah had heard, including Ivan Burton's murder.

Pete Hinds had just called the cops himself, apparently. Dave's reasoning had swayed him a little, too. He'd told Hinds the goodwill gesture wouldn't do any harm when the case came to trial. Sarah was well sceptical. Whichever way you looked at it, Hinds had taken a life in cold blood. As for the claim he'd been avenging his daughter's rape, Sarah didn't see that as a mitigating factor either. Burton, poor sod, was in no position to put forward a defence. Whereas Hinds had taken it upon himself to act as judge, juror and executioner. She'd be surprised if the courts didn't take a dim view of that.

'So what's happening now, Dave?' The Hinds were in the chalet still, but Dave she knew had a bird's-eye view from his previous vantage point. He certainly wasn't daft enough to watch them do another runner. Hinds had had it in mind though. He told Dave he'd intended on taking Natalie a lot further afield – out of the country, not just into another county.

'I'm waiting for the local cops to show before heading back, boss. I guess they'll bang him up in a cell till our guys arrive.' She turned her mouth down. Or Malik would ask West Mercia police to sort transport to Birmingham. She knew why Dave was hazy on detail – he'd had no contact with either force. He'd assured Hinds he'd stay well in the background so it wouldn't look as if the guy had been coerced into giving himself up. The more-than-generous offer hadn't been entirely altruistic. If his interfering presence on another patch came out he – and Sarah – would have a hell of a lot of explaining to do. She had more than a little to thank Dave for.

Ouch. She shuffled her numb bum.

'You OK?'

'I'm fine.' She'd have to get up though; her muscles were beginning to seize up. Bloody run. Never again. 'What about Natalie?'

'Her mum's on the way to drive her home. Ask me, the girl needs checking over by a doctor. Honest, boss, she's close to meltdown. Virtually catatonic. Poor kid was raped, don't forget.'

On her feet now, Sarah shooed away a couple of pigeons fighting over a burger bun. She'd like to know what Natalie had been doing in Burton's house in the first place. More to the point, how come her dad turned up? Raj Malik was going to have his work cut out.

'Did you get a chance to ask her about Lisa?' The initial reason for the entire jaunt.

'Barely. But one thing she did say – Lisa had been seeing some bloke. Older, dead good-looking.'

'Zach Fraser?'

'Nah. Natalie knows him, reckons he's quote, "a sweetie". Lisa was really secretive, wouldn't tell her the new guy's name.'

'That's bloody helpful. Do you think Natalie knows but won't say?'

'Not sure. I can't really make her out. Something there . . . I just can't put my finger on.'

'Maybe we can—'

'Sorry, boss. The cop car's arrived. I'd best make myself scarce.'

'OK, but Dave—' She glared at the phone. He'd gone. It was getting to be a habit. All she'd wanted to say was 'well done'.

A text pinged just as she arrived at the motor. 'No worries, boss. You can thank me later.' She curved a lip. If he was very good, she might even tell him how she felt.

FORTY-ONE

'Here.' Angela Webb shoved a large brown envelope in her husband's face before drifting off to the other side of the kitchen.

Webb glanced up from the back page of *The Sun*.

'Ta, love.' At least she was on speaking terms this morning. 'Post gets later and later these days, doesn't it?'

Just the one word out of her then – her shrugged response didn't really count. He watched her drop a slice of bread in the toaster, then cross to the window where she gazed out across the garden, arms folded across her chest. Through the spindly trees, the park lay grey and gloomy like her face in the glass, and probably her reflections.

Webb made heavy weather of a sigh before lifting the knife from his plate to use as a letter opener. Licking Marmite off the blade was a mistake: he nicked his tongue, winced, tasted blood. He ran the blade under the flap of the envelope then hurled the knife at the sink. The clash of steels sent a couple of magpies squawking off the fence. Angela hadn't flinched, didn't move an inch now, apart from gently parting her lips.

'Temper, temper.'

Piss off. He preferred the silent treatment to snippy digs any day. Glowering, he upended the envelope and gave it a shake. Papers spilled and fanned out across the table. It took him a second or two to realize they were press cuttings – photocopies mostly. He had to turn the sheets over, shuffle them round so he could see what was what. *Or, what the fuck?*

A headline leapt out, then another, a face in a photograph he'd seen before, a second alongside a similar story. His hands shook as he leafed through more sheets. When the toaster popped, he jumped a mile. But something less benign was making his blood run cold, turning his insides to ice.

They say it comes in threes, don't they?

Right. Jaw clenched, he sat up straight. The unexpected mail delivery – *make that, male delivery* – had forced the issue. Brought it to a head. Dither time was over. Doctor Google had provided a couple of addresses. No time like the present. Sneaking a glance at his wife, he gathered the sea of papers together, scraped back the chair, walked out of the kitchen.

'Ian. Mother of God. Look.'

Frowning he turned, framed in the doorway, arms laden.

Still standing in the same position, Angela stared wide-eyed pointing at the table with a wavering finger.

'How the hell did it get here?' she whispered.

'What? Where?' Nothing there. Christ, don't say she was losing it completely.

'By the plate.' He took a step closer, caught something glinting in the light.

'Move it then, you can see I've got my hands—'

'Don't put yourself out.' She lunged forward, swept away the plate which teetered on the edge before falling and smashing on the floor. He saw it too then.

A tangled silver chain with tiny letters caught up in the links.

'What the fuck are you doing?' Webb yelled. Stupid question: she had the phone in her hand.

'What does it look like?'

'We're not calling the police.'

'Damn right. *I* am.'

'No.' He shook his head. 'You're not.'

'Try and stop me.'

'Angie, Angie.' He off-loaded the papers on the side, smiled tentatively and held out his arms. 'Come here, love.' She met his gaze. Unsure. Voice even softer, he urged again. 'Please. Let's not fight anymore.' Perhaps she needed the hug, the human warmth. She nodded, let him hold her, kiss the top of her head. Making soothing sounds, he stroked her hair. They stayed like that for a minute or so until she gently pulled away.

'But the chain, Ian?' She bit her lip. 'Who sent it? What's going on?'

'I only wish I knew, love.' Big time. Whoever it was had a bunch of explaining to do. But he sure didn't want the old bill digging round, sticking their noses in. 'I'll find out, Angie. I promise.'

He stroked her face with the back of a finger. 'The cops have got the guy who killed Lisa. I don't want them here plodding round asking more stupid questions. And you know as well as me, love – nothing's going to bring her back.

'Besides, they'll take that away' – Webb tilted his head at the necklace – 'it could easily get lost in the system. We'd never see it again. You don't want that do you, love?' She shook her head, reached for the chain, gently untangled it before holding it up to catch the light. Her fond smile faded. 'There's a letter missing.' She scrabbled under *The Sun*, shifted broken pieces of plate round with her slippered foot. 'It's gone, Ian. There's no A.'

'Don't fret, love. That's something we can replace.' He slipped the cuttings back in the envelope.

'I guess.' She pocketed the chain. 'How will you find out where it's been? How it got here?'

'Only one way, isn't there?'

He'd be asking around.

'You must be Zoe? Is your dad in, love?' Webb was still unsure that coming to the house in Harborne was the best approach. That his suspicions were on the money he'd no doubt. The little he could see of the girl's face through the five-inch gap bore out the saying about apples and trees. The fact she'd left the chain on the door was pretty telling, too. Given what she'd been through, Webb reckoned the security measure was only common sense. He wasn't quite so enamoured with the way she was looking at him though. Like he was trying to flog dusters or double-glazing.

'May I ask who's calling?' Cut glass posh.

He toned down the Brummie accent a tad. 'Can you tell him an old friend?' Smiling, he offered a conspiratorial wink. 'We've not clapped eyes on each other in years. I'd love to give him a surprise.' *It'd be that all right.*

'I'll see if he's available.' She gave him the once-over – again. 'Wait there.' The door didn't quite slam.

Stepping back he gazed up at the three-storey double-fronted redbrick: all sparkly windows, glossy paintwork. Clearly Darby had gone up in the world. Minted, as the kids say. Webb swallowed, straightened his tie, glad he'd opted to put on a half-decent suit. His palms were damp, he ran them down his trousers, felt sweat cooling at the base of his spine.

Get a grip, man. He'd feel a lot feel easier once he knew how Darby was going to play it. Not that it was a game.

Well, the guy sure didn't look happy. His poker face and unblinking stare betrayed nothing. Not so much as a flicker in the hazel eyes. His hair looked damp from the shower, his skin smooth and lightly tanned. Like Caramac, Webb thought. He also reckoned that standing round listening to the birds wouldn't get them anywhere.

Hand outstretched he stepped forward and caught a waft of classy aftershave. Darby's Brut days long gone, if not forgotten. 'Remember me? It's been a while.'

He declined the handshake. 'You shouldn't have come here.' Joining Webb on the path, Darby pulled the door to behind him. 'Bad move. My wife and daughter—'

'We need to talk, *Nigel*.' He hoped the name-check would act as a wake-up call.

'I'm well aware of that. I've already spoken to the others.' Darby glanced at his watch. 'Give me an hour – we'll discuss it over a drink.'

He knew the pub Darby mentioned. Webb tapped a salute. 'Catch you there.'

Turned out Darby was well ahead.

FORTY-TWO

'You left your number.' No name, no polite pre-amble. Sarah would have recognized the voice even without its tell-tale sibilance. 'It's like this . . . I've been thinking.'

Could be dangerous in a woman with seriously depleted brain cells.

'Good of you to call, Mrs Vane.' Pottering round the kitchen, Sarah was partway through decanting a load of shopping, four bulging Tesco bags still to go. Shame there was no one to lend a hand. She'd half expected to find Dave home. Not home. *Back.* She knew what she meant. Still had no clue where Bridie Vane was coming from. 'You were saying? About the thinking?'

Another pause then, 'It's not easy this . . .'

Sarah heard the rasp of a match, then another then . . . thank God for that: third time lucky strike. Still listening, she used one hand to line up tins of tuna, chopped tomatoes, kidney beans ready to go on the shelf. Mrs Vane had dried up again.

'What's not easy?' Sarah asked. Lighting a fag? Splitting the atom? Thinking and talking at the same time?

'What you said about the reward?'

Poised tin in hand, Sarah frowned. *What had she said?* Oh yeah. If Bridie Vane's grasping daughter came up with the goods, she'd be looking to make a couple of grand. Utter bollocks, of course.

'I know it was a load of bollocks, Inspector . . .' *Got that right.* Sarah curved a lip. She'd also heard a tacit *but* which didn't take long for the woman to voice. 'But if someone thinks they know who killed Drake . . . could even give names . . .?'

Someone? Names plural? A tin hit the floor. Good job she'd
not been holding the eggs.

'Would that make a difference like? Cos if—'

'Where are you?' Sod the shopping. Dave could clear up
the mess.

She dashed off a quick note, and gathered her bag and keys.
Five minutes later, she was in the motor heading for Aston.

Darby was a few minutes late. Ian Webb sat at a table near a
fire door at the back nursing half a bitter. He reckoned the
pub's high-street prices were well stiff. Poncey place, too: all
'faux folksy' meets 'rustic charm' chic. The wood panelling,
bare floorboards and loud gingham put him in mind of an
upmarket log cabin. All it needed was a stuffed moose head
nailed to the wall and Michael Palin singing lumberjack songs.
Still, it'd be an improvement on the pap coming from the
speakers.

For the umpteenth time, Webb glanced up when the door
opened. Why the hell they let kids in these places, he'd never
know. And what was keeping Darby? He hoped the guy hadn't
got an attack of freezing feet. He patted his breast pocket: just
checking – he knew the papers had to be there. If what his
old *friend* – for want of a better word – said was true, they'd
be able to compare notes.

Looking down, Webb swirled his glass and watched the
beer slosh round the sides. Next time he glanced up, Darby
was coming through the door. *Friend* was clearly pushing it:
he headed straight for the bar, making no effort to seek Webb
out. He watched Darby swap banter with a bloke standing
next to him. Registered the flirting between Darby and the
barmaid while she sorted a gin and tonic. She'd not given
Webb the time of day, let alone that sort of sycophantic smile.
He just hoped Darby's G&T was a large one; he'd need at
least a double.

Webb looked away; he'd had enough of the floor show. He
had his head down pretending to find the *Guardian* fascinating
when Darby's brogues appeared in his sightline.

'I always had you down as a page three man. Young's,
wasn't it?' Webb glanced up to find Darby holding out a pint.

'Don't look so gormless. The girl remembered you from last time. It's not like I read minds or anything.'

'Shame.' Just as well actually, he was thinking the guy was an arrogant twat. 'Cheers.'

'Cheers.' Darby flopped in the chair opposite, unbuttoned his coat, then raised his glass. 'Here's to . . . let's not say "*old times*".' The fulsome smile was fleeting and fake, the words dripped with irony. 'We both know the reason we're here is *current* events.'

'Yeah and we're not the only ones keeping up.' Webb slipped a hand inside his jacket, slid some cuttings across the table. 'That lot came in the post.'

Sipping his drink, Darby took a closer look at a few, pushed them back in Webb's direction. 'I should've brought mine,' he drawled. 'We could've played snap.' Dead indifferent, but the glint darkening his eyes told a different story. 'I'll tell you something else, too.' He beckoned Webb nearer. 'We're not the only lucky recipients.' The men huddled together across the table as Darby shared more news. Top line being that media coverage of Jessica Silk's attack had first alerted him to the possibility the rapes weren't random.

'Terry and I have always kept in touch, you see.'

'Terry?'

'Terry Hatch. Goes by the name Silk now. Jonathan.'

Of course. Webb nodded slowly, beginning to see even more of the picture.

'Couple of days after Jessica's attack,' Darby said, 'Terry gets what you might call his "press pack" in the post.'

'And Winter?'

'Yes. I had to do a bit of detective work to track him down. But recognized him the minute I set eyes on him. You'd know him as Brian—'

'Wallace.' Webb nodded again, the picture was almost complete.

'We were gutted when we heard what happened to . . . your daughter.'

'Lisa.' He took a swig of beer. 'Her name's Lisa.'

Darby nodded. 'Terrible thing. Shocking. We were scared

it took it to a new level, but it's not the same guy, is it? Lisa's killer's confessed. It's been all over the news.'

Has he?

Darby was about to take a drink, the glass halted halfway to his mouth. 'You don't look convinced?'

Webb shrugged. Zach Fraser's demise was a path he'd no desire to go down. Apart from the fact Webb had played a major part in it, given what he knew now, Fraser's role was a diversion. Besides, a more pressing thought had just hit home.

'Hold on.' He slammed his glass on the table. 'If you knew what was going on, why the fucking hell didn't you warn me?'

'Calm down, for Christ's sake.' Darby glanced over his shoulder. Had to keep up appearances in his local, didn't he? Leaning in even closer, he lowered his voice. 'We only knew why he was doing it. We'd no way of knowing who'd be the next victim.'

'Or who'll be next.' Webb held Darby's gaze. 'It isn't going to stop here, is it?'

'I think we need a meet. The four of us.'

Webb nodded. They were all on *first* name terms. The names they used now were adopted. Assumed. Aliases. Whatever. The name they really needed to know was the attacker's. Finding out who'd targeted their daughters meant they could deal with the bastard, hopefully before he struck again. 'Take him out', as they say. Webb's lip curved. Have a nice little chat, while he was still capable of opening his mouth.

'Nearly forgot.' Darby pulled his wallet out of his coat pocket. 'Did you get one of these?'

Webb unfolded the paper: **I know what you are. How do you live with yourself? Call yourself a father?** Identical message.

'As you said, snap.'

Yet another thing the four had in common. Like a onetime communal address on the Isle of Wight. Not Osborne House, Queen Vic's old residence. No, the place Ian Webb had in mind used to be called Parkhurst. Nowadays it went by the name HM Prison.

FORTY-THREE

Stuck in football traffic on the Aston Expressway, Sarah hoped the Villa scarves streaming through car windows were colourfast. She hiked the speed of the wipers, beginning to think it might have made more sense staying on the phone to Bridie Vane. Then told herself not to be ridiculous. People's body language often said more unwittingly than any amount of carefully-chosen words on the end of a line.

Tapping the wheel, Sarah had a little smile to herself. Given Bridie's size, the body had a lot more going for it in terms of verbal fluency than her limited vocabulary.

Bee-atch. She slapped a mental wrist. No, nonverbal communication wasn't the only reason Sarah was keen to see Bridie in the flesh. Not a thought to hold. She curled a lip. It was more a case of what little the woman had uttered, speaking volumes.

For, 'if someone thinks they know Drake's killer' Sarah read: Bridie Vane has a bloody good idea who killed the guy. As for, 'could even give names' – only the inquiry team knew two people were implicated. Clearly that wasn't the case. The killers were well aware it was a joint effort. Question was, how come the small number in the loop appeared to include Bridie Vane?

An even bigger question in Sarah's book: how come all of a sudden the woman was keen to share?

Head cocked, Caroline froze, fingers poised over her keyboard. She couldn't abide extraneous noise, especially when she was approaching the end of a book – the writing needed total focus. Bang bloody bang. Again. *For fuck's sake.*

'Mark,' she yelled. 'Keep it down, will you?'

'Two ticks. Won't be a min.'

She sighed, didn't have high regard for tautology either. He was a reporter, for heaven's sake. After shuffling a few papers she took a sip of cold coffee then rolled her shoulders, shook her fingers. *Once more with feeling.* Hunched over the desk, she reread the last few lines on the screen then started pounding the keys.

Buggery bloody bollocks. She'd no idea what he was playing at, but she'd have to find out. She rolled back the swivel chair, marched out of the spare bedroom-stroke-office to find Mark outside his room wielding a screwdriver.

Hand slapped on hip she said, 'What the hell are you doing?'

'Thorry.' He took a screw or something from between his lips then, 'Sorry, Caro. I'll just finish up here and do the rest later.'

'Rest of what?' Running a hand through her hair she padded towards the door for a closer look. *Bloody cheek.* 'Why on earth do you need a lock?'

'Y' know that break-in over the road?'

'No.'

'What happened to those famous listening skills you're always banging on about?' Presumably the matey wink meant she was supposed to find that hilarious.

'The only one banging on round here right now—'

'I know, I know. Sorry.' He leaned forward, pecked her cheek. 'Anyway they robbed the guy's laptop.'

'Big deal, and don't try and get round me.'

'Round?' He raised a lascivious eyebrow. 'Thing is, I had a word with the cops. Apparently there's been three more since then. They reckon the area's being targeted.'

'OK, so we start using the burglar alarm.'

'Good thinking, captain. I'd still rather keep a few items under lock and key. The villains are mostly after laptops and tablets. With the amount of work on mine . . .?' He held out both palms.

Surely he duplicated everything? Caroline had memory sticks coming out of every orifice. Mostly what was on them was on The Cloud anyway. 'Even so, Mark, it's my house I—'

'Don't be cross, Caro. I bought one for your room too.' He pulled a little boy lost face.

'OK, OK. Just don't make a mess or damage the wood.' Gawd, she sounded like his bloody mother.

'Ah, ha.' Smiling, he jabbed the screwdriver at her. 'You have just hit the nail on the head.'

She gave a lop-sided smile. 'Back off, buster.'

'Sorry. True though. The other thing is: the cops say the robbers trash places – rip up books, pictures, clothes, piss in beds. My work's not the problem – it's backed up, natch, and other stuff's insured, but a lot of things in there are personal. Precious. Irreplaceable.' He dropped his gaze.

'I'm with you.' She stepped forward stroked his arm. 'Get on with it – before I change my mind.' She knew what would be on his mind: his mum's photos. He'd suggested Caroline tag along on the next visit. Mrs Slater was keen they met, apparently. Caroline wasn't convinced. Hospices were not her cup of Bovril. Besides, she might have the hots for Mark, but it wasn't like she wanted his babies or anything. 'And quit the whistling,' – as she reached the office she glanced over her shoulder, smiling –'or I'll shove that screwdriver where the sun don't even think about it.'

'Let's think about this. There's . . .' Smiling thinly, Sarah ticked a finger, held it there waiting while Bridie ripped open a packet of cheese and onion crisps. 'Ready?' she resumed. 'There's withholding information' – tick – 'incitement' – tick – 'perverting the course of justice' – tick – 'perjury' – she was out of fingers – 'and bearing false witness.'

'Big words.' Her jowls swayed along with the shake of her head. 'All boils down to threats in the end, don't it?'

Sarah sighed. The distressed leather creaked as she sat back on the sofa and crossed her legs. By rights it should be her fingers that were crossed; she'd stretched veracity with one or two of those potential charges. She just hoped Bridie Vane's grasp of the law was as tenuous as her grip on the economy. Fact was, soon as Bridie heard there was no big money in the offing, she'd hedged more bets than Paddy Power.

Sarah had little choice but to come on strong – she needed to budge the woman into opening her mouth. Though, watching Bridie stuff her face now, that wasn't a problem. For whatever reason, it seemed she was having second thoughts, not to mention third and fourth. It couldn't be down to cold feet. The Technicolor ice cream parlour, as Sarah still regarded the room, was sweltering and the woman's slippers looked like bits of dead sheep. Another animal image sprang to Sarah's mind, this time equine. As in dead horse and flog.

Plucking a hair off her skirt, she said, 'They're not threats, Mrs Vane.' Nor promises, more the pity.

Bridie upended the crisp packet and tipped what was left down her throat. Sarah stared agog. *Don't choke for God's sake. Not yet.*

'It's alright for you' – she wiped her mouth with a sleeve – 'people don't know where you live.'

They do actually. Sarah frowned. *Ah.* She was beginning to see the problem. Apart from Bridie's nervous glances, what was it she'd said a moment ago? '*All* boils down to threats . . .' Not just Sarah's bullet-pointed charge list then? 'Who're you afraid of, Mrs Vane?'

She dropped her head, brushed crisp bits off her chest. 'What if I was to say something and word got out like?'

'No one'll know.' The future tense sounded better, made the prospect appear more of a given. Sarah sat forward elbows on knees. 'I swear, until and unless a case goes to court, we'll keep your name out of the public domain.'

'Public what?'

'The media. Papers. Telly. Obviously if you give evidence in—'

'You think I might be on the telly?' Bridie angled her head, patted the thin, greying hair. Showing her best side, presumably. It'd be hard to tell. 'Yeah right, copper,' she drawled. 'I wasn't born yesterday.'

'Murder trials get lots of coverage. I wouldn't be at all surprised.' Stunned, maybe.

'Bollocks.' Her sigh lifted her chest a good two inches. 'Look, I might live to regret this but . . . thing is . . .' – she dropped her gaze, slowly twiddled her thumbs in her lap – 'they told me they'd only scare him. Put the wind up him, like.'

Not stunned. Blown away. Sarah felt her heart rate take a hike. 'Tell me more.'

They, she heard, were Bridie's ex-husband and an old mate – *cell* mate. Carl Vane, it transpired, hadn't long been let out of Stafford Prison. Wayne – Rowson? Rowley? – she couldn't remember, had been released from Winson Green nick a week or so earlier. They'd called on Bridie late one night out of the blue. Hammered.

Still fiddling with her thumbs, Bridie continued in the same even tone. 'I'd never seen Carl so crazy. I guess the anger must've festered while he was inside. He said Drake had fucked with the wrong girl. Him and Wayne were gonna teach the sicko a lesson. A lesson he'd never forget. Carl . . .' She paused. 'Carl's very . . . possessive when it comes to Em, see.'

Possessive? Had a funny way of showing it, walking out when she was a kid. Sarah wouldn't mind asking the girl a few questions, but according to Bridie she was in Bristol, staying with an aunt for the weekend.

'So what happened?' Sarah prompted.

'I begged him to leave it. People were making Drake's life a misery anyway. Why kill him? Why make it easy on the bastard?'

The image of Drake's butchered arms flashed before Sarah's eyes. Dead easy that. She tried not to show contempt in her voice.

'Have you any idea of the pain he suffered before he died?' The twiddling paused briefly. No answer. 'How did they know where to find him?' The pause was even longer. 'Mrs Vane how did they—?'

'Carl forced the address out of me.' That explained the delay.

'Forced?'

'I ain't proud of it. I had no choice.' Her fleeting glance caught Sarah's scepticism. 'Stuck-up bitch. Don't friggin' believe me do you?'

Her shrug was like a red rag.

Mrs Vane struggled forward, yanked her grubby hoodie almost up to the triple chin. 'This do you?'

Once she'd made sense of it, Sarah stifled a gasp. The lurid plum and damson shading wasn't a T-shirt, certainly wasn't a tattoo – a tat that size would cost an arm and leg. *What the hell had he hit her with?* Kicked the shit out of her too by the look of it. And round the nipples, cigarette burns.

'Pretty ain't it?' Tears glistened in her eyes as she covered the bruised flesh again. 'So you see, Mrs Detective, when I say "forced"?'

Sarah nodded. Nothing was ever black-and-white. But Bridie wasn't exactly driven snow material. Presumably she'd been a damn sight more terrified of another beating from her best beloved than anything the cops could inflict on her.

'We need to bring them in. Any idea where they are?'

Bridie Vane's word on its own wasn't enough, not for the courts. Sarah believed most of what she'd said, but even then it wasn't like the woman had never lied.

She shook her head. 'I'd tell you if I knew.'

Given what she'd revealed already, she probably would. Sarah held the woman's gaze, wondering why on earth she'd not spoken out before.

'I can see what you're thinking.' She dragged a hand through her hair. 'Look, I reckoned keeping my trap shut would protect Emma. Me too, if I'm honest.' She stared down at her lap again. 'I mean, if he was on the run, he'd have to lie low, not show his face round here for sure. But what's to say some time down the line he'd not be back? Start doing it all over again.'

'Beating you?'

'And Emma.' She met Sarah's gaze. 'Not just beating her either. He used to . . .'

Molest. Abuse. Fiddle. What a piece of work. What a warped, hypocritical bastard. Just listening to the story turned Sarah's stomach. If the allegations stood up, she'd be adding yet more charges to Vane's list. Quiet sobbing was all she could hear now as Bridie hunched forward, head in hands. Just as well, Sarah was finding it hard to mask her distaste for the woman. For the whole sordid sorry mess some people make of their lives.

'You've done the right thing, Mrs Vane.' *Eventually.*

'What Emma done was wrong though.'

Had she heard properly? Sarah's hand stilled as she reached for her bag. 'Wrong?'

'Drake was forever giving her a hand time at school.' Bridie made eye contact again. 'She only told me yesterday. She just wanted . . .'

'Wanted what?' Sarah snapped.

'To make him back off. Leave her alone.'

'So the allegations?' Had been a pack of lies. Sarah shook her head in sorrow and shocked disbelief; Bridie hung hers in what the DI sincerely hoped was shame. Drake had paid the ultimate price. But a successful prosecution this far down the line meant Emma would almost certainly get off scot free.

Sarah rose, couldn't trust herself to speak.

Bridie looked up eyes wide, face wet with tears. 'Where are you going?'

'I need to set wheels in motion.' The sooner Carl and his buddy were located the better.

'When you find him?' Her arm trembled as she reached out. 'Will he be locked up?'

'He'll certainly be in custody while we question him. We need to build a case. If we get the evid—'

'If?' Gasping for breath, she forced a hand down the cushion, chucked something at Sarah. 'There's your sodding evidence. Now do I get police protection?'

FORTY-FOUR

Still seated in the Audi outside Vane's house, Sarah tapped her phone's send button. The thirty-second vid now whizzed through to Twig's mobile. He was in the squad room, better placed than her to get it out on general release. Besides, she'd already had three private viewings. Still hadn't decided whether or not to charge Bridie Vane with withholding evidence. As it happened, the quality was crap with soft grainy footage jerking all over the place, but what's the saying about pictures and a thousand words?

'What do you think, Twig?' Hearing a low whistle on the line she curved a lip.

'It beats *Mission Impossible* any day. I reckon we're on to a winner.'

Not that he was watching an action movie: the stars of the show were almost dead to the world. The shaky camera work reflected the operator's nerves not artistic prowess. But then, Bridie had taken a hell of a risk. Phone in hand, she'd crept downstairs in the dead of night and videoed Carl Vane sprawled across a leather sofa in a drunken stupor.

Taken just hours after Drake was butchered, the snatched shots showed more than a pisshead surrounded by empty bottles and cans. They showed what looked like dark stains on his clothing. They showed a Dunhill lighter lying among the debris. And they showed a glint coming off Vane's knobbly wrist from a gold watch. A Rolex. The close up even captured the crack in the glass. Sarah saw it as a case split wide open.

With both men's dabs and DNA already on the database, it'd be a piece of cake matching them with samples from the crime scene. A matter of seconds. Twig would start assigning tasks the minute they were off the phone.

'I'm heading back now.' Squinting, she pulled down the visor; the sun had made a comeback, too. 'Should be with you by four.'

'Tea-time. I'll get kettle on.' She heard a smile in his voice. 'And ma'am? Well done.'

The mug shots were up on a white board in the squad room. Carl Vane and Benny Rowley: faces bathed in a shaft of sunlight streaming through the window. With DNA and fingerprint matches now confirmed, an APW had been issued for their arrest of Lawrence Drake's murder. Cops across the country would be looking to collar them. Their scowling faces were the first things Sarah saw when she walked in.

Glancing round, she clocked Doug Spencer with his head down and Jed Holmes with a phone clamped to his ear. Paul Wood was on a call too, but gave her a thumbs' up. Smiling, she raised a palm, then slung her coat and bag on a desk before striding over for a closer look at the images.

Even without the names scrawled underneath, she'd know which of the charmers was Vane. Not because of the video where only his profile was in shot, but because of the striking resemblance she could see between the guy and his daughter. He was striking in other ways too, according to the written info on the board. Same went for his buddy, Rowley. Her eyebrow rose as she ran her gaze down their list of offences: disorder, affray, assault, illegal wounding, ABH, GBH. What you might call career progression.

'They're only the highlights, ma'am.' Twig had turned up alongside with a cuppa in hand. 'We'd need another white board to get everything down.'

Sarah turned and gave him a full-on smile. 'Nice work either way.'

'We all chipped in.' He nodded at the other guys. They both knew Sarah's team would be bigger if Starr hadn't siphoned it off to keep Brody happy. Mind, had she not been landed with Spencer in a limited quid pro quo, it'd be even sparser. The young detective had only cocked-up once, but it was enough for Brody to want shot of him. Twig said he'd tasked Spencer with the database stuff and he was now arranging the release of Bridie's video's to other forces, Jed was talking to staff at Stafford and Winson Green prisons trying to get a steer on forwarding addresses, Twig had just been liaising with the probation people.

Nodding she turned back and, arms folded, studied the faces again. 'So all we have to do now is find the bastards.'

'Shouldn't be too hard.' Twig took a sip of tea, told her he'd browsed their records and police reports. 'If you ask me – they love porridge, can't get enough of the stuff.'

Still staring at the pictures she murmured, 'Oh yeah?'

'Well they've been caught more times than flu.'

Her smile faded as she narrowed her eyes. Something about Rowley struck a faint chord, she was pretty sure she'd seen the heavy-set features, dark tightly-curled hair before. She tapped a finger against her lip running through recent deposits in the memory bank. A slightly louder chord went off in her head. *Where'd she left her phone?*

'Won't be a tick.' She walked to the desk where she'd

dumped her coat, found the phone in a pocket. Wandering
back, she scrolled through Dave's emails from the last week
or so. Got it. He'd headed it 'rogues' gallery' – though his
stab at an amusing subject line didn't look so funny now. And
the apostrophe was in the wrong place. The attached pics
showed the rubberneckers opposite Drake's house the morning
after the murder. As far as she knew the line-up only held one
rogue. She curved a lip. What had Dave said about the ghouls?
*'Surely anyone with something to hide wouldn't be dense
enough to show their face?'*

'What do you think?' She handed the phone to Twig,
watched his eyes as he quickly took in the scene, then saw
the slow smile spreading across his face.

'I think, DI Quinn, unless Benny Boy has a double . . . he's
even thicker than I'd given him credit for.'

'I'll second that.' Apart from Rowley's immensely stupid
proximity to the crime scene, the pictures actually proved
jack-shit – on their own. *Hold on.* She took the phone back,
studied the line up again: Rowley had no missus, no family
round these parts and he'd been inside for eighteen months.
So how come he was pally enough with the woman next in
line to have an arm round her? Sarah tapped a fingernail on
the screen. 'I'd like to know who he's with, Twig.'

And more to the point, if they were still together – where.

Armed with pictures of the happy couple, Jed and Spencer
were out knocking on doors in Aston. Sarah was just about
ready for home after virtuously completing an hour's worth
of admin – updating the action log, signing leave forms, initial-
ling expenses. Leaning back now, she linked hands on top of
her head and cast a smug glance at the almost empty in-tray.
Yeah, time well spent.

On the other hand, the call to Starr could've gone better.
Not that she'd expected him to belt out a rendition of *For
She's A Jolly Good Fellow*, but he might've sounded a touch
less grudging and as for carping on about how much time
could've been saved if she'd drawn out Bridie Vane's revelation
first time round . . .?

Thanks for that, sir. Like anyone could've had the faintest idea the bloody woman had shots of Sleeping Beastie on a phone up her metaphorical sleeve. Bridie's tipping point had been realizing, finally, she held the means of getting Vane sent down for life. The key word being life because then, unlike the ubiquitous bad penny, the bastard wouldn't be popping up in Bridie – or Emma's – life anytime soon.

She'd told Sarah she'd clung on to the pictures as some sort of bargaining chip with Vane: mess with me again and I'll . . . The reality had only gradually dawned. If he ever saw her hand, she'd end up like Drake – dead meat.

Which reminded her, Dave was doing steak tonight. When he'd called half an hour ago she could've murdered a rare sirloin. Now? She turned her mouth down. Maybe not so much. It'd be good catching up with the chef though. Dave could fill her in on the juicy bits of his jaunt to Hereford.

She sat up, stretched her arms towards the ceiling, felt a twinge in her lower back. Mind, it went with the sore calf muscles. Obviously God's way of saying exercise isn't all it's cracked up to be. Smiling, she logged off and gathered her bits. Shucking into her coat, she opened the door to find Brody standing there, knuckles about to rap on wood.

'DI Quinn. Not off already are we?'

'Got it in one.' She completed the coat manoeuvre, couldn't be arsed to tell him she didn't have to be in at all on a day off. Nor mention the cut on his cheek had opened. It wasn't like blood was gushing out. Hunt was right though, Joel Price's ring had taken out quite a chunk of skin.

'Shame,' Brody said stroking his jaw. 'The governor's standing a few rounds in The Queen's Head later. I know you've not so much cause to celebrate, but you're welcome to join the lads.'

Bloody nerve. Only one reason Brody had shown his face: he'd come to gloat. A game two could play. 'Had you not heard? There's an alert out for—'

'Yeah. Vane and Rowley.' The shrug was dismissive. She suspected he was about to up his game. 'I've got Fraser and Price. And y'know what they say about birds and hands. Your two are still out in the bush, aren't they?' She could almost hear the ner-ner-ner-nerner.

Bully for you. He could interpret her cocked head whichever way he wanted. As for his tame birds, he was pushing it given Zach Fraser's permanent position on a slab. But Joel Price was definitely putty in Brody's palm.

After six hours of questioning the guy had apparently broken down and admitted all three rape charges. Brody told her he'd be calling the victims with the news before setting off to the pub. 'So if you want to party there's time to powder your nose, slap on the war paint, whatever it is women do these days.'

I'd rather slap yours. She pulled the door to. 'Thanks, but no thanks. I'll let you get on with it.' *The gloating.*

The guy couldn't take a hint; he walked her down the corridor. 'Raj Malik'll be there. Soon as he finishes interviewing.' Raj was in with Pete Hinds. She'd taken a brief nose through the two-way mirror. Curiosity more than anything. It wasn't like Hinds was giving Raj a hard time.

'And when *charges* have been laid, of course.' Brody smiled as he held the fire door for her. Boy, was he laying her lack of a collar on with a trowel.

She sniffed. Those teeth of his really did need attention. 'Congrats all round then.'

'Nearly a full house. Still, I'm sure you'll have the charge book out before long, Sarah. And two out of three ain't bad.'

'Not bad at all.' *You patronizing git.* Thank God they'd run out of corridor. 'I'll say good night here, George. Just one thing,' – smiling she handed him a tissue from her pocket – 'you need a wipe. There's something on your face.'

Shame it was only blood. Not half-a-dozen eggs as well.

FORTY-FIVE

'Forget it. It's off.'

'Who the fuck's this?' Webb snapped. The call had given him a rude awakening. He'd fallen asleep on the sofa and answered on autopilot in Mr Grumpy mode. Besides, the bloke on the other end sounded like a heavy breather in a slasher movie.

'Shut it and listen up. I haven't got long.'

The superior sneer was more than enough for Webb to go on this time.

'Get on with it then.' He sat up straight, ran a hand through his mussed hair. Darby had always been an arrogant sod, reckoned he was a cut above even in Parkhurst. *Cut?* Webb smirked. Yeah, well Darby had been well known for carrying a knife.

'The meet's off. No call any more. They've caught the bastard.'

Phone clamped to ear, Webb wandered through to the kitchen, scratching his chest. 'And?' He felt the paper he'd shoved in his pocket prickle his skin. He was wide awake now and quickly learned from Darby that a DI Brody had called twenty minutes ago with breaking news: a man would appear in court first thing on Monday charged with Zoe's rape. The cop had wanted Darby to hear first-hand before the media got wind of the story.

Webb leaned against the sink, legs crossed at the ankles, took a slug of red wine straight from the bottle. 'This bloke's admitting it, is he?'

'Put his hand up to all three.' Darby said he'd already talked to Silk and Winter who'd both had Brody on the line with the same tidings. 'Bastard'll go down big time.'

Webb paused, gave it some thought. 'Right.'

'Is that it?' Darby's sigh sounded less than happy. 'Thought you'd be pleased.'

He necked another mouthful, then said, 'You telling me cops never cock-up?'

'Course they do, but the man's confessed.'

'So? What if it's false? Forced? Like that'd be a first.'

'Amazing.' He snorted. 'You should be relieved, not looking for—'

'This DI Brody. Got evidence as well, has he?' Webb sank the last mouthful and tipped the bottle over the sink.

'Yeah, talked me through every skin cell, every drop of . . . fuck's sake, man, we didn't go into detail.'

Webb ran cold water to disperse the dregs. They reminded him of blood. Damson teardrops of blood.

'I think we should go ahead anyway,' he said. 'Just in case.' Darby pooh-poohed the suggestion, told Webb he and the others had already called the meeting off.

'Is that wise?' Webb felt the paper's rough edges as he slipped it out of his pocket. 'You never know what's down the line.'

'The heat's off. Relax, man.'

'What if it goes pear-shaped?'

'Look, matey, I haven't a bloody clue what your problem is, but you need to chill.'

Temper, temper. And he'd buggered off. No worries. Webb had already decided he'd leave Darby's bubble intact. The guy might have no clue, but Webb had one. One he was looking at.

Maybe I should tell Angela what you did? Next time you two bump into each other – ask Nigel what he thinks.

Smart-arsed git. Webb reckoned his pen pal must be so busy coming up with lines like that, he no longer had the time to bother cutting words from newspapers. The latest note was scribbled in biro on lined paper torn from a pad. Webb had found it shoved through the door no more than an hour ago, which strongly suggested that whoever the cops had banged up in a police cell hadn't been out on a special delivery. The post might be late these days, but even junk mail didn't come at night.

Lip curved, he walked to the bin where he painstakingly tore the paper over and over again. He gave a thin smile as he sprinkled the tiny shreds over a load of used tea bags, peelings and cracked egg shell. The white lacy bits could almost be confetti. Except the last thing on Webb's mind was a wedding. The latest threat had been too close to home, even more personal. And it had planted a seed in his head.

FORTY-SIX

Sunday morning and there were a few thick heads round the nick. Sarah had spotted a couple earlier in the canteen shovelling fatty fry-ups down their neck. She'd heard about last night's celebrations via the grapevine, though 'distillery' might be more apt. From what she gathered, the party had gone on until the early hours and the Brody bunch had allegedly downed their combined bodyweight in Scotch.

Sipping coffee, Sarah stood gazing through a window in the squad room trying not to look smug. She'd been tucked up in bed by midnight. Not that DI Goody Two Shoes had necessarily been sleeping. Awake for quite a while as it happened. She curved a lip: give her indoor exercise any day. Didn't even need any gear for it, though Dave had made the odd suggestion. She'd have to think about it – could never really see herself in red lace. Or a basque.

'Gold top was it, ma'am?'

'I'm sorry?' Turning, she broadened her smile. 'Huntie. Good to see you.'

'Actually you look more like a cat that got a churn full of cream.'

'I was miles away for a minute. What you up to anyway?' She assumed he'd still be at Brody's brief. She'd wound hers up a while ago – Spencer and Holmes were en route to Aston again armed with the mystery woman's pic. Sarah had other officers on the phone dealing with possible sightings of the wanted men. If half the calls were genuine, Rowley and Vane needed to be members of the magic circle or have their own personal TARDIS.

'I'm around if you need a hand.'

She frowned. 'I'd have thought Brody—?'

'Nah. He's not in today.'

'A no show?' They started walking towards the white board.

'I dare say he's nursing a sore head but no, scheduled day off. I'm getting the paperwork ready for Price's court appearance tomorrow, but apart from that I'm all yours.'

'Well if you're offering?' She talked him through the visuals pointing out the main players, gave him a rundown on the latest state of play, said she needed someone to take Bridie Vane's statement. The woman was due at the station late morning. Though her co-operation was late, given its level, charges wouldn't be pressed.

'Get all the good jobs, don't I?' Hunt winked. 'Yeah, no worries.'

Another thought struck as she reached the door. Turning back she called, 'John, if the media are sniffing round, can you field the calls?'

'Sure. We've not released anything yet though.'

Maybe not but it hadn't stopped Slater ringing her at home last night. The guy had a nerve. Said he'd heard a whisper, tried checking it out with Brody who wasn't picking up. No surprise there then. Brody would have had a glass in one hand and the other would have been too busy slapping backs. Either way Slater had been out of order trying to trade on the old pals' act. Sarah wouldn't be surprised if Caroline had put him up to it – anything to help her latest lapdog scoop a juicy bone exclusive.

Not that he had. Sarah had given Slater short shrift wrapped in bum's-rush-schtum.

Snout down and frantically barking, the dog failed to respond when its name was called. Oblivious to its elderly owner's increasingly querulous commands, the Border collie burrowed feverishly near the trees and hedges lining the side of the canal. The woman called again, with the same negative result. Sighing, she started to retrace her steps. Maybe she should have kept him on the lead, but on the days when there was time to venture a little further afield, it was lovely to let him have his head for a while. Beyond the tourist section of the canal it was almost rural, the towpath held far more interesting smells for a four-legged creature. Though from where she stood, the only thing visible were his quivering hindquarters.

'Bentley! Bentley! Come away now.'

The swishing black tail was a blur and suggested to Mrs Marlow that Bentley had found something only the greediest dog could judge edible. She recalled the time he'd gorged on a bird's putrid remains. The vet took a guess at a young seagull. Either way, Bentley's free meal had cost her a small fortune.

'Come on, Bentley, there's a good boy.' The old woman had no option but to investigate further. She picked her way gingerly along a path now rutted with gnarled tree roots and strewn with all manner of litter: rubble, half house bricks, plastic bags. Recent rain had left the uneven earth squelchy in places, adding to the hazards for the slightly unsteady on their feet. After her nasty fall nine months ago, the last thing Mrs Marlow wanted was to trip and injure herself. Anybody could lie here undiscovered for hours, maybe days.

Bentley failed to register her presence even when she stood inches away. Leaning down she patted his back, softly spoke his name. Nothing. She shook her head. Only one thing for it then. She reached in her pocket for a doggie treat. Not, she told herself, that he currently deserved one. 'Here boy, look what I've got.'

Doggy chocs never failed. Smiling indulgently, she watched Bentley back out from the undergrowth. She didn't notice his nose twitching, didn't see the dry leaves stuck in his fur, the thing she registered was Bentley's glistening red muzzle. The smell made her gag but she could barely tear her gaze away It was only when she realized he was unharmed that she sank slowly and painfully to her knees to find out where the blood had come from.

FORTY-SEVEN

'The victim was stabbed, ma'am. Young woman.'

Sarah nodded briskly at the police community support officer holding up the Do Not Cross tape. *Tell me something I don't know,* she thought ducking under the cordon. As she started walking down the towpath, the same route she'd run only yesterday, he called her back, then presumably so the gawpers wouldn't be privy, lowered the volume.

'I'm told she's still alive. Just.'

'Thanks.' She gave a thin smile, wondering why she'd not heard. The triple-nine hadn't long come in though. Details from control were pretty scant: girl's body, stab wounds, signs of sexual assault. It was the latter that had sent the DI's antenna into overdrive. With Joel Price under lock and key, it looked as if they might have another sex attacker on the patch, a copycat even. Always a danger when a case attracted a lot of media coverage. Either way Sarah had expected to see the pathologist working on the victim, not two paramedics bent over the body.

She homed in on the forensics guys who stood a respectful distance away. One was pouring something hot from a flask. The other had clocked her approach and handed over a spare white suit.

'Thanks, Lynne.' Lynne Holdsworth, mid-thirties, sharp as a lance. 'There's no weapon lying around. No ID that I could see. Faintest of heartbeats.'

'Any idea who found her?' Kitting up, Sarah listened to Lynne's succinct account. The postscript being that a uniformed officer had given the old dear a lift home where he'd try and take a proper statement; she'd not been fit for much at the scene.

'I tell you DI Quinn,' Lynne raked a gloved hand through a glossy auburn bob, 'we could've done without the bloody dog. And I mean literally bloody.'

Sarah lifted a corner of her mouth. 'I hear what you're saying – canine contamination and all that. But Lassie just might have saved a life here.' Well, lent a paw. From what she could see the paramedics were doing the lion's share.

'Lassie? You mean, Bentley. What a name.' Smiling, she shook her head. 'Bentley the bloody Border collie.'

An old woman and a sheepdog? Sarah reckoned she might have spotted them from her apartment window yesterday morning. She'd mentally summed up the motley crew down by the canal as *all human life.* Grimacing, she glanced across at what little she could see of the victim, hoping the young woman was still clinging on to hers.

'What's the score then, boss?'

Eyebrow raised, she turned to find Dave heading her way, rubbing his hands together.

'Good though it is to see you, I thought you were a lad of leisure today?' She'd left him curled up in bed.

'With all this kicking off?' He told her he'd heard the sirens, clocked the police activity, put in a call to the squad room. Rocking on the balls of his feet, he looked like he was dying to get cracking.

They walked away a few paces while she filled him in on the few details she'd picked up. Clearly they were waiting on the medicos before getting a closer look at the scene. Beyond the immediate area, uniform had already started searching. Officers with heads down could be seen studying the path, others used beaters to separate hedges, undergrowth. Sarah doubted they'd find the weapon – whatever it was – ditched in the greenery. Not when the attacker had the murky depths of the Birmingham and Worcester canal at his disposal. Doubtless she'd be looking to call in divers before too long. She shuddered: the sludge-coloured water looked *so* inviting. Dave's gaze was down there too.

'Bet I know what you're thinking,' he said.

'Go on then.'

'Sooner them than me?'

'Clever dick.' She smiled. 'Still, we'd best get the underwater team on standby.'

'Consider it done.' He flashed a grin along with his mobile. 'And are you thinking what I'm thinking?'

'Try me.'

His pause was telling. 'What if Brody's got the wrong guy banged up?'

She pursed her lips, the thought had crossed her mind. It was a no-brainer that Joel Price had raped Zoe Darby – the evidence was irrefutable. Not so with the other two. As far as she knew, all Brody had so far was Price's confession.

'Bridges, cross. Let's wait and see what we have here eh, Dave?'

'You're the boss.' He tapped a salute. 'I'll just put that call in to the frog squad then have a wander, see if I can rustle up any witnesses.'

Frog squad. She rolled her eyes. 'You'd better not let the lads catch you say . . .?'

'What is it?'

'What you said about witnesses. I think you'll be bloody lucky to find any, Dave.' She narrowed her eyes. Like finding the victim so quickly had been pure chance, all down to a nosy mutt. Lynne had told her the victim hadn't been visible from the path, the old woman needed to crouch before she saw what was what. It also appeared that the girl had been forced through a gap in the bushes. So had the attacker been fortuitous with his choice of location? Or had that gap been carefully selected? She voiced the theory to Dave who nodded, clearly on board.

'You're thinking he reccied it?'

'Has to be a possibility, doesn't it?'

There had to be another outside chance – that he'd been spotted hanging about.

'DI Quinn?'

She turned at Lynne's call, followed the FSI's gaze. Sarah felt her heart sink. Peeling off a blood-stained latex glove, a paramedic walked slowly away from the crime scene. His face told her they'd done everything they could, a tear about to trickle from the corner of his eye told her it hadn't been enough.

'I hope you nail the bastard pretty damn quick.' He slipped the hand, still gloved, into a pocket of his dark green combats and pulled out a driving licence – provisional. 'At least we know who she is. Sorry – was.'

FORTY-EIGHT

Charlotte Flinn. 18. Dave had an address via the PNC within minutes. Edgbaston. Temple Street.

'Want me to go round, boss?'

She shook her head. The offer was to go and break the

bad news to whoever might be there, possibly waiting for someone who'd never walk through the door again. Ideally, Sarah preferred delivering the death knock personally, but the girl might not even live with her parents. She'd be more use here. So would Dave. Besides, the pathologist was on his way, she needed words with him at least before she left.

'Give Huntie a bell, Dave.' There must be a spare bod in the squad room he could send. She wanted Dave to question the old woman with the dog. If the towpath was a favourite haunt, it was just feasible she might have spotted someone hanging around recently. 'And call the boat trip people.' Another long shot, but there was a regular one-hour service. She'd watched the narrow boats sail past her window enough. In terms of anyone seeing anything dodgy, she was thinking crew rather than passengers. But who knew?

'On it, captain.'

Her smile faded when she turned. The paramedics were packing their gear, they'd be pulling out any minute. All she could see of the girl was a grubby foot. She knew it was ridiculous, illogical, whatever, but she hated the idea of the girl lying there alone. Sod it.

She called to Lynne, 'Can you get the tent ready while I take a look?' The body wouldn't be going anywhere for hours, it needed protection from the elements as much as prying eyes. Gun metal grey clouds loomed on the horizon. Sarah couldn't see the rain holding off much longer.

Taking a deep breath, then swallowing hard, she approached the victim and squatted at her side. The red blanket covering the body couldn't hide the smells: blood and human waste – olfactory warnings of what lay ahead. Steeling herself further, she gently removed the blanket, slowly ran an assessing gaze over the body. The head was to the side and the one blue eye open seemed to stare at Sarah. The girl looked young for her age, small and slight. And violated: bruised, battered, broken. Given the blood loss, God knew how she'd survived as long as she had. Churned earth streaked her naked flesh, fingernails were caked with mud, twigs and leaves caught in her hair. *You poor, poor child.*

Sarah felt tears well in her eyes, longed to comfort the girl, make it all better. Crazy, stupid notions. Emotional diarrhoea wouldn't help. One thing might help Sarah though. She reached out, gently stroked a strand of hair away from the girl's face and whispered, 'Trust me, Charlotte. I'll get the bastard who did this. I promise.'

The call came as Sarah strode through Brindleyplace heading back to the motor. Sunday mid-morning still, but wine bars and coffee shops were already filling up. She was vaguely aware of a busker playing saxophone somewhere nearby: the strains of Baker Street competed with clanging church bells. Neither appealed. Sarah had a bunch of other stuff to contend with.

She'd left it with Richard Patten that he'd let her know the minute he could about the extent of the sex attack on Charlotte Flinn. All the signs suggested rape, but it needed confirming. From what Patten had said, the murder weapon was definitely a knife, short with a serrated blade. Provisional cause of death, blood loss brought on by traumatic injury.

He'd pointed out defence wounds across one of the girl's arms and broken skin across her knuckles. Indications were that she'd put up a hell of a fight. Patten thought it likely she'd scratched her attacker. Sarah hoped she'd scratched his bloody eyes out. As for the driving licence, she could only imagine it had come adrift during the scuffle. A bag or purse was something else they'd yet to locate. The frog squad, as Dave put it, would start dragging the canal in an hour or so. All this, plus a million other things, buzzed in her head when she answered the phone.

'DC Spencer here, ma'am. We got him.' The glee tone bordered on smug.

Frowning, she broke her stride momentarily, thought for a crazy second or two he meant Charlotte's attacker. The initial elation then sank faster than a concrete duck. And what was Spencer waiting for – a round of applause?

'Go on then.' She'd not meant to snap, but on top of the disappointment – however baseless – she could do without guessing games.

'Benny Rowley, ma'am. He's in custody. We found him holed up at Aston.'

No wonder he'd sounded chuffed. Not now though – chastened more like. She'd pissed on his parade big time and felt pretty churlish. And this deserved her full attention.

'Sorry, Doug,' she said perching on a bench outside a pub. 'Talk me through it.'

'When I say "holed up", ma'am – I mean it.' They'd found him skulking in a cubby hole under the no-longer mystery woman's stairs. Sarah heard how an elderly couple living a few doors down from a Sharon Dent in South Street had immediately recognized the woman in the photograph. The oldies had told Spencer and Jed Holmes exactly where they could find that 'bloody trollop' and her latest 'waste-of-space creep'.

'They reckoned Dent and Rowley made the neighbours from hell look like Margo and Jerry from *The Good Life*. Tell the truth, ma'am, I hadn't got a clue what they were going on about at first but then I got the picture.' So did Sarah – she'd watched the Seventies sit-com often enough.

Spencer sniffed. 'Even more so when we laid eyes on them. Honest, ma'am, Jeremy Kyle'd pay a fortune to have them on the show.'

She told him to get on with it, but this time had a smile in her voice. Dent, he said, had been first to get the once over. Rowley, having heard an increasingly hostile altercation between his lady friend and detectives at the front door, decided to squirrel himself away.

'I tell you, ma'am, we could have booked her for offensive behaviour.'

'Why didn't you?'

'Cos she upped the ante. Took a swing at Jed. I got the cuffs out, threatened to run her in for assault and she caved.' Dent initiated what Spencer called a little pre-emptive plea-bargaining. As in, 'put the cuffs away – I'll show you where he's hiding his hairy arse'.

'Her words, ma'am, not mine.'

She curved a lip. 'And Vane?'

'Rowley couldn't dob him in fast enough apparently. Blamed

the lot on him. Rowley claimed he'd never have lifted a finger against Drake had he not been coerced.'

Sarah snorted. 'I'll bet he didn't use that word.'

'Bet on that, ma'am and you'd clean up. Anyway, he's cooling his heels in a cell now. DS Hunt told me to tell you he's happy to do the interview.'

'Great. And Vane? Rowley have any ideas where we can find him?'

'Better than that, ma'am.'

He'd told them exactly where Carl Vane was lying low: in a condemned tower block in Weoley Castle. Spencer said uniformed officers and a dog handler were on site and about ready to move in.

'Dog's not called Daimler, is it?' she quipped.

'Sorry?'

'Forget it. You had to be there. Anyway bloody good work, Doug. Pass big thanks on to Jed, too.' She ended the call with the widest smile she'd had in a while.

FORTY-NINE

Slumped in a police cell, Carl Vane looked as miserable as clinically depressed sin. Benny Rowley cowered in the far corner of the furthest cell, well out of harm's way. If Vane got anywhere near the guy he'd rip his fucking head off then shove it up his ass. It was the most charming threat he'd voiced in the last half hour.

Sarah could still hear Vane's dulcet tones as she mounted the stairs outside the custody suite. Still smell the stink of stale body odour and grimy flesh. Glancing back, she thought – to coin a Dave-ism – *sooner them than me*. The lucky individuals in this instance being Shona Bruce and John Hunt to whom she'd had to delegate the questioning of the men. Compared with the new inquiry, the Drake case was all over, bar the shouting. Though now she came to think of it, the shouting was still on-going. Whatever. Curiosity had got the better of her and before the interviews got underway, she'd popped down to grab a quick butcher's. She shuddered. Given what they'd meted out to Drake, make that a quick gawp.

At the top of the flight she glanced at her watch and decided to carry on up to the canteen. The news conference wasn't until half one. She could fit in coffee and a bite to eat and still have time to brief the Flinns when they arrived.

Once they'd established Charlotte did live with her parents at the Edgbaston address, Sarah had asked Dave to drive out there and try and persuade them to do an appeal. Insensitive and intrusive it might be, but the sad fact is people are often more willing to talk on camera in the immediate aftermath of a loved one's death than when they'd had time to think about it. Ask any reporter, they'd say the same.

Anyway, Dave's magic had worked on the Flinns. He might yet charm Mrs Marlow, but she'd not been at home when he dropped by. He'd pay another visit later.

Back at her desk, Sarah had a mouthful of chicken and avocado sandwich when her phone rang, and it must've sounded that way when she answered.

'Lucky for some, isn't it? Can't remember when I had my last morsel. Must be great to have a break every now and again.' She smiled at the pathologist's laboured sigh.

'Sorry, Dr Patten, didn't catch what you said. Must be all the violins in the background.'

'Watch it, DI Quinn.' She pictured him pointing a mock-admonishing finger, to go with the faux censorious tone.

'Right.' She laid the sandwich to one side, picked up a pen. 'What can I do for you?'

'It's more a case of what I might be able to do for you.' He told her he saw it when he turned Charlotte's body, even then almost missed it because of all the blood and muck. It was small and he had no idea of its significance.

She tapped the pen on her desk. *Come on, spit out.*

'He carved a number at the base of her spine, Sarah.'

She drew her eyebrows together. 'A number?'

'A four.'

She wrote it down, added Charlotte Flinn alongside.

'You still there, Sarah?'
She paused, still considering, then, 'Was she raped, Richard?'
'Unquestionably.'
Christ on a bike. She was beginning to see it now.

'What's it telling you, Dave?' He stood in front of Sarah's
desk holding a sheet of notepaper in one hand. She'd called
him in the minute he got back to the station, desperate to hear
his take on the number carved on the body. If it matched
Sarah's reading, everything changed and she'd have to steel
herself to call Starr again.

Sitting back in the chair, fingers laced in her lap, she studied
his face as he ran his gaze down the list she'd written. She
ran hers down an identical list in her head.

Charlotte Flinn 4
Lisa Webb 3
Jessica Silk 2
Hannah Winter 1

Sarah's laid-back pose hid heightened tension. She was almost
certain now that her interpretation was correct. Loath to point
it out, she was willing Dave to see it for himself. Either way
they didn't have much time. The media were already milling
round downstairs.

'My God.' He held her gaze then slung the paper on her
desk. 'What an arrogant tosser.' *One way of putting it.*

'And?' She raised an eyebrow.

'He's telling us we've got the wrong man.'

Nodding she gave a thin smile. *That's my boy.*

'Zoe Darby's rape doesn't count,' he said, 'because whoever
the arrogant dickhead is didn't commit it. So now the bastard's
making his mark.' In the cruellest fashion: gouging it into
Charlotte's smooth young skin.

'Exactly.'

They knew Zoe's attack was down to Joel Price, the evidence
proved it. Not so in the other cases: Price's confession didn't
say it all.

'He doesn't want anyone taking his limelight, Dave. Doesn't

like it at all. But I think I do.' Standing, she reached for her jacket, nodded at the door. 'Before this he's not put so much as a toe wrong.'

Dave nodded. 'And now he's showing his hand.'

Making it more likely another cock-up would be on the cards. All they need do now was find the rest of him, before he notched up number five.

Reading between the lines had narrowed the field down: a green shoot had emerged from the seed in Ian Webb's head. He could be wrong. It was more than twenty years since he'd set eyes on the girl. In all that time he'd never given her a second thought. He snorted. Who was he trying to kid? She haunted his subconscious, drifted bare-foot and wraith-like through countless dreams. Even now when he closed his eyes he could picture her. He'd rarely seen a more beautiful woman. Leaning heavily on the sink, he stared at his reflection in the bathroom mirror. Not a pretty sight. He ran the cold tap, splashed water over his face.

'Ian, are you up there? Dinner's on the table.'

'I'm nipping out, Ange. I'll warm it up later.' She muttered something, he wasn't really listening. Dabbing his cheeks with a towel, his thoughts were back on the girl. He'd heard about the baby when he was inside. The date fitted, he knew it could be his. He'd certainly not made contact on his release and couldn't see her welcoming him with open arms. All day it had taken him to find out where she lived. He doubted she'd be overjoyed to see him, probably run a mile if she could. He hoped he was wrong about the kid, really hoped that. He had to know one way or the other.

Angie finding out was one of the things he feared most. And whoever wrote the last note knew that. Christ, the threat hadn't even been veiled.

Maybe I should tell Angela what you did?

He slipped the first note out of his wallet.

I know what you are. How do you live with yourself? Call yourself a father?

Lip curled, he screwed the paper into a tight ball then flushed the loo. He watched the paper whirl and bob up and down a

few times, stayed watching until he was absolutely sure it had
gone for good.

FIFTY

'Are we gonna watch the news then?' Tea-towel tucked
in waistband, Dave stood at the stove sweating
onions and garlic in a pan. Glass in hand, Sarah was
overseeing gastronomic proceedings from her perch on the
side. Overseeing was pushing it given she was a distinctly
sous-chef.

'Why? Are you hoping you'll be on?' Sarah masked a
smile with a sip of wine. He might at that though, he'd
metaphorically held the Flinns' hands during the filming that
afternoon.

'Ha, ha.' Pointing the spatula at her. 'Nah, just interested
how it'll come across. I thought she was really good.'

Sarah nodded. Couldn't argue with that. Dignified and
unflinching, Patricia Flinn had delivered a heartfelt appeal
straight to camera. The husband, Tom, had slumped next to
her sobbing.

'Let's hope we get some decent leads off the back of it.'
She topped up his dwindling Merlot. The appeal had already
aired on local radio, the story appeared on news websites and
the police Twitter feed. Squad members staffing phones would
contact her with anything significant.

'Can you reach the tomatoes?'

'Sure. Want a crisp?'

'No.' More spatula pointing. 'And neither should you.'

'Right, boss.' Smiling, she took another. As for the real
boss, it was a bloody shame she'd not been able to reach Starr.
The DCS really needed to know they almost certainly had the
wrong bloke banged up for three rapes. She'd left copious
messages on Starr's voicemail asking him to get back ASAP.
Christ. She'd even tried calling Brody. Couldn't do much more
than that.

'Still,' Dave said, studiously stirring the pan. 'I s'pose you can pig out all you like now you've taken up jogging.'

Had she hell. She'd lost the taste for it after the trial run. She narrowed her eyes.

'How do you know—?'

He shrugged. 'Saw your kit in the wash.'

'Smarty pants.'

'They're certainly fetching.'

'Cheeky boy.' Smiling, she flicked his wrist. 'You'll be fetching something in a minute.' He'd certainly helped fetch Pete Hinds back. The guy would appear before magistrates in the morning on murder and arson charges. As for Natalie, Sarah knew Dave still harboured vague reservations about the girl. Felt she knew far more than she was saying. If anyone could draw her out, it would be Shona. Sarah made a mental note.

'I know something you can fetch.' He winked.

'What's that then?'

'TV remote?'

'All right, all right. Don't panic.' She flapped a hand. 'I'll make sure it's on in time.' She doubted he'd even make the cut. Either way the news certainly wouldn't feature the numbers' angle. Releasing it to the media was the last thing she'd do. Talk about field day? They'd camp outside police HQ if they knew about the carving on Charlotte's body.

On the other hand, hinting at a sensational twist like that might have prompted a bigger turnout at the news conference. She'd expected to see a few more faces, especially Slater's given it was his patch and crime stories were supposed to be his baby. Playing catch-up, he'd called afterwards begging for a quote but if he couldn't be bothered to show, tough. Why should she do him any favours?

Especially when she'd bet her pension the reporter had been too busy running round servicing Caroline.

Frowning, Caroline tucked a pen behind her ear then scooted the office chair back from her desk. She needed to see the stuff Mark had been working on. Now the new book was done, if not dusted, she might as well pull the case studies into some sort of sequence. She knew he had cracking material lying around, she'd read some already.

He might be back by now of course. Bull elephants on a stag night could conga through the house and Caroline wouldn't notice if she had her head down. She padded along the landing, knocked none too gently on his bedroom door. *Stupid woman.* Course he wasn't in there. The lock was on so unless he'd taken a crash course from Houdini . . .?

She checked the time on her phone, slipped it back in her pocket. In her book, half-six was 'sun over the yardarm' o'clock. If she recalled right, there was a decent little Soave in the fridge. If Mark wasn't downstairs, she'd have a drink and a shower by which time he should be in-house and she'd be able to get stuck in. She snorted when she opened the drawer saw the spare padlock still lying next to the cork-screw. Her stuff wasn't as precious as his, huh? Thank you so much.

Or . . . she pursed her lips. How about looking at it another way?

Blessing in disguise and all that. She'd been in Mark's room enough times, it wasn't like he'd mind. Besides it was his fault, he should've been back long before now. She ripped open the packaging and tipped out the keys.

Who needed Houdini?

Shoot. Mark certainly needed a Hoover and a bigger bin at the very least. She stood in the doorway hands on hips, surveying the mess. How he worked in it, she'd never know. It looked like the bomb squad had turned up too late. She started picking her way over a carpet strewn with clothes, shoes, books, papers, cuttings. She knew the file she wanted, just couldn't spot it among the crap.

Momentarily she stopped in her tracks. Caroline gasped when she saw the photograph on the pillow. Why the hell had he taken it? She perched on the bed and took the picture in her hands. His mother looked to be as near death as almost made no difference – lying in the foetal position on a high metal-railed bed, she looked little more than a bag of sallow skin and bones, light bounced from a billiard ball skull, pain etched on every line of her ravaged face.

Caroline shook her head. The image bore no relation to other photographs she'd seen of Mrs Slater. Mark had loads of her in her prime. Why on earth not remember her like that? Not this wizened, pathetic creature.

She sighed, placed it back exactly where she'd found it. No way on God's earth would she want to see the woman in the flesh. Standing, she swept her gaze round the room again, walked over to check the desk drawers, the shelves. *Think laterally woman.* Suppose he'd fallen asleep reading it.

Only one way to find out and it was a hands and knees job, ably assisted by a little light from the lamp. Bingo. The file was propped between the bed and the back wall. *God, it's hard being a genius.* She still needed to lie on her front and shuffle under before she could get hold of it though. *Gotcha.* File in hand, she reversed out then sat back on her heels smiling.

Dusty under there or what? When she brushed her sleeve, something small and shiny dropped on the carpet. Cufflink? Nah, Mark didn't wear cufflinks. Right size though and it looked like silver. Frowning she picked it up, examined it more closely in her palm.

Shit. Quickly she closed her fingers. Felt her scalp tingle, heartbeat increase. This was no cufflink. And even if it was – the initial wouldn't be A.

Stumbling to her feet, she ran towards the door.

Mark stood on the landing. 'Looking for something, Caro?'

Smiling, Sarah aimed the remote and zapped it at the screen. 'Better luck next time, eh?'

Never mind fifteen minutes of fame, Dave hadn't bagged fifteen seconds. The news report had carried a fleeting shot of Sarah then majored almost exclusively on the Flinns.

'Very funny.'

'They're always after people for *MasterChef.*' She patted her full stomach, pushed away the empty plate. 'Maybe find that's more your forte?'

'Knock it on the head, or I'll—'

Still smiling, she lifted a finger and reached for her phone. Could be Starr. Caller display read Baker. *Close.* She frowned.

Not like him to call on a Sunday night. 'Chief to what do I
owe the pleas—?'

'It's business, Quinn. I just caught the news.'

'Go on.'

'The murdered girl's father?'

'Tom Flinn?'

'Not when I nailed him years ago, he wasn't.'

He'd been called Gordon Heath, the chief told her, and the
judge had sentenced him to three years prison.

She had a feeling she knew the answer but asked anyway,
'What for?'

'Rape.'

She nodded, already there.

'Think about it, Quinn. Was she the target or her old man?'

Eyes narrowed, Sarah ended the call. The bigger question
was whether the other girls had paid for their fathers' criminal
pasts.

'What is it, boss?'

'Dave. We need to do some digging.'

FIFTY-ONE

The day's digging had led to a dead end, or as good as.
A helpful neighbour had pointed Ian Webb in the
direction of the hospice. The sister on duty wouldn't
let him pay a visit, of course. Not that she'd spelt it out, but
the signals weren't hard to read: the patient wouldn't be
talking to anyone, even if she could.

He'd gone back, learned a bit more from the neighbour.
They'd lived next door for years apparently. The old man
had been like a father to the boy when he'd been growing
up. Even now the son popped in from time to time, mostly
when he had to pick up the post. They'd have a chinwag
over a cuppa and that. Webb had nodded and enthused, like
he'd known about the boy all along. Getting the forwarding
address had been like taking candy from a baby. Shame he'd

not been able to pass on the neighbour's well wishes at the hospice.

Maybe he'd have better luck handing them to her son.

Caroline flashed the file and what she hoped was a convincing smile. 'Hi Mark. Found it thanks.'

'Clever girl. You deserve an A star. Give. Now.' Unsmiling, he held out a palm.

Hers was closed so tight, she felt the silver edges piercing her skin. Saw beads of blood oozing from long scratches on one of his cheeks.

'Not with you. How'd you mean?' Pathetic. There was no point bullshitting. She sounded like an idiot and he was clearly no fool, he certainly didn't have his sights set on the bloody file.

'You know exactly what I mean.' Underlining the point, he drew a knife from his breast pocket.

'It's the girl's, isn't it?' Her hand shook as she let the letter drop from her fingers into his open palm. 'And, no, I don't know, Mark. I don't know *why.*' Not even half of it.

'Always the reporter eh, Caro? Don't tell me you're after the story?'

'Why not?'

'Because then I'd have to kill you.' He stroked the blade along her jaw line. The smile didn't reach his eyes. 'Still want to hear?'

Anything to buy time. 'Sure. If you want to.' She saw the temptation in his eyes.

He held her gaze for a few seconds more then, 'As you say, "why not?".' Sighing, he rubbed a hand over his face. 'It's over now anyway. She's dead. Christ, I need a drink.'

He pointed the knife towards a chair in the kitchen. She did as bid, watching him pour Scotch into a tumbler. He drank as he paced the floor. His mother had died an hour ago. He'd idolized her, worshipped her, everything had been for her. In between his wracking sobs, Caroline heard it all. She almost felt sorry for the guy, almost. Her hand had been in her pocket most of the time. She prayed her fingers had found the right letters in the text she'd sent Sarah. Prayed harder, she'd live to tell the tale.

*   *   *

Seated in the back of a cab, Sarah raked her fingers through her hair. She probably wasn't over the limit but couldn't afford to take the risk. Dave had gone on ahead to question Jonathan Silk.

The thinking was: if someone was out to exact revenge for rape, what would most hurt the rapist? It had to be living with the knowledge that a daughter had been violated in the same way. If Jessica, Hannah and Lisa had paid for their fathers' crimes, the men had to have changed their names or police background checks should have picked up the link. Only the men could confirm what looked increasingly like the rapist's motive. One might have an idea about the perp. The only way to find out was to ask and given the attacks were becoming more frequent – the sooner the better. Sarah was en route to Selly Oak to tackle Ian Webb.

Until a text came through.

Sarah got the cabbie to drop her a few doors down from Caroline's. As she approached on foot, she couldn't see lights on in the house which probably meant they were in a back room. Thank God she'd been heading to Webb's place anyway – it was ten minutes since Caroline's message came in. Sarah had called Dave to tell him the score and he'd join her soon as he could. Her fear was that they didn't have a lot of time to play with. Reading between the lines of the text, neither did Caroline.

a-killer gouse now help

Not a killer. The killer. The man who'd raped and murdered Lisa Webb, the man almost certainly behind the attacks on Jessica, Hannah and Charlotte. A man with nothing to lose.

So why was Ian Webb's motor parked outside?

Webb would've knocked, gone inside for a nice little chat. Christ, he'd have hammered the door down if need be. Force hadn't been necessary. When he tried the handle, the door gave. Slipping in quietly, he heard voices from down the hallway. Ears pricked, Webb held his breath listening out for a tell-tale pause or change in tone. The bloke spouted on as before. Given the volume and intensity of the voice, the fact they'd heard nothing was no surprise. Unlike what was being said. He was talking to some woman – and the content was tell-tale alright. Webb tiptoed down the hall towards the source, felt his gorge rise as he heard even more home truths.

'*It ruined her. The shame, disgust, revulsion, fear, guilt. She kept it secret all these years. Even when she found out she was pregnant, she didn't tell anyone. And even if it hadn't been too late, she'd never have got rid of the baby. She loved me from the moment I was born. It says so – in her diaries. It's how I found out who he was – it's all in there.*'

Webb tightened his fists into balls: snivelling little bastard. Barely taking a breath, he padded closer taking vocal cover under the woman's bloody stupid question.

'*So Lisa is – was – your half-sister?*'

'*Nothing like keeping it in the family, eh? Not quite next of kin but yeah, her dad's my fucking father. And I made him pay.*'

'*And the other girls?*'

'*Rapists are animals so their precious daughters are fair game. I'm only sorry some sleaze bag got to Zoe Darby before me. I marked her father's card weeks ago – along with all the other doting daddies.*'

The woman screamed when Webb kicked the door open. 'Is that so, *son*?' His glance fell immediately on the table where light glinted off Lisa's missing letter. To the right, he caught a brighter flash a split second before the blade sliced across his neck.

'Never take your eye off the ball, *Dad.*'

Staggering back, Webb clamped a hand to the wound. Whether adrenalin or white-hot rage, he felt no pain just hot blood spurting through his fingers. This time he saw the blade coming, fended the blow, lashed out with a foot. The knife clattered to the floor as Slater gasping for breath hunched over, hands cupped round his crotch.

'Nor you, you murdering bastard.' Webb gritted his teeth then slammed his fist down on Slater's head again and again and again.

White-faced and trembling, Caroline backed against the side. If blood loss didn't fell Webb first, she reckoned she had less than a minute before he turned on her. Keeping her gaze on the men, she slowly reached a hand behind her back, felt along the surface until her fingers wrapped round the cork-screw. She almost gave the game away when she glimpsed Sarah.

Sarah heard Webb and the first blow land as she dashed down the hall. Within seconds, she took in the scene. Knife. Blood. Neck wound. Webb's ragged breathing. If the men weren't separated fast, she'd have two bodies on her hands. Holding Caroline's gaze, she willed her not to react. Then she held up five fingers and mouthed two words.

'Bloody good job I can lip read, isn't it?' Despite the quip, Caroline still looked pale. Her hand shook as she poured wine into a glass. She'd distracted Webb alright. Jabbing a corkscrew into someone's hand will do that.

Leaning against the side, Sarah raised a palm to turn down a drink. 'That and teamwork's what it boiled down to, Caroline.'

Teamwork and timing. Sarah had cuffs ready and pounced on a count of five. Fact that Webb was woozy and slipped on his own blood helped. The ambulance would arrive any minute. Webb was still sprawled unconscious on the floor. Both men were. They lay next to each other, virtually touching hands.

Like father, like son.

FIFTY-TWO

'Were you close to your dad?' Sarah and Dave were walking home along the canal after dinner in Brindleyplace. In mellow mood, she watched the dark water shimmer with the reflections of a million coloured lights. He'd had the day off, but she'd been tying loose ends back at the nick. It was Saturday evening, almost a week since Webb and Slater very nearly killed each other. Slater wouldn't be out of hospital for a while: his skull was fractured in three places. Webb had needed a blood transfusion. He'd already been remanded in custody. They'd both be sent down in due course.

'What's brought this on, Sarah?' She let him take her hand. 'Just interested.' Not surprising. Family bonds – and blood feuds – had kept them both busy recently. The entire workload had revolved round the case. She'd written God knows how many reports, interviewed Webb three times, read Mrs Slater's diaries. Caroline had provided a pretty comprehensive write-up on what Slater told her that night in the kitchen. He'd still be interviewed extensively when he was fit enough. Even if he denied every word, it wouldn't matter. The evidence they'd found at his mother's house in Bearwood was conclusive: clothes, bags, jewellery. The surviving victims would get everything back after the trial – assuming they wanted it. Knowing why they'd been raped meant they'd never look at their fathers in the same way again.

'I still miss him,' Dave said, 'if that answers your question.'

'I miss mine, too.' She smiled, squeezed his hand. 'Maybe that's what drove Slater. Partly. Missing out on a father's love only to discover the man he'd fantasized about had raped the mother he adored.'

'Really Sigmund? Well he had a bloody funny way of showing it.' Dave tucked her hand under his arm. 'Dead funny.'

'Yeah OK.' *Like Pete Hinds.* They now knew he'd been prepared to take the rap for a murder the daughter he loved had committed. Natalie had finally confessed, not prepared to see her dad get a life sentence. He'd still go down for the arson attack. Natalie would use the rape in mitigation, but they only had her word for the fact Burton had attacked her.

Like they'd only had Webb's word initially that he'd been tipped off about Zach Fraser's arrest in connection with Lisa's murder. They'd not have known at all if it hadn't been for Webb Junior. Anthony had given the cops chapter and verse after finding out his father was a rapist. A check on Webb's phone records found Brody's number listed and the date and time tallied with the tip-off. If Baker took the Internal Affairs job – he could well find himself looking into Brody's suspension.

'The chief was on good form, wasn't he?' She smiled, as she put the key in the door. They'd left Baker and Caroline in Carluccio's having dessert. Caroline had certainly dined out on her role in helping nail Webb. As Baker put it: she'd given the bastard a damn good corkscrewing.

'He sure was,' Dave said. 'And I'm glad you're in a good mood.'

'Why's that?' The smile turned arctic the instant she stepped inside. 'What the bloody hell's that doing here?'

Curled up in a basket by the radiator, Drake's cat didn't even lift its head, just opened one eye then dropped off back to sleep.

'Trial run you said. And look he already feels at home. Just like—'

'If you say "one of the family", Dave – I swear I'll kill you.'

Lightning Source UK Ltd.
Milton Keynes UK
UKOW01f1149120816

280561UK00001B/3/P